BATTLE ON THE STEPS!

His hand came out of the dark and caught Valeria's wrist as she stumbled blindly on the steps. She felt herself half-dragged, half-lifted up the winding stair, while Conan released her and turned on the steps, his ears and instincts telling him their foes were hard at their backs. *And the sounds were not all those of human feet.*

Something came writhing up the steps, something that slithered and rustled and brought a chill in the air with it. Conan lashed down with his great sword and felt the blade shear through something that might have been flesh and bone, and cut deep into the stair beneath. Something touched his foot that chilled like the touch of frost, and then the darkness beneath him was disturbed by a frightful thrashing and lashing, and a man cried out in agony.

The next moment Conan was racing up the winding staircase, and through a door that stood open at the head . . .

BLACK HOUNDS OF DEATH

Robert E. Howard

COSMOS BOOKS

BLACK HOUNDS OF DEATH

Published by
Dorchester Publishing Co., Inc.
200 Madison Ave.
New York, NY 10016
in collaboration with Wildside Press LLC

ISBN-10: 0-8439-5946-0
ISBN-13: 978-0-8439-5946-8

The name "Cosmos Books" and the Cosmos logo
are the property of Wildside Press, LLC.

Printed in the United States of America.

CONTENTS

BLACK CANAAN

Weird Tales, June 1936

1. Call from Canaan

"Trouble on Tularoosa Creek!"

A warning to send cold fear along the spine of any man who was raised in that isolated back country, called Canaan, that lies between Tularoosa and Black River — to send him racing back to that swamp-bordered region, wherever the word might reach him.

It was only a whisper from the withered lips of a shuffling black crone, who vanished among the throng before I could seize her; but it was enough. No need to seek confirmation; no need to inquire by what mysterious, black-folk way the word had come to her. No need to inquire what obscure forces worked to unseal those wrinkled lips to a Black River man. It was enough that the warning had been given — and understood.

Understood? How could any Black River man fail to understand that warning? It could have but one meaning — old hates seething again in the jungle-deeps of the swamplands, dark shadows slipping through the cypress, and massacre stalking out of the black, mysterious village that broods on the moss-festooned shore of sullen Tularoosa.

Within an hour New Orleans was falling further behind me with every turn of the churning wheel. To every man born in Canaan, there is always an invisible tie that draws him back whenever his homeland is imperiled by the murky shadow that has lurked in its jungled recesses for more than half a century.

The fastest boats I could get seemed maddeningly slow for that race up the big river, and up the smaller, more turbulent stream. I was burning with impatience when I stepped off on the Sharpsville landing, with the last fifteen miles of my journey yet to make. It was past midnight, but I hurried to the livery stable where, by tradition half a century old, there is always a Buckner horse, day or night.

As a sleepy black boy fastened the cinches, I turned to the owner of the stable, Joe Lafely, yawning and gaping in the light of the lantern he upheld. "There are rumors of trouble on Tularoosa?"

He paled in the lantern-light.

"I don't know. I've heard talk. But you people in Canaan are a shut-mouthed clan. No one *outside* knows what goes on in there —"

The night swallowed his lantern and his stammering voice as I headed west along the pike.

The moon set red through the black pines. Owls hooted away off in the woods, and somewhere a hound howled his ancient wistfulness to the night. In the darkness that foreruns dawn I crossed Nigger Head Creek, a streak of shining black fringed by walls of solid shadows. My horse's hoof splashed through the shallow water and clinked on the wet stones, startlingly loud in the stillness. Beyond Nigger Head Creek began the country men called Canaan.

Heading in the same swamp, miles to the north, that gives birth to Tularoosa, Nigger Head flows due south to join Black River a few miles west of Sharpsville, while the Tularoosa runs westward to meet the same river at a higher point. The trend of Black River is from northwest to southeast; so these three streams form the great irregular triangle known as Canaan.

In Canaan lived the sons and daughters of the white frontiersmen who first settled the country, and the sons and daughters of their slaves. Joe Lafely was right; we were an isolated, shut-mouthed breed, self-sufficient, jealous of our seclusion and independence.

Beyond Nigger Head the woods thickened, the road narrowed, winding through unfenced pinelands, broken by live oaks and cypresses. There was no sound except the soft clop-clop of hoofs in the thin dust, the creak of the saddle. Then someone laughed throatily in the shadows.

I drew up and peered into the trees. The moon had set and dawn was not yet come, but a faint glow quivered among the trees, and by it I made out a dim figure under the moss-hung branches. My hand instinctively sought the butt of one of the dueling-pistols I wore, and the action brought another low, musical laugh, mocking yet seductive. I glimpsed a brown face, a pair of scintillant eyes, white teeth displayed in an insolent smile.

"Who the devil are you?" I demanded.

"Why do you ride so late, Kirby Buckner?" Taunting laughter bubbled in the voice. The accent was foreign and unfamiliar; a faintly Negroid twang was there, but it was rich and sensuous as the rounded body of its owner. In the lustrous pile of dusky hair a great white blossom glimmered palely in the darkness.

"What are you doing here?" I demanded. "You're a long way from any darky cabin. And you're a stranger to me."

"I came to Canaan since you went away," she answered. "My cabin is on the Tularoosa. But now I've lost my way. And my poor brother has hurt his leg and cannot walk."

"Where is your brother?" I asked, uneasily. Her perfect English was disquieting to me, accustomed as I was to the dialect of the black folk.

"Back in the woods, there — far back!" She indicated the black depths with a swaying motion of her supple body rather than a gesture of her hand, smiling audaciously as she did so.

I knew there was no injured brother, and she knew I knew it, and laughed at me. But a strange turmoil of conflicting emotions stirred in me. I had never before paid any attention to a black or brown woman. But this quadroon girl was different from any I had ever seen. Her features were regular as a white woman's, and her speech was not that of a common wench. Yet she was barbaric, in the open lure of her smile, in the gleam of her eyes, in the shameful posturing of her voluptuous body. Every gesture, every motion she made set her apart from the ordinary run of women; her beauty was untamed and lawless, meant to madden rather than to soothe, to make a man blind and dizzy, to rouse in him all the unreined passions that are his heritage from his ape ancestors.

I hardly remember dismounting and tying my horse. My blood pounded suffocatingly through the veins in my temples as I scowled down at her, suspicious yet fascinated.

"How do you know my name? Who *are* you?"

With a provocative laugh, she seized my hand and drew me deeper into the shadows. Fascinated by the lights gleaming in her dark eyes, I was hardly aware of her action.

"Who does not know Kirby Buckner?" she laughed. "All the people of Canaan speak of you, white or black. Come! My poor brother longs to look upon you!" And she laughed with malicious triumph.

It was this brazen effrontery that brought me to my senses. Its cynical mockery broke the almost hypnotic spell in which I had fallen.

I stopped short, throwing her hand aside, snarling: "What devil's game are you up to, wench?"

Instantly the smiling siren was changed to a blood-mad jungle cat. Her eyes flamed murderously, her red lips writhed in a snarl as she leaped back, crying out shrilly. A rush of bare feet answered her call. The first faint light of dawn struck through the branches, revealing my assailants, three gaunt black giants. I saw the gleaming whites of their eyes, their bare glistening teeth, the sheen of naked steel in their hands.

My first bullet crashed through the head of the tallest man, knocking him dead in full stride. My second pistol snapped — the cap had somehow slipped from the nipple. I dashed it into a black face, and as the man fell, half-stunned, I whipped out my bowie knife and closed with the other. I parried his stab and my counterstroke ripped across his belly-muscles. He screamed like a swamp-panther and made a wild grab for my knife wrist, but I struck him in the mouth with my clenched left fist, and felt his lips split and his teeth crumble under the impact as he reeled backward, his knife waving wildly. Before he could regain his balance I was after him, thrusting, and got home under his ribs. He groaned and slipped to the ground in a puddle of his own blood.

I wheeled about, looking for the other. He was just rising, blood streaming down his face and neck. As I started for him he sounded a panicky yell and plunged into the underbrush. The crashing of his blind flight came back to me, muffled with distance. The girl was gone.

2. The Stranger on Tularoosa

The curious glow that had first showed me the quadroon girl had vanished. In my confusion I had forgotten it. But I did not waste time on vain conjecture as to its source, as I groped my way back to the road. Mystery had come to the pinelands and a ghostly light that hovered among the trees was only part of it.

My horse snorted and pulled against his tether, frightened by the smell of blood that hung in the heavy damp air. Hoofs clattered down the road, forms bulked in the growing light. Voices challenged.

"Who's that? Step out and name yourself, before we shoot!"

"Hold on, Esau!" I called. "It's me — Kirby Buckner!"

"Kirby Buckner, by thunder!" ejaculated Esau McBride, lowering his pistol. The tall rangy forms of the other riders loomed behind him.

"We heard a shot," said McBride. "We was ridin' patrol on the roads around Grimesville like we've been ridin' every night for a week now — ever since they killed Ridge Jackson."

"Who killed Ridge Jackson?"

"The swamp niggers. That's all we know. Ridge come out of the woods early one mornin' and knocked at Cap'n Sorley's door. Cap'n says he was the color of ashes. He hollered for the Cap'n for God's sake to let him in, he had somethin' awful to tell him. Well, the Cap'n started down to open the door, but before he'd got down the stairs he heard an awful row among the dogs outside, and a man screamed he reckoned was Ridge. And when he got to the door, there wasn't nothin' but a dead dog layin' in the yard with his head knocked in, and the others all goin' crazy. They found Ridge later, out in the pines a few hundred yards from the house. From the way the ground and the bushes was tore up, he'd been dragged that far by four or five men. Maybe they got tired of haulin' him along. Anyway, they beat his head into a pulp and left him layin' there."

"I'll be damned!" I muttered. "Well, there's a couple of niggers lying back there in the brush. I want to see if you know them. I don't."

A moment later we were standing in the tiny glade, now white in the growing dawn. A black shape sprawled on the matted pine needles, his head in a pool of blood and brains. There were wide smears of blood on the ground and bushes on the other side of the little clearing, but the wounded black was gone.

McBride turned the carcass with his foot.

"One of them niggers that came in with Saul Stalk," he muttered.

"Who the devil's that?" I demanded.

"Strange nigger that moved in since you went down the river last time. Come from South Carolina, he says. Lives in that old cabin in the Neck — you know, the shack where Colonel Reynolds' niggers used to live."

"Suppose you ride on to Grimesville with me, Esau," I said, "and tell me about this business as we ride. The rest of you might scout around and see if you can find a wounded nigger in the brush."

They agreed without question; the Buckners have always been tacitly considered leaders in Canaan, and it came natural for me to offer suggestions. Nobody gives *orders* to white men in Canaan.

"I reckoned you'd be showin' up soon," opined McBride, as we rode along the whitening road. "You usually manage to keep up with what's happenin' in Canaan."

"What *is* happening?" I inquired. "I don't know anything. An old black woman dropped me the word in New Orleans that there was trouble. Naturally I came home as fast as I could. Three strange niggers waylaid me —" I was curiously disinclined to mention the woman. "And now you tell me somebody killed Ridge Jackson. What's it all about?"

"The swamp niggers killed Ridge to shut his mouth," announced McBride. "That's the only way to figure it. They must have been close behind him when he knocked on Cap'n Sorley's door. Ridge worked for Cap'n Sorley most of his life; he thought a lot of the old man. Some kind of deviltry's bein' brewed up in the swamps, and Ridge wanted to warn the Cap'n. That's the way I figure."

"Warn him about what?"

"We don't know," confessed McBride. "That's why we're all on edge. It must be an uprisin'."

That word was enough to strike chill fear into the heart of any Canaan-dweller. The blacks had risen in 1845, and the red terror of that revolt was not forgotten, nor the three lesser rebellions before it, when the slaves rose and spread fire and slaughter from Tularoosa to the shores of Black River. The fear of a black uprising lurked forever in the depths of that forgotten back country; the very children absorbed it in their cradles.

"What makes you think it might be an uprising?" I asked.

"The niggers have all quit the fields, for one thing. They've all got business in Goshen. I ain't seen a nigger nigh Grimesville for a week. *The town niggers have pulled out.*"

In Canaan we still draw a distinction born in antebellum days. "Town-niggers" are descendants of the house-servants of the old days, and most of them live in or near Grimesville. There are not many, compared to the mass of "swamp-niggers" who dwell on tiny farms along the creeks and the edge of the swamps, or in the black village of Goshen, on the Tularoosa. They are descendants of the field hands of other days, and, untouched by the mellow civilization which refined the natures of the house-servants, they remain as primitive as their African ancestors.

"Where have the town-niggers gone?" I asked.

"Nobody knows. They lit out a week ago. Probably hidin' down on Black River. If we win, they'll come back. If we don't, they'll take refuge in Sharpsville."

I found his matter-of-factness a bit ghastly, as if the actuality of the uprising were an assured fact.

"Well, what have you done?" I demanded.

"Ain't much we could do," he confessed. "The niggers ain't made no open move, outside of killin' Ridge Jackson; and we couldn't prove who done that, or why they done it.

"They ain't done nothin' but clear out. But that's mighty suspicious. We can't keep from thinkin' Saul Stark's behind it."

"Who is this fellow?" I asked.

"I told you all I know, already. He got permission to settle in that old deserted cabin on the Neck; a great big black devil that talks better English than I like to hear a nigger talk. But he was respectful enough. He had three or four big South Carolina bucks with him, and a brown wench which we don't know whether she's his daughter, sister, wife or what. He ain't been in to Grimesville but that one time, and a few weeks after he came to Canaan, the niggers begun actin' curious. Some of the boys wanted to ride over to Goshen and have a showdown, but that's takin' a desperate chance."

I knew he was thinking of a ghastly tale told us by our grandfathers of how a punitive expedition from Grimesville was once ambushed and butchered among the dense thickets that masked Goshen, then a rendezvous for runaway slaves, while another red-handed band devastated Grimesville, left defenseless by that reckless invasion.

"Might take all the men to get Saul Stark," said McBride. "And we don't dare leave the town unprotected. But we'll soon have to — hello, what's this?"

We had emerged from the trees and were just entering the village of Grimesville, the community center of the white population of Canaan. It was not pretentious. Log cabins, neat and white-washed, were plentiful enough. Small cottages clustered about big, old-fashioned houses which sheltered the rude aristocracy of that backwoods democracy. All the "planter" families lived "in town." "The country" was occupied by their tenants, and by the small independent farmers, white and black.

A small log cabin stood near the point where the road wound out of the deep forest. Voices emanated from it, in accents of menace, and a tall lanky figure, rifle in hand, stood at the door.

"Howdy, Esau!" this man hailed us. "By golly, if it ain't Kirby Buckner! Glad to see you, Kirby."

"What's up, Dick?" asked McBride.

"Got a nigger in the shack, tryin' to make him talk. Bill Reynolds seen him sneakin' past the edge of town about daylight, and nabbed him."

"Who is it?" I asked.

"Tope Sorley. John Willoughby's gone after a blacksnake."

With a smothered oath I swung off my horse and strode in, followed by McBride. Half a dozen men in boots and gun-belts clustered about a pathetic figure cowering on an old broken bunk. Tope Sorley (his forebears had adopted the name of the family that owned them, in slave days) was a pitiable sight just then. His skin was ashy, his teeth chattered spasmodically, and his eyes seemed to be trying to roll back into his head.

"Here's Kirby!" ejaculated one of the men as I pushed my way through the group. "I'll bet he can make this coon talk!"

"Here comes John with the blacksnake!" shouted someone, and a tremor ran through Tope Sorley's shivering body.

I pushed aside the butt of the ugly whip thrust eagerly into my hand.

"Tope," I said, "you've worked one of my father's farms for years. Has any Buckner ever treated you any way but square?"

"Nossuh," came faintly.

"Then what are you afraid of? Why don't you speak up? Something's going on in the swamps. *You* know, and I want you to tell us — why the town niggers have all run away, why Ridge Jackson was killed, why the swamp niggers are acting so mysteriously."

"And what kind of devilment that cussed Saul Stark's cookin' up over on Tularoosa!" shouted one of the men.

Tope seemed to shrink into himself at the mention of Stark.

"I don't dast," he shuddered. "He'd put me in de swamp!"

"Who?" I demanded. "Stark? Is Stark a conjer man?"

Tope sank his head in his hands and did not answer. I laid my hand on his shoulder.

"Tope," I said, "you know if you'll talk, we'll protect you. If you don't talk, I don't think Stark can treat you much rougher than these men are likely to. Now spill it — what's it all about?"

He lifted desperate eyes.

"You-all got to lemme stay here," he shuddered. "And guard me, and gimme money to git away on when de trouble's over."

"We'll do all that," I agreed instantly. "You can stay right here in this cabin, until you're ready to leave for New Orleans or wherever you want to go."

He capitulated, collapsed, and words tumbled from his livid lips.

"Saul Stark's a conjer man. He come here because it's way off in back country. He aim to kill all de while folks in Canaan —"

A growl rose from the group, such a growl as rises unbidden from the throat of the wolf-pack that scents peril.

"He aim to make hisself king of Canaan. He sent me to spy dis mornin' to see if Mistah Kirby got through. He sent men to waylay him on de road, cause he knowed Mistah Kirby was comin' back to Canaan. Niggers makin' voodoo on Tularoosa, for weeks now. Ridge Jackson was goin' to tell Cap'n Sorley; so Stark's niggers foller him and kill him.

That make Stark mad. He ain't want to *kill* Ridge; he want to put him in de swamp with Tunk Bixby and de others."

"What are you talking about?" I demanded.

Far out in the woods rose a strange, shrill cry, like the cry of a bird. But no such bird ever called before in Canaan. Tope cried out as if in answer, and shriveled into himself. He sank down on the bunk in a veritable palsy of fear.

"That was a signal!" I snapped. "Some of you go out there."

Half a dozen men hastened to follow my suggestion, and I returned to the task of making Tope renew his revelations. It was useless. Some hideous fear had sealed his lips. He lay shuddering like a stricken animal, and did not even seem to hear our questions. No one suggested the use of the blacksnake. Anyone could see the Negro was paralyzed with terror.

Presently the searchers returned empty-handed. They had seen no one, and the thick carpet of pine needles showed no footprints. The men looked at me expectantly. As Colonel Buckner's son, leadership was expected of me.

"What about it, Kirby?" asked McBride. "Breckinridge and the others have just rode in. They couldn't find that nigger you cut up."

"There was another nigger I hit with a pistol," I said. "Maybe he came back and helped him." Still I could not bring myself to mention the brown girl. "Leave Tope alone. Maybe he'll get over his scare after a while. Better keep a guard in the cabin all the time. The swamp niggers may try to get him as they got Ridge Jackson. Better scour the roads around the town, Esau; there may be some of them hiding in the woods."

"I will. I reckon you'll want to be gettin' up to the house, now, and seein' your folks."

"Yes. And I want to swap these toys for a couple of .44s. Then I'm going to ride out and tell the country people to come into Grimesville. If it's to be an uprising, we don't know when it will commence."

"You're not goin' alone!" protested McBride.

"I'll be all right," I answered impatiently. "All this may not amount to anything, but it's best to be on the safe side. That's why I'm going after the country folks. No, I don't want anybody to go with me. Just in case the niggers do get crazy enough to attack the town, you'll need every man you've got. But if I can get hold of some of the swamp niggers and talk to them, I don't think there'll be any attack."

"You won't get a glimpse of them," McBride predicted.

3. Shadows Over Canaan

It was not yet noon when I rode out of the village westward along the old road. Thick woods swallowed me quickly. Dense walls of pines marched with me on either hand, giving way occasionally to fields enclosed with straggling rail fences, with the log cabins of the tenants or owners close by, with the usual litters of tow-headed children and lank hound dogs.

Some of the cabins were empty. The occupants, if white, had already gone into Grimesville; if black they had gone into the swamps, or fled to the hidden refuge of the town niggers, according to their affiliations. In any event, the vacancy of their hovels was sinister in its suggestion.

A tense silence brooded over the pinelands, broken only by the occasional wailing call of a plowman. My progress was not swift, for from time to time I turned off the main road to give warnings to some lonely cabin huddled on the bank of one of the many thicket-fringed creeks. Most of these families were south of the road; the white settlements did not extend far to the north; for in that direction lay Tularoosa Creek with its jungle-grown marshes that stretched inlets southward like groping fingers.

The actual warning was brief; there was no need to argue or explain. I called from the saddle: "Get into town; trouble brewing on Tularoosa." Face paled, and people dropped whatever they were doing: the men to grab guns and jerk mules from the plow to hitch to the wagons, the women to bundle necessary belongings together and shrill the children in from their play. As I rode I heard the cow-horns blowing up and down the creeks, summoning men from distant fields — blowing as they had not blown for a generation, a warning and a defiance which I knew carried to such ears as might be listening in the edges of the swamplands. The country emptied itself behind me, flowing in thin but steady streams toward Grimesville.

The sun was swinging low among the topmost branches of the pines when I reached the Richardson cabin, the westernmost "white" cabin in Canaan. Beyond it lay the Neck, the angle formed by the junction of Tularoosa with Black River, a jungle-like expanse occupied only by scattered Negro huts.

Mrs. Richardson called to me anxiously from the cabin stoop.

"Well, Mr. Kirby, I'm glad to see you back in Canaan! We been hearin' the horns all evenin', Mr. Kirby. What's it mean? It — it ain't —"

"You and Joe better get the children and light out for Grimesville," I answered. "Nothing's happened yet, and may not, but it's best to be on the safe side. All the people are going."

"We'll go right now!" she gasped, paling as she snatched off her apron. "Lord, Mr. Kirby, you reckon they'll cut us off before we can git to town?"

I shook my head. "They'll strike at night, if at all. We're just playing safe. Probably nothing will come of it."

"I bet you're wrong there," she predicted, scurrying about in desperate activity. "I been hearin' a drum beatin' off toward Saul Stark's cabin, off and on, for a week now. They beat drums back in the Big

Uprisin'. My pappy's told me about it many's the time. The niggers skinned his brother alive. The horns was blowin' all up and down the creeks, and the drums was beatin' louder'n the horns could blow. You'll be ridin' back with us, won't you, Mr. Kirby?"

"No; I'm going to scout down along the trial a piece."

"Don't go too far. You're liable to run into old Saul Stark and his devils. Lord! *Where* is that man? Joe! *Joe!*"

As I rode down the trail her shrill voice followed me, thin-edged with fear.

Beyond the Richardson farm pines gave way to live oaks. The underbrush grew ranker. A scent of rotting vegetation impregnated the fitful breeze. Occasionally I sighted a nigger hut, half hidden under the trees, but always it stood silent and deserted. Empty nigger cabins meant but one thing: the blacks were collecting at Goshen, some miles to the east on the Tularoosa; and that gathering, too, could have but one meaning.

My goal was Saul Stark's hut. My intention had been formed when I heard Tope Sorley's incoherent tale. There could be no doubt that Saul Stark was the dominant figure in this web of mystery. With Saul Stark I meant to deal. That I might be risking my life was a chance any man must take who assumes the responsibility of leadership.

The sun slanted through the lower branches of the cypresses when I reached it — a log cabin set against a background of gloomy tropical jungle. A few steps beyond it began the uninhabitable swamp in which Tularoosa emptied its murky current into Black River. A reek of decay hung in the air; gray moss bearded the trees, and poisonous vines twisted in rank tangles.

I called: "Stark! Saul Stark! Come out here!"

There was no answer. A primitive silence hovered over the tiny clearing. I dismounted, tied my horse and approached the crude, heavy door. Perhaps this cabin held a clue to the mystery of Saul Stark; at least it doubtless contained the implements and paraphernalia of his noisome craft. The faint breeze dropped suddenly. The stillness became so intense it was like a physical impact. I paused, startled; it was as if some inner instinct had shouted urgent warning.

As I stood there every fiber of me quivered in response to that subconscious warning; some obscure, deep-hidden instinct sensed peril, as a man senses the presence of the rattlesnake in the darkness, or the swamp panther crouching in the bushes. I drew a pistol, sweeping the trees and bushes, but saw no shadow or movement to betray the ambush I feared. But my instinct was unerring; what I sensed was not lurking in the woods about me; it was inside the cabin — *waiting*. Trying to shake off the feeling, and irked by a vague half-memory that kept twitching at the back of my brain, I again advanced. And again I stopped short, with one foot on the tiny stoop, and a hand half-advanced to pull open the door. A chill shivering swept over me, a sensation like that which shakes a man to whom a flicker of lightning has revealed the black abyss into which another blind step would have hurled him. For the first time in my life I knew the meaning of fear; I knew that black horror lurked in that sullen cabin under the moss-bearded cypresses — a horror against which every primitive instinct that was my heritage cried out in panic.

And that insistent half-memory woke suddenly. It was the memory of a story of how voodoo men leave their huts guarded in their absence by a powerful ju-ju spirit to deal madness and death to the intruder. White men ascribed such deaths to superstitious fright and hypnotic suggestion. But in that instant I understood my sense of lurking peril; I comprehended the horror that breathed like an invisible mist from that accursed hut. I sensed the reality of the ju-ju, of which the grotesque wooden images which voodoo men place in their huts are only a symbol.

Saul Stark was gone; but he had left a Presence to guard his hut.

I backed away, sweat beading the backs of my hands. Not for a bag of gold would I have peered into the shuttered windows or touched that unbolted door. My pistol hung in my hand, useless I knew against the *Thing* in that cabin. What it was I could not know, but I knew it was some brutish, soulless entity drawn from the black swamps by the spells of voodoo. Man and the natural animals are not the only sentient beings that haunt this planet. There are invisible *Things* — black spirits of the deep swamps and the slimes of the river beds — the Negroes know of them. . . .

My horse was trembling like a leaf and he shouldered close to me as if seeking security in bodily contact. I mounted and reined away, fighting a panicky urge to strike in the spurs and bolt madly down the trail.

I breathed an involuntary sigh of relief as the somber clearing fell away behind me and was lost from sight. I did not, as soon as I was out of sight of the cabin, revile myself for a silly fool. My experience was too vivid in my mind. It was not cowardice that prompted my retreat from that empty hut; it was the natural instinct of self-preservation, such as keeps a squirrel from entering the lair of a rattlesnake.

My horse snorted and shied violently. A gun was in my hand before I saw what had startled me. Again a rich musical laugh taunted me.

She was leaning against a bent tree-trunk, her hands clasped behind her sleek head, insolently posing her sensuous figure. The barbaric fascination of her was not dispelled by daylight; if anything, the glow of the low-hanging sun enhanced it.

"Why did you not go into the ju-ju cabin, Kirby Buckner?" she mocked, lowering her arms and moving insolently out from the tree.

She was clad as I had never seen a swamp woman, or any other woman, dressed. Snakeskin sandals were on her feet, sewn with tiny sea-shells that were never gathered on this continent. A short silken skirt of flaming crimson molded her full hips, and was upheld by a broad bead-worked girdle. Barbaric anklets and armlets clashed as she moved, heavy ornaments of crudely hammered gold that were as African as her loftily piled coiffure. Nothing else she wore, and on her bosom, between her arching breasts, I glimpsed the faint lines of tattooing on her brown skin.

She posed derisively before me, not in allure, but in mockery. Triumphant malice blazed in her dark eyes; her red lips curled with cruel mirth. Looking at her then I found it easy to believe all the tales I had heard of torture and mutilations inflicted by the women of savage races on wounded enemies. She was alien, even in this primitive setting; she needed a grimmer, more bestial background, a background of steaming jungle, reeking black swamps, flaring fires and cannibal feasts, and the bloody altars of abysmal tribal gods.

"Kirby Buckner!" She seemed to caress the syllables with her red tongue, yet the very intonation was an obscene insult. "Why did you not enter Saul Stalk's cabin? It was not locked! Did you fear what you might see there? Did you fear you might come out with your hair white like an old man's, and the drooling lips of an imbecile?"

"What's in that hut?" I demanded.

She laughed in my face, and snapped her fingers with a peculiar gesture.

"One of the ones which come oozing like black mist out of the night when Saul Stark beats the ju-ju drum and shrieks the black incantation to the gods that crawl on their bellies in the swamp."

"What is he doing here? The black folk were quiet until he came."

Her red lips curled disdainfully. "Those black dogs? They are his slaves. If they disobey he kills them, *or puts them in the swamp*. For long we have looked for a place to begin our rule. We have chosen Canaan. You whites must go. And since we know that white people can never be driven away from their land, we must kill you all."

It was my turn to laugh, grimly.

"They tried that, back in '45."

"They did not have Saul Stark to lead them, then," she answered calmly.

"Well, suppose they won? Do you think that would be the end of it? Other white men would come into Canaan and kill them all."

"They would have to cross water," she answered. "We can defend the rivers and creeks. Saul Stark will have many *servants in the swamps* to do his bidding. He will be king of black Canaan. No one can cross the waters to come against him. He will rule his tribe, as his fathers ruled their tribes in the Ancient Land."

"Mad as a loon!" I muttered. Then curiosity impelled me to ask: "Who is this fool? What are you to him?"

"He is the son of a Kongo witch-finder, and he is

the greatest voodoo priest out of the Ancient Land," she answered, laughing at me again. "I? You shall learn who *I* am, tonight in the swamp, in the House of Damhallah."

"Yes?" I grunted. "What's to prevent me from taking you into Grimesville with me? You know the answers to questions I'd like to ask."

Her laughter was like the slash of a velvet whip.

"*You* drag me to the village of the whites? Not all death and Hell could keep me from the Dance of the Skull, tonight in the House of Damballah. You are *my* captive, already." She laughed derisively as I started and glared into the shadows about me. "No one is hiding there. I am alone, and you are the strongest man in Canaan. Even Saul Stark fears you, for be sent me with three men to kill you before you could reach the village. Yet you are my captive. I have but to beckon, so" — she crooked a contemptuous finger — "and you will follow to the fires of Dumallah and the knives of the torturers."

I laughed at her, but my mirth rang hollow. I could not deny the incredible magnetism of this brown enchantress; it fascinated and impelled, drawing me toward her, beating at my willpower. I could not fail to recognize it any more than I could fail to recognize the peril in the ju-ju hut.

My agitation was apparent to her, for her eyes flashed with unholy triumph.

"Black men are fools, all but Saul Stark," she laughed. "White men are fools, too. I am the daughter of a white man, who lived in the hut of a black king and mated with his daughters. I know the strength of white men, and their weakness. I failed last night when I met you in the woods, but now I cannot fail!" Savage exultation thrummed in her voice. "By the blood in your veins I have snared you. The knife of the man you killed scratched your hand — seven drops of blood that fell on the pine needles have given me your soul! I took that blood, and Saul Stark gave me the man who ran away. Saul Stark hates cowards. With his hot, quivering heart, and seven drops of your blood, Kirby Buckner, deep in the swamps I have made such magic as none but a Bride of Damballah can make. Already you feel its urge! Oh, you are strong! The man you fought with the knife died less than an hour later. But you cannot fight me. Your blood makes you my slave. I have put a conjurement upon you."

By heaven, it was not mere madness she was mouthing! Hypnotism, magic, call it what you will, I felt its onslaught on my brain and will — blind, senseless impulse that seemed to be rushing me against my will to the brink of some nameless abyss.

"I have made a charm you cannot resist!" she cried. "When I call you, you will come! Into the deep swamps you will follow me. You will see the Dance of the Skull, and you will see the doom of a poor fool who sought to betray Saul Stark — who dreamed he could resist the Call of Damballah when it came. Into the swamp he goes tonight, with Tunk Bixby and the other four fools who opposed Saul Stark. You shall see that. You shall know and understand your own doom. And then you too shall go into the swamp, into darkness and silence deep as the darkness of nighted Africa! But before the darkness engulfs you there will be sharp knives, and little fires — oh, you will scream for death, even for the death that is beyond death!"

With a choking cry I whipped out a pistol and leveled it full at her breast. It was cocked and my finger was on the trigger. At that range I could not miss. But she looked full into the black muzzle and laughed — laughed — laughed, in wild peals that froze the blood in my veins.

And I sat there like an image pointing a pistol I could not fire! A frightful paralysis gripped me. I knew, with numbing certainty, that my life depended on the pull of that trigger, but I could not crook my finger — not though every muscle in my body quivered with the effort and sweat broke out on my face in clammy beads.

She ceased laughing, then, and stood looking at me in a manner indescribably sinister.

"You cannot shoot me, Kirby Buckner," she said quietly. "I have enslaved your soul. You cannot understand my power, but it has ensnared you. It is the Lure of the Bride of Damballah — the blood I have mixed with the mystic waters of Africa drawing the blood in your veins. Tonight you will come to me, in the House of Damballah."

"You lie!" My voice was an unnatural croak bursting from dry lips. "You've hypnotized me, you she-devil, so I can't pull this trigger. But you can't drag me across the swamps to you."

"It is you who lie," she returned calmly. "You know you lie. Ride back toward Grimesville or wherever you will, Kirby Buckner. But when the sun sets and the black shadows crawl out of the swamps, you will see me beckoning you, and you will follow me. Long I have planned your doom, Kirby Buckner, since first I heard the white men of Canaan talking of you. It was I who sent the word down the river that brought you back to Canaan. Not even Saul Stark knows of my plans for you.

"At dawn Grimesville shall go up in flames, and the heads of the white men will be tossed in the blood-running streets. But tonight is the Night of Damballah, and a white sacrifice shall be given to the black gods. Hidden among the trees you shall watch the Dance of the Skull — and then I shall call you forth — to die! And now, go fool! Run as far and as fast as you will. At sunset, wherever you are, you will turn your footsteps toward the House of Damballah!"

And with the spring of a panther she was gone into the thick brush, and as she vanished the strange paralysis dropped from me. With a gasped oath I fired blindly after her, but only a mocking laugh floated back to me.

Then in a panic I wrenched my horse about and spurred him down the trail. Reason and logic had momentarily vanished from my brain, leaving me in the grasp of blind, primitive fear. I had confronted sorcery beyond my power to resist. I had felt my will mastered by the mesmerism in a brown woman's eyes. And now one driving urge overwhelmed me — a wild desire to cover as much distance as I could before that low-hanging sun dipped below the horizon and the black shadows came crawling from the swamps.

And yet I knew I could not outrun the grisly specter that menaced me. I was like a man fleeing in a nightmare, trying to escape from a monstrous phantom which kept pace with me despite my desperate speed.

I had not reached the Richardson cabin when above the drumming of my flight I heard the clop of hoofs ahead of me, and an instant later, sweeping around a kink in the trail, I almost rode down a tall, lanky man on an equally gaunt horse.

He yelped and dodged back as I jerked my horse to its haunches, my pistol presented at his breast.

"Look out, Kirby! It's me — Jim Braxton! My God, you look like you'd seen a ghost! What's chasin' you?"

"Where are you going?" I demanded, lowering my gun.

"Lookin' for you. Folks got worried as it got late and you didn't come in with the refugees. I 'lowed I'd light out and look for you. Miz Richardson said you rode into the Neck. Where in tarnation you been?"

"To Saul Stark's cabin."

"You takin' a big chance. What'd you find there?"

The sight of another white man had somewhat steadied my nerves. I opened my mouth to narrate my adventure, and was shocked to hear myself saying, instead: "Nothing. He wasn't there."

"Thought I heard a gun crack, a while ago," he remarked, glancing sharply at me, sidewise.

"I shot at a copperhead," I answered, and shuddered. This reticence regarding the brown woman was compulsory; I could no more speak of her than I could pull the trigger of the pistol aimed at her. And I cannot describe the horror that beset me when I realized this. The conjer spells the black men feared were not lies, I realized sickly; demons in human form *did* exist who were able to enslave men's will and thoughts.

Braxton was eyeing me strangely.

"We're lucky the woods ain't full of black copperheads," he said. "Tope Sorley's pulled out."

"What do you mean?" By an effort I pulled myself together.

"Just that. Tom Breckinridge was in the cabin with him. Tope hadn't said a word since you talked to him. Just laid on that bunk and shivered. Then a kind of holler begun way out in the woods, and Tom went to the door with his rifle-gun, but couldn't see nothin'. Well, while he was standin' there he got a lick on the head from *behind*, and as he fell he seen that crazy nigger Tope jump over him and light out for the woods. Tom he taken a shot at him, but missed. Now what you make of that?"

"The Call of Damballah!" I muttered, a chill perspiration beading my body. "God! The poor devil!"

"Huh? What's that?"

"For God's sake let's not stand here mouthing! The sun will soon be down!" In a frenzy of impatience I kicked my mount down the trail. Braxton followed me, obviously puzzled. With a terrific effort I got a grip on myself. How madly fantastic it was that Kirby Buckner should be shaking in the grip of unreasoning terror! It was so alien to my whole nature that it was no wonder Jim Braxton was unable to comprehend what ailed me.

"Tope didn't go of his own free will," I said. "That call was a summons he couldn't resist. Hypnotism, black magic, voodoo, whatever you want to call it, Saul Stark has some damnable power that enslaves men's willpower. The blacks are gathered somewhere in the swamp, for some kind of a devilish voodoo ceremony, which I have reason to believe will culminate in the murder of Tope Sorley. We've got to get to Grimesville if we can. I expect an attack at dawn."

Braxton was pale in the dimming light. He did not ask me where I got my knowledge.

"We'll lick 'em when they come; but it'll be a slaughter."

I did not reply. My eyes were fixed with savage

intensity on the sinking sun, and as it slid out of sight behind the trees I was shaken with an icy tremor. In vain I told myself that no occult power could draw me against my will. If she had been able to compel me, why had she not forced me to accompany her from the glade of the ju-ju hut? A grisly whisper seemed to tell me that she was but playing with me, as a cat allows a mouse almost to escape, only to be pounced upon again.

"Kirby, what's the matter with you?" I scarcely heard Braxton's anxious voice. "You're sweatin' and shakin' like you had the aggers. What — hey, what you stoppin' for?"

I had not consciously pulled on the rein, but my horse halted, and stood trembling and snorting, before the mouth of a narrow trail which meandered away at right angles from the road we were following — a trail that led north.

"Listen!" I hissed tensely.

"What is it?" Braxton drew a pistol. The brief twilight of the pinelands was deepening into dusk.

"Don't you hear it?" I muttered. "Drums! Drums beating in Goshen!"

"I don't hear nothin'," he mumbled uneasily. "If they was beatin' drums in Goshen you couldn't hear 'em this far away."

"Look there!" My sharp sudden cry made him start. I was pointing down the dim trail, at the figure which stood there in the dusk less than a hundred yards away. There in the dusk I saw her, even made out the gleam of her strange eyes, the mocking smile on her red lips. "Saul Stark's brown wench!" I raved, tearing at my scabbard. "My God, man, are you stone-blind? Don't you see her?"

"I don't see nobody!" he whispered, livid. "What are you talkin' about, Kirby?"

With eyes glaring I fired down the trail, and fired again, and yet again. This time no paralysis gripped my arm. But the smiling face still mocked me from the shadows. A slender, rounded arm lifted, a finger beckoned imperiously; and then she was gone and I was spurring my horse down the narrow trail, blind, deaf and dumb, with a sensation as of being caught in a black tide that was carrying me with it as it rushed on to a destination beyond my comprehension.

Dimly I heard Braxton's urgent yells, and then he drew up beside me with a clatter of hoofs, and grabbed my reins, setting my horse back on its haunches. I remember striking at him with my gun-barrel, without realizing what I was doing. All the black rivers of Africa were surging and foaming within my consciousness, roaring into a torrent that was sweeping me down to engulf me in an ocean of doom.

"Kirby, are you crazy? This trail leads to Goshen!"

I shook my head dazedly. The foam of the rushing waters swirled in my brain, and my voice sounded far away. "Go back! Ride for Grimesville! I'm going to Goshen."

"Kirby, you're mad!"

"Mad or sane, I'm going to Goshen this night," I answered dully. I was fully conscious. I knew what I was saying, and what I was doing. I realized the incredible folly of my action, and I realized my inability to help myself. Some shred of sanity impelled me to try to conceal the grisly truth from my companion, to offer a rational reason for my madness. "Saul Stark is in Goshen. He's the one who's responsible for all this trouble. I'm going to kill him. That will stop the uprising before it starts."

He was trembling like a man with the ague.

"Then I'm goin' with you."

"You must go on to Grimesville and warn the people," I insisted, holding to sanity, but feeling a strong urge begin to seize me, an irresistible urge to be in motion — to be riding in the direction toward which I was so horribly drawn.

"They'll be on their guard," he said stubbornly. "They won't need my warnin'. I'm goin with you. I don't know what's got in you, but I ain't goin' to let you die alone among these black woods."

I did not argue. I could not. The blind rivers were sweeping me on — on — on! And down the trail, dim in the dusk, I glimpsed a supple figure, caught the gleam of uncanny eyes, the crook of a lifted finger. . . . Then I was in motion, galloping down the trail, and I heard the drum of Braxton's horse's hoofs behind me.

4. *The Dwellers in the Swamp*

Night fell and the moon shone through the trees, blood-red behind the black branches. The horses were growing hard to manage.

"They got more sense'n us, Kirby," muttered Braxton.

"Panther, maybe," I replied absently, my eyes searching the gloom of the trail ahead.

"Naw, t'ain't. Closer we get to Goshen, the worse they git. And every time we swing nigh to a creek they shy and snort."

The trail had not yet crossed any of the narrow, muddy creeks that crisscrossed that end of Canaan, but several times it had swung so close to one of them that we glimpsed the black streak that was water glinting dully in the shadows of the thick growth. And each time, I remembered, the horses showed signs of fear.

But I had hardly noticed, wrestling as I was with the grisly compulsion that was driving me. Remember, I was not like a man in a hypnotic trance. I was fully awake, fully conscious. Even the daze in which I had seemed to hear the roar of black rivers had passed, leaving my mind clear, my thoughts lucid. And that was the sweating hell of it: to realize my folly clearly and poignantly, but to be unable to conquer it. Vividly I realized that I was riding to torture and death, and leading a faithful friend to the same end. But on I went. My efforts to break the spell that gripped me almost unseated my reason, but on I went. I cannot explain my compulsion, any more than I can explain why a sliver of steel is drawn to a magnet. It was a black power beyond the ring of white man's knowledge; a basic, elemental thing of which formal hypnotism is but scanty crumbs, spilled at random. A power beyond my control was drawing me to Goshen, and beyond; more I cannot explain, any more than the rabbit could explain why the eyes of the swaying serpent draw him into its gaping jaws.

We were not far from Goshen when Braxton's horse unseated its rider, and my own began snorting and plunging.

"They won't go no closer!" gasped Braxton, fighting at the reins.

I swung off, threw the reins over the saddle horn.

"Go back, for God's sake, Jim! I'm going on afoot."

I heard him whimper an oath, then his horse was galloping after mine, and he was following me on foot. The thought that he must share my doom sickened me, but I could not dissuade him; and ahead of me a supple form was dancing in the shadows, luring me on — on — on. . . .

I wasted no more bullets on that mocking shape. Braxton could not see it, and I knew it was part of my enchantment, no real woman of flesh and blood, but a hell-born will-o'-the-wisp, mocking me and leading me through the night to a hideous death. A "sending," the people of the Orient, who are wiser than we, call such a thing.

Braxton peered nervously at the black forest walls about us, and I knew his flesh was crawling with the fear of sawed-off shotguns blasting us suddenly from the shadows. But it was no ambush of lead or steel I feared as we emerged into the moonlit clearing that housed the cabins of Goshen.

The double line of log cabins faced each other across the dusty street. One line backed against the bank of Tularoosa Creek. The back stoops almost overhung the black waters. Nothing moved in the moonlight. No lights showed, no smoke oozed up from the stick-and-mud chimneys. It might have been a dead town, deserted and forgotten.

"It's a trap!" hissed Braxton, his eyes blazing slits. He bent forward like a skulking panther, a gun in each hand. "They're layin' for us in them huts!"

Then he cursed, but followed me as I strode down the street. I did not hail the silent huts. I *knew* Goshen was deserted. I felt its emptiness. Yet there was a contradictory sensation as of spying eyes fixed upon us. I did not try to reconcile these opposite convictions.

"They're gone," muttered Braxton, nervously. "I can't smell 'em. I can always smell niggers, if they're a lot of 'em, or if they're right close. You reckon they've gone to raid Grimesville?"

"No," I muttered. "They're in the House of Damballah."

He shot a quick glance at me.

"That's a neck of land in the Tularoosa about three miles west of here. My grandpap used to talk about it. The niggers held their heathen palavers there back in slave times. You ain't — Kirby — you —"

"Listen!" I wiped the icy sweat from my face. *"Listen!"*

Through the black woodlands the faint throb of a drum whispered on the wind that glided up the shadowy reaches of the Tularoosa.

Braxton shivered. "It's them, all right. But for God's sake, Kirby — *look out!*"

With an oath he sprang toward the houses on the bank of the creek. I was after him just in time to glimpse a dark clumsy object scrambling or tumbling down the sloping bank into the water. Braxton threw up his long pistol, then lowered it, with a baffled curse. A faint splash marked the disappearance of the creature. The shiny black surface crinkled with spreading ripples.

"What was it?" I demanded.

"A nigger on his all-fours!" swore Braxton. His face was strangely pallid in the moonlight. "He was crouched between them cabins there, watchin' us!"

"It must have been an alligator." What a mystery is the human mind! I was arguing for sanity and logic, I, the blind victim of a compulsion beyond sanity and logic. "A nigger would have to come up for air."

"He swum under the water and come up in the shadder of the bresh where we couldn't see him," maintained Braxton. "Now he'll go warn Saul Stark."

"Never mind!" The pulse was thrumming in my temples again, the roar of foaming waters rising irresistibly in my brain. "I'm going — straight through the swamp. For the last time, go back!"

"No! Sane or mad, I'm goin' with you!"

The pulse of the drum was fitful, growing more distinct as we advanced. We struggled through jungle-thick growth; tangled vines tripped us; our boots sank in scummy mire. We were entering the fringe of the swamp which grew deeper and denser until it culminated in the uninhabitable morass where the Tularoosa flowed into Black River, miles farther to the west.

The moon had not yet set, but the shadows were black under the interlacing branches with their mossy beards. We plunged into the first creek we must cross, one of the many muddy streams flowing into the Tularoosa. The water was only thigh-deep, the moss-clogged bottom fairly firm. My foot felt the edge of a sheer drop, and I warned Braxton: "Look out for a deep hole; keep right behind me."

His answer was unintelligible. He was breathing heavily, crowding close behind me. Just as I reached the sloping bank and pulled myself up by the slimy, projecting roots, the water was violently agitated behind me. Braxton cried out incoherently, and hurled himself up the bank, almost upsetting me. I wheeled, gun in hand, but saw only the black water seething and whirling after his thrashing rush through it.

"What the devil, Jim?"

"Somethin' grabbed me!" he panted. "Somethin' out of the deep hole. I tore loose and busted up the bank. I tell you, Kirby, something's follerin' us! Somethin' that swims under the water."

"Maybe it was that nigger you saw. These swamp people swim like fish. Maybe he swam up under the water to try to drown you."

He shook his head, staring at the black water, gun in hand.

"It *smelt* like a nigger, and the little I saw of it *looked* like a nigger. But it didn't *feel* like any kind of a human."

"Well, it was an alligator then," I muttered absently as I turned away. As always when I halted, even for a moment, the roar of peremptory and imperious rivers shook the foundations of my reason.

He splashed after me without comment. Scummy puddles rose about our ankles, and we stumbled over moss-grown cypress knees. Ahead of us there loomed another, wider creek, and Braxton caught my arm.

"Don't do it, Kirby!" he gasped. "If we go into that water, it'll git us sure!"

"What?"

"I don't know. Whatever it was that flopped down that bank back there in Goshen. The same thing that grabbed me in that creek back yonder. Kirby, let's go back."

"Go back?" I laughed in bitter agony. "I wish to God I could! I've got to go on. Either Saul Stark or I must die before dawn."

He licked dry lips and whispered. "Go on, then; I'm with you, come heaven or Hell." He thrust his pistol back into its scabbard, and drew a long keen knife from his boot. "Go ahead!"

I climbed down the sloping bank and splashed into the water that rose to my hips. The cypress branches bent a gloomy, moss-trailing arch over the creek. The water was black as midnight. Braxton was a blur, toiling behind me. I gained the first shelf of the opposite bank and paused, in water knee-deep, to turn and look back at him.

Everything happened at once, then. I saw Braxton halt short, staring at something on the bank behind me. He cried out, whipped out a gun and fired, just as I turned. In the flash of the gun I glimpsed a supple form reeling backward, a brown face fiendishly contorted. Then in the momentary blindness that followed the flash, I heard Jim Braxton scream.

Sight and brain cleared in time to show me a sudden swirl of the murky water, a round, black object breaking the surface behind Jim — and then Braxton gave a strangled cry and went under with a frantic thrashing and splashing. With an incoherent yell I sprang into the creek, stumbled and went to my knees, almost submerging myself. As I struggled up I saw Braxton's head, now streaming blood, break the surface for an instant, and I lunged toward it. It went under and another head appeared in its place, a shadowy black head. I stabbed at it ferociously, and my knife cut only the blank water as the thing dipped out of sight.

I staggered from the wasted force of the blow, and when I righted myself, the water lay unbroken about me. I called Jim's name, but there was no answer. Then panic laid a cold hand on me, and I splashed to the bank, sweating and trembling. With the water no higher than my knees I halted and waited, for I knew not what. But presently, down the creek a short distance, I made out a vague object lying in the shallow water near the shore.

I waded to it, through the clinging mud and crawling vines. It was Jim Braxton, and he was dead. It was not the wound in his head which had killed him. Probably he had struck a submerged rock when he was dragged under. But the marks of strangling fingers showed black on his throat. At the sight a nameless horror oozed out of that black swamp water and coiled itself clammily about my soul; for no human fingers ever left such marks as those.

I had seen a head rise in the water, a head that looked like that of a Negro, though the features had been indistinct in the darkness. But no man, white or black, ever possessed the fingers that had crushed the life out of Jim Braxton. The distant drum grunted as if in mockery.

I dragged the body up on the bank and left it. I could not linger longer, for the madness was foaming in my brain again, driving me with white-hot spurs. But as I climbed the bank, I found blood on the bushes, and was shaken by the implication.

I remembered the figure I had seen staggering in the flash of Braxton's gun. *She* had been there, waiting for me on the bank, then — not a spectral illusion, but the woman herself, in flesh and blood! Braxton had fired at her, and wounded her. But the wound could not have been mortal; for no corpse lay among the bushes, and the grim hypnosis that dragged me onward was unweakened. Dizzily I wondered if she could be killed by mortal weapons.

The moon had set. The starlight scarcely penetrated the interwoven branches. No more creeks barred my way, only shallow streams, through which I splashed with sweating haste. Yet I did not expect to be attacked. Twice the dweller in the depths had passed me by to attack my companion. In icy despair I knew I was being saved for a grimmer fate. Each stream I crossed might be hiding the monster that killed Jim Braxton. Those creeks were all connected in a network of winding waterways. It could follow me easily. But my horror of it was less than the horror of the jungle-born magnetism that lucked in a witch-woman's eyes.

And as I stumbled through the tangled vegetation, I heard the drum rumbling ahead of me, louder and louder, in demoniacal mockery. Then a human voice mingled with its mutter, in a long-drawn cry of horror and agony that set every fiber of me quivering with sympathy. Sweat coursed down my clammy flesh; soon my own voice might be lifted like that, under unnamable torture. But on I went, my feet moving like automatons, apart from my body, motivated by a will not my own.

The drum grew loud, and a fire glowed among the black trees. Presently, crouching among the bushes, I stared across the stretch of black water that separated me from a nightmare scene. My halting there was as compulsory as the rest of my actions had been. Vaguely I knew the stage for horror had been set, but the time for my entry upon it was not yet. When the time had come, I would receive my summons.

A low, wooded island split the black creek, connected with the shore opposite me by a narrow neck of land. At its lower end the creek split into a network of channels threading their way among hummocks and rotting logs and moss-grown, vine-tangled clumps of trees. Directly across from my refuge the shore of the island was deeply indented by an arm of open, deep black water. Bearded trees walled a small clearing, and partly hid a hut. Between the hut and the shore burned a fire that sent up weird twisting snake-tongues of green flames. Scores of black people squatted under the shadows of the overhanging branches. When the green fire lit their faces it lent them the appearance of drowned corpses.

In the midst of the glade stood a giant Negro, an awesome statue in black marble. He was clad in ragged trousers, but on his head was a band of beaten gold set with a huge red jewel, and on his feet were barbaric sandals. His features reflected titanic vitality no less than his huge body. But he was all Negro — flaring nostrils, thick lips, ebony skin. I knew I looked upon Saul Stark, the conjure man.

He was regarding something that lay in the sand before him, something dark and bulky that moaned feebly. Presently, lifting his head, he rolled out a sonorous invocation across the black waters. From the blacks huddled under the trees came a shuddering response, like a wind wailing through midnight branches. Both invocation and response were framed in an unknown tongue — a guttural, primitive language.

Again he called out, this time a curious high-pitched wail. A shuddering sigh swept the black people. All eyes were fixed on the dusky water. And presently an object rose slowly from the depths. A sudden trembling shook me. It looked like the head of a Negro. One after another it was followed by similar objects until five heads reared above the black, cypress-shadowed water. They might have been five Negroes submerged except for their heads — but I knew this was not so. There was something diabolical here. Their silence, motionlessness, their whole aspect was unnatural. From the trees came the hysterical sobbing of women, and someone whimpered a man's name.

Then Saul Stark lifted his hands, and the five heads silently sank out of sight. Like a ghostly whisper I seemed to hear the voice of the African witch: *"He puts them in the swamp!"*

Stark's deep voice rolled out across the narrow water: "And now the Dance of the Skull, to make the conjer sure!"

What had the witch said? *"Hidden among the trees you shall watch the Dance of the Skull!"*

The drum struck up again, growling and rumbling. The blacks swayed on their haunches, lifting a wordless chant. Saul Stark paced measuredly about the figure on the sand, his arms weaving cryptic patterns. Then he wheeled and faced toward the other end of the glade. By some sleight of hand he now grasped a grinning human skull, and this he cast upon the wet sand beyond the body. "Bride of Damballah!" he thundered. "The sacrifice awaits!"

There was an expectant pause; the chanting sank. All eyes were glued on the farther end of the glade. Stark stood waiting, and I saw him scowl as if puzzled. Then as he opened his mouth to repeat the call, a barbaric figure moved out of the shadows.

At the sight of her a chill shuddering shook me. For a moment she stood motionless, the firelight glinting on her gold ornaments, her head hanging on her breast. A tense silence reigned and I saw Saul Stark staring at her sharply. She seemed to be detached, somehow, standing aloof and withdrawn, head bent strangely.

Then, as if rousing herself, she began to sway with a jerky rhythm, and presently whirled into the mazes of a dance that was ancient when the ocean drowned the black kings of Atlantis. I cannot describe it. It was bestiality and diabolism set to motion, framed in a writhing, spinning whirl of posturing and gesturing that would have appalled a dancer of the Pharaohs. And that cursed skull danced with her; rattling and clashing on the sand, it bounded and spun like a live thing in time with her leaps and prancings.

But there was something amiss. I sensed it. Her arms hung limp, her drooping head swayed. Her legs bent and faltered, making her lurch drunkenly and out of time. A murmur rose from the people, and bewilderment etched Saul Stark's black countenance. For the domination of a conjer man is a thing hinged on a hair-trigger. Any trifling dislocation of formula or ritual may disrupt the whole web of his enchantment.

As for me, I felt the perspiration freeze on my flesh as I watched the grisly dance. The unseen shackles that bound me to that gyrating she-devil were strangling, crushing me. I knew she was approaching a climax, when she would summon me from my hiding-place, to wade through the black waters to the House of Damballah, to my doom.

Now she whirled to a floating stop, and when she

halted, poised on her toes, she looked toward the spot where I lay hidden, and I knw that she could see me as plainly as if I stood in the open; knew, too, somehow, that only she knew of my presence. I felt myself toppling on the edge of the abyss. She raised her head and I saw the flame of her eyes, even at that distance. Her face was lit with awful triumph. Slowly she raised her hand, and I felt my limbs begin to jerk in response to that terrible magnetism. She opened her mouth —

But from that open mouth sounded only a choking gurgle, and suddenly her lips were dyed crimson. And suddenly, without warning, her knees gave way and she pitched headlong into the sands.

And as she fell, so I too fell, sinking into the mire. Something burst in my brain with a shower of flame. And then I was crouching among the trees, weak and trembling, but with such a sense of freedom and lightness of limb as I never dreamed a man could experience. The black spell that gripped me was broken; the foul incubus lifted from my soul. It was as if light had burst upon a night blacker than African midnight.

At the fall of the girl a wild cry arose from the blacks, and they sprang up, trembling on the verge of panic. I saw their rolling white eyeballs, their bared teeth glistening in the firelight. Saul Stark had worked their primitive natures up to a pitch of madness, meaning to turn this frenzy, at the proper time, into a fury of battle. It could as easily turn into a hysteria of terror. Stark shouted sharply at them.

But just then the girl in a last convulsion, rolled over on the wet sand, and the firelight shone on a round hole between her breasts, which still oozed crimson. Jim Braxton's bullet had found its mark.

From the first I had felt that she was not wholly human; some black jungle spirit sired her, lending her the abysmal subhuman vitality that made her what she was. She had said that neither death nor Hell could keep her from the Dance of the Skull. And, shot through the heart and dying, she had come through the swamp from the creek where she had received her death-wound to the House of Damballah. And the Dance of the Skull had been her death dance.

Dazed as a condemned man just granted a reprieve, at first I hardly grasped the meaning of the scene that now unfolded before me.

The blacks were in a frenzy. In the sudden, and to them inexplicable, death of the sorceress they saw a fearsome portent. They had no way of knowing that she was dying when she entered the glade. To them, their prophetess and priestess had been struck down under their very eyes, by an invisible death. This was magic blacker than Saul Stark's wizardry — and obviously hostile to them.

Like fear-maddened cattle they stampeded. Howling, screaming, tearing at one another they blundered through the trees, heading for the neck of land and the shore beyond. Saul Stark stood transfixed, heedless of them as he stared down at the brown girl, dead at last. And suddenly I came to myself, and with my awakened manhood came cold fury and the lust to kill. I drew a gun, and aiming in the uncertain fire-light, pulled the trigger. Only a click answered me. The powder in the cap-and-ball pistols was wet.

Saul Stark lifted his head and licked his lips. The sounds of flight faded in the distance, and he stood alone in the glade. His eyes rolled whitely toward the black woods around him. He bent, grasped the man-like object that lay on the sand, and dragged it into the hut. The instant he vanished I started toward the island, wading through the narrow channels at the lower end. I had almost reached the shore when a mass of driftwood gave way with me and I slid into a deep hole.

Instantly the water swirled about me, and a head rose beside me; a dim face was close to mine — the face of a Negro — *the face of Tunk Bixby.* But now it was inhuman; as expressionless and soulless as that of a catfish; the face of a being no longer human, and no longer mindful of its human origin.

Slimy, misshapen fingers gripped my throat, and I drove my knife into that sagging mouth. The features vanished in a wave of blood; mutely the thing sank out of sight, and I hauled myself up the bank, under the thick bushes.

Stark had run from his hut, a pistol in his hand. He was staring wildly about, alarmed by the noise he had heard, but I knew he could not see me. His ashy skin glistened with perspiration. He who had ruled by fear was now ruled by fear. He feared the unknown hand that had slain his mistress; feared the Negroes who had fled from him; feared the abysmal swamp which had sheltered him, and the monstrosities he had created. He lifted a weird call that quavered with panic. He called again as only four heads broke the water, but he called in vain.

But the four heads began to move toward the shore and the man who stood there. He shot them one after another. They made no effort to avoid the bullets. They came straight on, sinking one by one. He had fired six shots before the last head vanished. The shots drowned the sounds of my approach. I was close behind him when he turned at last.

I know he knew me; recognition flooded his face and fear went with it, at the knowledge that he had a human being to deal with. With a scream he hurled his empty pistol at me and rushed after it with a lifted knife.

I ducked, parried his lunge and countered with a thrust that bit deep into his ribs. He caught my wrist and I gripped his, and there we strained, breast to breast. His eyes were like a mad dog's in the starlight, his muscles like steel cords.

I ground my heel down on his bare foot, crushing the instep. He howled and lost balance, and I tore my knife hand free and stabbed him in the belly. Blood spurted and he dragged me down with him. I jerked loose and rose, just as he pulled himself up on his elbow and hurled his knife. It sang past my ear, and I stamped on his breast. His ribs caved in under my heel. In a red killing-haze I knelt, jerked back his head and cut his throat from ear to ear.

There was a pouch of dry powder in his belt. Before I moved further I reloaded my pistols. Then I went into the hut with a torch. And there I understood the doom the brown witch had meant for me. Tope Sorley lay moaning on a bunk. The transmutation that was to make him a mindless, soulless semi-human dweller in the water was not complete, but his mind was gone. Some of the physical changes had been made — by what godless sorcery out of Africa's black abyss I have no wish to know. His body was rounded and elongated, his legs dwarfed; his feet were flattened and broadened, his fingers horribly long, and *webbed*. His neck was inches longer than it should be. His features were not altered, but the expression was no more human than that of a great fish. And there, but for the loyalty of Jim Braxton, lay Kirby Buckner. I placed my pistol muzzle against Tope's head in grim mercy and pulled the trigger.

And so the nightmare closed, and I would not drag out the grisly narration. The white people of Canaan never found anything on the island except the bodies of Saul Stark and the brown woman. They think to this day that a swamp Negro killed Jim Braxton, after he had killed the brown woman, and that I broke up the threatening uprising by killing Saul Stark. I let them think it. They will never know the shapes the black water of Tularoosa hides. That is a secret I share with the cowed and terror-haunted black people of Goshen and of it neither they not I have ever spoken.

ALWAYS COMES EVENING

The Pantagraph, August 1936

*Riding down the road at evening with the stars for steed and
      shoon
I have heard an old man singing underneath a copper moon;
"God, who gemmed with topaz twilights, opal portals of the day,
"On your amaranthine mountains, why make human souls of clay?*

*"For I rode the moon-mare's horses in the glory of my youth,
"Wrestled with the hills at sunset—till I met brass-tinctured
       Truth.
"Till I saw the temples topple, till I saw the idols reel,
"Till my brain had turned to iron, and my heart had turned to steel.*

*"Satan, Satan, brother Satan, fill my soul with frozen fire;
"Feed with hearts of rose-white women ashes of my dead desire.
"For my road runs out in thistles and my dreams have turned to
       dust.
"And my pinions fade and falter to the raven-wings of rust.*

*"Truth has smitten me with arrows and her hand is in my hair—
"Youth, she hides in yonder mountains—go and seek her, if you
       dare!
"Work your magic, brother Satan, fill my brain with fiery spells.
"Satan, Satan, brother Satan, I have known your fiercest Hells."*

*Riding down the road at evening when the wind was on the sea,
I have heard an old man singing, and he sang most drearily.
Strange to hear, when dark lakes shimmer to the wailing of the
       loon,
Amethystine Homer singing under evening's copper moon.*

RED NALS

Weird Tales: **Part 1, July 1936;
Part 2, August-September 1936;
Part 3, October 1936**

1. *The Skull on the Crag*

The woman on the horse reined in her weary steed. It stood with its legs wide-braced, its head drooping, as if it found even the weight of the gold-tassled, red-leather bridle too heavy. The woman drew a booted foot out of the silver stirrup and swung down from the gilt-worked saddle. She made the reins fast to the fork of a sapling, and turned about, hands on her hips, to survey her surroundings.

They were not inviting. Giant trees hemmed in the small pool where her horse had just drunk. Clumps of undergrowth limited the vision that quested under the somber twilight of the lofty archs formed by intertwining branches. The woman shivered with a twitch of her magnificent shoulders, and then cursed.

She was tall, full-bosomed and large-limbed, with compact shoulders. Her whole figure reflected an unusual strength, without detracting from the femininity of her appearance. She was all woman, in spite of her bearing and her garments. The latter were incongruous, in view of her present environs. Instead of a skirt she wore short, wide-legged silk breeches, which ceased a hand's breadth short of her knees, and were upheld by a wide silken sash worn as a girdle. Flaring-topped boots of soft leather came almost to her knees, and a low-necked, wide-collared, wide-sleeved silk shirt completed her costume. On one shapely hip she wore a straight double-edged sword, and on the other a long dirk. Her unruly golden hair, cut square at her shoulders, was confined by a band of crimson satin.

Against the background of somber, primitive forest she posed with an unconscious picturesqueness, bizarre and out of place. She should have been posed against a background of sea-clouds, painted masts, and wheeling gulls. There was the color of the sea in her wide eyes. And that was at it should have been, because this was Valeria of the Red Brotherhood, whose deeds are celebrated in song and ballad wherever seafarers gather.

She strove to pierce the sullen green roof of the arched branches and see the sky which presumably lay above it, but presently gave it up with a muttered oath.

Leaving her horse tied, she strode off toward the east, glancing back toward the pool from time to time in order to fix her route in her mind. The silence of the forest depressed her. No birds sang in the lofty boughs, nor did any rustling in the bushes indicate the presence of small animals. For leagues she had traveled in a realm of brooding stillness, broken only by the sounds of her own flight.

She had slaked her thirst at the pool, but now felt the gnawings of hunger and began looking about for some of the fruit on which she had sustained herself since exhausting the food originally in her saddle-bags.

Ahead of her, presently, she saw an outcropping of dark, flint-like rock that sloped upward into what looked like a rugged crag rising among the trees. Its summit was lost to view amidst a cloud of encircling leaves. Perhaps its peak rose above the treetops, and from it she could see what lay beyond — if, indeed, anything lay beyond but more of this apparently illimitable forest through which she had ridden for so many days.

A narrow ridge formed a natural ramp that led up the steep face of the crag. After she had ascended some fifty feet, she came to the belt of leaves that surrounded the rock. The trunks of the trees did not crowd close to the crag, but the ends of their lower branches extended about it, veiling it with their foliage. She groped on in leafy obscurity, not able to see either above or below her; but presently she glimpsed blue sky, and a moment later came out in the clear, hot sunlight and saw the forest roof stretching away under her feet.

She was standing on a broad shelf which was about even with the treetops, and from it rose a spire-like jut that was the ultimate peak of the crag she had climbed. But something else caught her attention at the moment. Her foot had struck something in the litter of blown dead leaves which carpeted the shelf. She kicked them aside and looked down on the skeleton of a man. She ran an experienced eye over the bleached frame, but saw no broken bones nor any sign of violence. The man must have died a natural death; though why he should have climbed a tall crag to die she could not imagine.

She scrambled up to the summit of the spire and looked toward the horizons. The forest roof — which looked like a floor from her vantage point — was just as impenetrable as from below. She could not even see the pool by which she had left her horse. She glanced northward, in the direction from which she had come. She saw only the rolling green ocean stretching away and away, with just a vague blue line in the distance to hint of the hill-range she had crossed days before, to plunge into this leafy waste.

West and east the view was the same; though the blue hill-line was lacking in those directions. But when she turned her eyes southward she stiffened and caught her breath. A mile away in that direction the forest thinned out and ceased abruptly, giving way to a cactus-dotted plain. And in the midst of that plain rose the walls and towers of a city. Valeria swore in amazement. This passed belief. She would not have been surprised to sight human habitations of another sort — the beehive-shaped huts of the black people, or the cliff-dwellings of the mysterious brown race which legends declared inhabited some country of this unexplored region. But it was a startling experience to come upon a walled city here so many long weeks' march from the nearest outposts of any sort of civilization.

Her hands tiring from clinging to the spire-like pinnacle, she let herself down on the shelf, frowning in indecision. She had come far — from the camp of the mercenaries by the border town of Sukhmet amidst the level grasslands, where desperate adventurers of many races guard the Stygian frontier against the raids that come up like a red wave from Darfar. Her flight had been blind, into a country of which she was wholly ignorant. And now she wavered between an urge to ride directly to that city in the plain, and the instinct of caution which prompted her to skirt it widely and continue her solitary flight.

Her thoughts were scattered by the rustling of the leaves below her. She wheeled catlike, snatched at her sword; and then she froze motionless, staring wide-eyed at the man before her.

He was almost a giant in stature, muscles rippling smoothly under his skin which the sun had burned brown. His garb was similar to hers, except that he wore a broad leather belt instead of a girdle. Broadsword and poniard hung from his belt.

"Conan, the Cimmerian!" ejaculated the woman. "What are *you* doing on my trail?"

He grinned hardly, and his fierce blue eyes burned with a light any woman could understand as they ran over her magnificent figure, lingering on the swell of her splendid breasts beneath the light shirt, and the clear white flesh displayed between breeches and boot-tops.

"Don't you know?" he laughed. "Haven't I made my admiration for you plain ever since I first saw you?"

"A stallion could have made it no plainer," she answered disdainfully. "But I never expected to encounter you so far from the ale-barrels and meat-pots of Sukhmet. Did you really follow me from Zarallo's camp, or were you whipped forth for a rogue?"

He laughed at her insolence and flexed his mighty biceps.

"You know Zarallo didn't have enough knaves to whip me out of camp," he grinned. "Of course I followed you. Lucky thing for you, too, wench! When you knifed that Stygian officer, you forfeited Zarallo's favor and protection, and you outlawed yourself with the Stygians."

"I know it," she replied sullenly. "But what else could I do? You know what my provocation was."

"Sure," he agreed. "If I'd been there, I'd have knifed him myself. But if a woman must live in the war-camps of men, she can expect such things."

Valeria stamped her booted foot and swore.

"Why won't men let me live a man's life?"

"That's obvious!" Again his eager eyes devoured her. "But you were wise to run away. The Stygians would have had you skinned. That officer's brother followed you; faster than you thought, I don't doubt. He wasn't far behind you when I caught up with him. His horse was better than yours. He'd have caught you and cut your throat within a few more miles."

"Well?" she demanded.

"Well what?" He seemed puzzled.

"What of the Stygian?"

"Why, what do you suppose?" he returned impatiently. "I killed him, of course, and left his carcass for the vultures. That delayed me, though, and I almost lost your trail when you crossed the rocky spurs of the hills. Otherwise I'd have caught up with you long ago."

"And now you think you'll drag me back to Zarallo's camp?" she sneered.

"Don't talk like a fool," he grunted. "Come, girl, don't be such a spitfire. I'm not like that Stygian you knifed, and you know it."

"A penniless vagabond," she taunted.

He laughed at her.

"What do you call yourself? You haven't enough money to buy a new seat for your breeches. Your disdain doesn't deceive me. You know I've commanded bigger ships and more men than you ever did in your life. As for being penniless — what rover isn't, most of the time? I've squandered enough gold in the seaports of the world to fill a galleon. You know that, too."

"Where are the fine ships and the bold lads you commanded, now?" she sneered.

"At the bottom of the sea, mostly," he replied cheerfully. "The Zingarans sank my last ship off the Shemite shore — that's why I joined Zarallo's Free Companions. But I saw I'd been stung when we marched to the Darfar border. The pay was poor and the wine was sour, and I don't like black women. And that's the only kind that came to our camp at Sukhmet — rings in their noses and their teeth filed — bah! Why did you join Zarallo? Sukhmet's a long way from salt water."

"Red Ortho wanted to make me his mistress," she answered sullenly. "I jumped overboard one night and swam ashore when we were anchored off the Kushite coast. Off Zabhela, it was. There was a Shemite trader told me that Zarallo had brought his Free Companies south to guard the Darfar border. No better employment offered. I joined an east-bound caravan and eventually came to Sukhmet."

"It was madness to plunge southward as you did," commented Conan, "but it was wise, too, for Zarallo's patrols never thought to look for you in this direction. Only the brother of the man you killed happened to strike your trail."

"And now what do you intend doing?" she demanded.

"Turn west," he answered. "I've been this far south, but not this far east. Many days' traveling to the west will bring us to the open savannas, where the black tribes graze their cattle. I have friends among them. We'll get to the coast and find a ship.

I'm sick of the jungle."

"Then be on your way," she advised. "I have other plans."

"Don't be a fool!" He showed irritation for the first time. "You can't keep on wandering through this forest."

"I can if I choose."

"But what do you intend doing?"

"That's none of your affair," she snapped.

"Yes, it is," he answered calmly. "Do you think I've followed you this far, to turn around and ride off empty-handed? Be sensible, wench. I'm not going to harm you."

He stepped toward her, and she sprang back, whipping out her sword.

"Keep back, you barbarian dog! I'll spit you like a roast pig!"

He halted, reluctantly, and demanded: "Do you want me to take that toy away from you and spank you with it?"

"Words! Nothing but words!" she mocked, lights like the gleam of the sun on blue water dancing in her reckless eyes.

He knew it was the truth. No living man could disarm Valeria of the Brotherhood with his bare hands. He scowled, his sensations a tangle of conflicting emotions. He was angry, yet he was amused and filled with admiration for her spirit. He burned with eagerness to seize that splendid figure and crush it in his iron arms, yet he greatly desired not to hurt the girl. He was torn between a desire to shake her soundly, and a desire to caress her. He knew if he came any nearer her sword would be sheathed in his heart. He had seen Valeria kill too many men in border forays and tavern brawls to have any illusions about her. He knew she was as quick and ferocious as a tigress. He could draw his broadsword and disarm her, beat the blade out of her hand, but the thought of drawing a sword on a woman, even without intent of injury, was extremely repugnant to him.

"Blast your soul, you hussy!" he exclaimed in exasperation. "I'm going to take off your —"

He started toward her, his angry passion making him reckless, and she poised herself for a deadly thrust. Then came a startling interruption to a scene at once ludicrous and perilous.

"What's that?"

It was Valeria who exclaimed, but they both started violently, and Conan wheeled like a cat, his great sword flashing into his hand. Back in the forest had burst forth an appalling medley of screams — the screams of horses in terror and agony. Mingled with their screams there came the snap of splintering bones.

"Lions are slaying the horses!" cried Valeria.

"Lions, nothing!" snorted Conan, his eyes blazing. "Did you hear a lion roar? Neither did I! Listen to those bones snap — not even a lion could make that much noise killing a horse."

He hurried down the natural ramp and she followed, their personal feud forgotten in the adventurers' instinct to unite against common peril. The screams had ceased when they worked their way downward through the green veil of leaves that brushed the rock.

"I found your horse tied by the pool back there," he muttered, treading so noiselessly that she no longer wondered how he had surprized her on the crag. "I tied mine beside it and followed the tracks of your boots. Watch, now!"

They had emerged from the belt of leaves, and stared down into the lower reaches of the forest. Above them the green roof spread its dusky canopy. Below them the sunlight filtered in just enough to make a jade-tinted twilight. The giant trunks of trees less than a hundred yards away looked dim and ghostly.

"The horses should be beyond that thicket, over there," whispered Conan, and his voice might have been a breeze moving through the branches. "Listen!"

Valeria had already heard, and a chill crept through her veins; so she unconsciously laid her white hand on her companion's muscular brown arm. From beyond the thicket came the noisy crunching of bones and the loud rending of flesh, together with the grinding, slobbering sounds of a horrible feast.

"Lions wouldn't make that noise," whispered Conan. "Something's eating our horses, but it's not a lion — Crom!"

The noise stopped suddenly, and Conan swore

softly. A suddenly risen breeze was blowing from them directly toward the spot where the unseen slayer was hidden.

"Here it comes!" muttered Conan, half-lifting his sword.

The thicket was violently agitated, and Valeria clutched Conan's arm hard. Ignorant of jungle-lore, she yet knew that no animal she had ever seen could have shaken the tall brush like that.

"It must be as big as an elephant," muttered Conan, echoing her thought. "What the devil —" His voice trailed away in stunned silence.

Through the thicket was thrust a head of nightmare and lunacy. Grinning jaws bared rows of dripping yellow tusks; above the yawning mouth wrinkled a saurian-like snout. Huge eyes, like those of a python a thousand times magnified, stared unwinkingly at the petrified humans clinging to the rock above it. Blood smeared the scaly, flabby lips and dripped from the huge mouth.

The head, bigger than that of a crocodile, was further extended on a long scaled neck on which stood up rows of serrated spikes, and after it, crushing down the briars and saplings, waddled the body of a titan, a gigantic, barrel-bellied torso on absurdly short legs. The whitish belly almost raked the ground, while the serrated backbone rose higher than Conan could have reached on tiptoe. A long spiked tail, like that of a gargantuan scorpion, trailed out behind.

"Back up the crag, quick!" snapped Conan, thrusting the girl behind him. "I don't think he can climb, but he can stand on his hind legs and reach us —"

With a snapping and rending of bushes and saplings the monster came hurtling through the thickets, and they fled up the rock before him like leaves blown before a wind. As Valeria plunged into the leafy screen a backward glance showed her the titan rearing up fearsomely on his massive hinder legs, even as Conan had predicted. The sight sent panic racing through her. As he reared, the beast seemed more gigantic than ever; his snouted head towered among the trees. Then Conan's iron hand closed on her wrist and she was jerked headlong into the blinding welter of the leaves, and out again into the hot sunshine above, just as the monster fell forward with his front feet on the crag with an impact that made the rock vibrate.

Behind the fugitives the huge head crashed through the twigs, and they looked down for a horrifying instant at the nightmare visage framed among the green leaves, eyes flaming, jaws gaping. Then the giant tusks clashed together futilely, and after that the head was withdrawn, vanishing from their sight as if it had sunk in a pool.

Peering down through broken branches that scraped the rock, they saw it squatting on its haunches at the foot of the crag, staring unblinkingly up at them.

Valeria shuddered.

"How long do you suppose he'll crouch there?"

Conan kicked the skull on the leaf-strewn shelf.

"That fellow must have climbed up here to escape him, or one like him. He must have died of starvation. There are no bones broken. That thing must be a dragon, such as the black people speak of in their legends. If so, it won't leave here until we're both dead."

Valeria looked at him blankly, her resentment forgotten. She fought down a surging of panic. She had proved her reckless courage a thousand times in wild battles on sea and land, on the blood-slippery decks of burning warships, in the storming of walled cities, and on the trampled sandy beaches where the desperate men of the Red Brotherhood bathed their knives in one another's blood in their fights for leadership. But the prospect now confronting her congealed her blood. A cutlass stroke in the heat of battle was nothing; but to sit idle and helpless on a bare rock until she perished of starvation, besieged by a monstrous survival of an elder age — the thought sent panic throbbing through her brain.

"He must leave to eat and drink," she said helplessly.

"He won't have to go far to do either," Conan pointed out. "He's just gorged on horse-meat and, like a real snake, he can go for a long time without eating or drinking again. But he doesn't sleep after eating, like a real snake, it seems. Anyway, he can't climb this crag."

Conan spoke imperturbably. He was a barbarian,

and the terrible patience of the wilderness and its children was as much a part of him as his lusts and rages. He could endure a situation like this with a coolness impossible to a civilized person.

"Can't we get into the trees and get away, traveling like apes through the branches?" she asked desperately.

He shook his head. "I thought of that. The branches that touch the crag down there are too light. They'd break with our weight. Besides, I have an idea that devil could tear up any tree around here by its roots."

"Well, are we going to sit here on our rumps until we starve, like that?" she cried furiously, kicking the skull clattering across the ledge. "I won't do it! I'll go down there and cut his damned head off —"

Conan had seated himself on a rocky projection at the foot of the spire. He looked up with a glint of admiration at her blazing eyes and tense, quivering figure, but, realizing that she was in just the mood for any madness, he let none of his admiration sound in his voice.

"Sit down," he grunted, catching her by her wrist and pulling her down on his knee. She was too surprised to resist as he took her sword from her hand and shoved it back in its sheath. "Sit still and calm down. You'd only break your steel on his scales. He'd gobble you up at one gulp, or smash you like an egg with that spiked tail of his. We'll get out of this jam some way, but we shan't do it by getting chewed up and swallowed."

She made no reply, nor did she seek to repulse his arm from about her waist. She was frightened, and the sensation was new to Valeria of the Red Brotherhood. So she sat on her companion's — or captor's — knee with a docility that would have amazed Zarallo, who had anathematized her as a she-devil out of Hell's seraglio.

Conan played idly with her curly yellow locks, seemingly intent only upon his conquest. Neither the skeleton at his feet nor the monster crouching below disturbed his mind or dulled the edge of his interest.

The girl's restless eyes, roving the leaves below them, discovered splashes of color among the green. It was fruit, large, darkly crimson globes suspended from the boughs of a tree whose broad leaves were a peculiarly rich and vivid green. She became aware of both thirst and hunger, though thirst had not assailed her until she knew she could not descend from the crag to find food and water.

"We need not starve," she said. "There is fruit we can reach."

Conan glanced where she pointed.

"If we ate that we wouldn't need the bite of a dragon," he grunted. "That's what the black people of Kush call the Apples of Derketa. Derketa is the Queen of the Dead. Drink a little of that juice, or spill it on your flesh, and you'd be dead before you could tumble to the foot of this crag."

"Oh!"

She lapsed into dismayed silence. There seemed

no way out of their predicament, she reflected gloomily. She saw no way of escape, and Conan seemed to be concerned only with her supple waist and curly tresses. If he was trying to formulate a plan of escape he did not show it.

"If you'll take your hands off me long enough to climb up on that peak," she said presently, "you'll see something that will surprise you."

He cast her a questioning glance, then obeyed with a shrug of his massive shoulders. Clinging to the spire-like pinnacle, he stared out over the forest roof.

He stood a long moment in silence, posed like a bronze statue on the rock.

"It's a walled city, right enough," he muttered presently. "Was that where you were going, when you tried to send me off alone to the coast?"

"I saw it before you came. I knew nothing of it when I left Sukhmet."

"Who'd have thought to find a city here? I don't believe the Stygians ever penetrated this far. Could black people build a city like that? I see no herds on the plain, no signs of cultivation, or people moving about."

"How can you hope to see all that, at this distance?" she demanded.

He shrugged his shoulders and dropped down on the shelf.

"Well, the folk of the city can't help us just now. And they might not, if they could. The people of the Black Countries are generally hostile to strangers.

Probably stick us full of spears —"

He stopped short and stood silent, as if he had forgotten what he was saying, frowning down at the crimson spheres gleaming among the leaves.

"Spears!" he muttered. "What a blasted fool I am not to have thought of that before! That shows what a pretty woman does to a man's mind."

"What are you talking about?" she inquired.

Without answering her question, he descended to the belt of leaves and looked down through them. The great brute squatted below, watching the crag with the frightful patience of the reptile folk. So might one of his breed have glared up at their troglodyte ancestors, treed on a high-flung rock, in the dim dawn ages. Conan cursed him without heat, and began cutting branches, reaching out and severing them as far from the end as he could reach. The agitation of the leaves made the monster restless. He rose from his haunches and lashed his hideous tail, snapping off saplings as if they had been toothpicks. Conan watched him warily from the corner of his eye, and just as Valeria believed the dragon was about to hurl himself up the crag again, the Cimmerian drew back and climbed up to the ledge with the branches he had cut. There were three of these, slender shafts about seven feet long, but not larger than his thumb. He had also cut several strands of tough, thin vine.

"Branches too light for spear-hafts, and creepers no thicker than cords," he remarked, indicating the foliage about the crag. "It won't hold our weight — but there's strength in union. That's what the Aquilonian renegades used to tell us Cimmerians when they came into the hills to raise an army to invade their own country. But we always fight by clans and tribes."

"What the devil has that got to do with those sticks?" she demanded.

"You wait and see."

Gathering the sticks in a compact bundle, he wedged his poniard hilt between them at one end. Then with the vines he bound them together, and when he had completed his task, he had a spear of no small strength, with a sturdy shaft seven feet in length.

"What good will that do?" she demanded. "You told me that a blade couldn't pierce his scales —"

"He hasn't got scales all over him," answered Conan. "There's more than one way of skinning a panther."

Moving down to the edge of the leaves, he reached the spear up and carefully thrust the blade through one of the Apples of Derketa, drawing aside to avoid the darkly purple drops that dripped from the pierced fruit. Presently he withdrew the blade and showed her the blue steel stained a dull purplish crimson.

"I don't know whether it will do the job or not," quoth he. "There's enough poison there to kill an elephant, but — well, we'll see."

Valeria was close behind him as he let himself down among the leaves. Cautiously holding the poisoned pike away from him, he thrust his head through the branches and addressed the monster.

"What are you waiting down there for, you misbegotten offspring of questionable parents?" was one of his more printable queries. "Stick your ugly head up here again, you long-necked brute — or do you want me to come down there and kick you loose from your illegitimate spine?"

There was more of it — some of it couched in eloquence that made Valeria stare, in spite of her profane education among the seafarers. And it had its effect on the monster. Just as the incessant yapping of a dog worries and enrages more constitutionally silent animals, so the clamorous voice of a man rouses fear in some bestial bosoms and insane rage in others. Suddenly and with appalling quickness, the mastodonic brute reared up on its mighty hind legs and elongated its neck and body in a furious effort to reach this vociferous pigmy whose clamor was disturbing the primeval silence of its ancient realm.

But Conan had judged his distance with precision. Some five feet below him the mighty head crashed terribly but futilely through the leaves. And as the monstrous mouth gaped like that of a great snake, Conan drove his spear into the red angle of the jawbone hinge. He struck downward with all the strength of both arms, driving the long poniard blade to the hilt in flesh, sinew and bone.

Instantly the jaws clashed convulsively together, severing the triple-pieced shaft and almost precipitating Conan from his perch. He would have fallen but for the girl behind him, who caught his sword-belt in a desperate grasp. He clutched at a rocky projection, and grinned his thanks back at her.

Down on the ground the monster was wallowing like a dog with pepper in its eyes. He shook his head from side to side, pawed at it, and opened his mouth repeatedly to its widest extent. Presently he got a huge front foot on the stump of the shaft and managed to tear the blade out. Then he threw up his head, jaws wide and spouting blood, and glared up at the crag with such concentrated and intelligent fury that Valeria trembled and drew her sword. The scales along his back and flanks turned from rusty brown to a dull lurid red. Most horribly the monster's silence was broken. The sounds that issued from his blood-streaming jaws did not sound like anything that could have been produced by an earthly creation.

With harsh, grating roars, the dragon hurled himself at the crag that was the citadel of his enemies. Again and again his mighty head crashed upward through the branches, snapping vainly on empty air. He hurled his full ponderous weight against the rock until it vibrated from base to crest. And rearing upright he gripped it with his front legs like a man and tried to tear it up by the roots, as if it had been a tree.

This exhibition of primordial fury chilled the blood in Valeria's veins, but Conan was too close to the primitive himself to feel anything but a comprehending interest. To the barbarian, no such gulf existed between himself and other men, and the animals, as existed in the conception of Valeria. The monster below them, to Conan, was merely a form of life differing from himself mainly in physical shape. He attributed to it characteristics similar to his own, and saw in its wrath a counterpart of his rages, in its roars and bellowings merely reptilian equivalents to the curses he had bestowed upon it. Feeling a kinship with all wild things, even dragons, it was impossible for him to experience the sick horror which assailed Valeria at the sight of the brute's ferocity.

He sat watching it tranquilly, and pointed out the various changes that were taking place in its voice and actions.

"The poison's taking hold," he said with conviction.

"I don't believe it." To Valeria it seemed preposterous to suppose that anything, however lethal, could have any effect on that mountain of muscle and fury.

"There's pain in his voice," declared Conan. "First he was merely angry because of the stinging in his jaw. Now he feels the bite of the poison. Look! He's staggering. He'll be blind in a few more minutes. What did I tell you?"

For suddenly the dragon had lurched about and went crashing off through the bushes.

"Is he running away?" inquired Valeria uneasily.

"He's making for the pool!" Conan sprang up, galvanized into swift activity. "The poison makes him thirsty. Come on! He'll be blind in a few moments, but he can smell his way back to the foot of the crag, and if our scent's here still, he'll sit there until he dies. And others of his kind may come at his cries. Let's go!"

"Down there?" Valeria was aghast.

"Sure! We'll make for the city! They may cut our heads off there, but it's our only chance. We may run into a thousand more dragons on the way, but it's sure death to stay here. If we wait until he dies, we may have a dozen more to deal with. After me, in a hurry!"

He went down the ramp as swiftly as an ape, pausing only to aid his less agile companion, who, until she saw the Cimmerian climb, had fancied herself the equal of any man in the rigging of a ship or on the sheer face of a cliff.

They descended into the gloom below the branches and slid to the ground silently, though Valeria felt as if the pounding of her heart must surely be heard from far away. A noisy gurgling and lapping beyond the dense thicket indicated that the dragon was drinking at the pool.

"As soon as his belly is full he'll be back," muttered Conan. "It may take hours for the poison to kill him — if it does at all."

Somewhere beyond the forest the sun was sinking to the horizon. The forest was a misty twilight place of black shadows and dim vistas. Conan gripped Valeria's wrist and glided away from the foot of the crag. He made less noise than a breeze blowing among the tree-trunks, but Valeria felt as if her soft boots were betraying their flight to all the forest.

"I don't think he can follow a trail," muttered Conan. "But if a wind blew our body-scent to him, he could smell us out."

"Mitra, grant that the wind blow not!" Valeria breathed.

Her face was a pallid oval in the gloom. She gripped her sword in her free hand, but the feel of the shagreen-bound hilt inspired only a feeling of helplessness in her.

They were still some distance from the edge of the forest when they heard a snapping and crashing behind them. Valeria bit her lip to check a cry.

"He's on our trail!" she whispered fiercely.

Conan shook his head.

"He didn't smell us at the rock, and he's blundering about through the forest trying to pick up our scent. Come on! It's the city or nothing now! He could tear down any tree we'd climb. If only the wind stays down —"

They stole on until the trees began to thin out ahead of them. Behind them the forest was a black impenetrable ocean of shadows. The ominous crackling still sounded behind them, as the dragon blundered in his erratic course.

"There's the plain ahead," breathed Valeria. "A little more and we'll —"

"Crom!" swore Conan.

"Mitra!" whispered Valeria.

Out of the south a wind had sprung up.

It blew over them directly into the black forest behind them. Instantly a horrible roar shook the woods. The aimless snapping and crackling of the bushes changed to a sustained crashing as the dragon came like a hurricane straight toward the spot from which the scent of his enemies was wafted.

"Run!" snarled Conan, his eyes blazing like those of a trapped wolf. "It's all we can do!"

Sailor's boots are not made for sprinting, and the life of a pirate does not train one for a runner. Within a hundred yards Valeria was panting and reeling in her gait, and behind them the crashing gave way to a rolling thunder as the monster broke out of the thickets and into the more open ground.

Conan's iron arm about the woman's waist half-lifted her; her feet scarcely touched the earth as she was borne along at a speed she could never have attained herself. If he could keep out of the beast's way for a bit, perhaps that betraying wind would shift — but the wind held, and a quick glance over his shoulder showed Conan that the monster was almost upon them, coming like a war-galley in front of a hurricane. He thrust Valeria from him with a force that sent her reeling a dozen feet to fall in a crumpled heap at the foot of the nearest tree, and the Cimmerian wheeled in the path of the thundering titan.

Convinced that his death was upon him, the Cimmerian acted according to his instinct, and hurled himself full at the awful face that was bearing down on him. He leaped, slashing like a wildcat, felt his sword cut deep into the scales that sheathed the mighty snout — and then a terrific impact knocked him rolling and tumbling for fifty feet with all the wind and half the life battered out of him.

How the stunned Cimmerian regained his feet, not even he could have ever told. But the only thought that filled his brain was of the woman lying dazed and helpless almost in the path of the hurtling fiend, and before the breath came whistling back into his gullet he was standing over her with his sword in his hand.

She lay where he had thrown her, but she was struggling to a sitting posture. Neither tearing tusks nor trampling feet had touched her. It had been a shoulder or front leg that struck Conan, and blind monster rushed on, forgetting the victims whose scent it had been following, in the sudden agony of its death throes. Headlong on its course it thundered until its low-hung head crashed into a gigantic tree in its path. The impact tore the tree up by the roots and must have dashed the brains from the misshapen skull. Tree and monster fell together, and the dazed humans saw the branches and leaves shaken by the convulsions of the creature they covered — and then grow quiet.

Conan lifted Valeria to her feet and together they started away at a reeling run. A few moments later they emerged into the still twilight of the treeless plain.

Conan paused an instant and glanced back at the ebon fastness behind them. Not a leaf stirred, nor a bird chirped. It stood as silent as it must have stood before Man was created.

"Come on," muttered Conan, taking his companion's hand. "It's touch and go now. If more dragons come out of the woods after us —"

He did not have to finish the sentence.

The city looked very far away across the plain, farther than it had looked from the crag. Valeria's heart hammered until she felt as if it would strangle her. At every step she expected to hear the crashing of the bushes and see another colossal nightmare bearing down upon them. But nothing disturbed the silence of the thickets.

With the first mile between them and the woods, Valeria breathed more easily. Her buoyant self-confidence began to thaw out again. The sun had set and darkness was gathering over the plain, lightened a little by the stars that made stunted ghosts out of the cactus growths.

"No cattle, no plowed fields," muttered Conan. "How do these people live?"

"Perhaps the cattle are in pens for the night," suggested Valeria, "and the fields and grazing-pastures are on the other side of the city."

"Maybe," he grunted. "I didn't see any from the crag, though."

The moon came up behind the city, etching walls and towers blackly in the yellow glow. Valeria shivered. Black against the moon the strange city had a somber, sinister look.

Perhaps something of the same feeling occurred to Conan, for he stopped, glanced about him, and grunted: "We'll stop here. No use coming to their gates in the night. They probably wouldn't let us in. Besides, we need rest, and we don't know how they'll receive us. A few hours' sleep will put us in better shape to fight or run."

He led the way to a bed of cactus which grew in a circle — a phenomenon common to the southern desert. With his sword he chopped an opening, and motioned Valeria to enter.

"We'll be safe from the snakes here, anyhow."

She glanced fearfully back toward the black line that indicated the forest some six miles away.

"Suppose a dragon comes out of the woods?"

"We'll keep watch," he answered, though he made no suggestion as to what they would do in such an event. He was staring at the city, a few miles away. Not a light shone from spire or tower. A great black mass of mystery, it reared cryptically against the moonlit sky.

"Lie down and sleep. I'll keep the first watch."

She hesitated, glancing at him uncertainly, but he sat down cross-legged in the opening, facing toward the plain, his sword across his knees, his back to her. Without further comment she lay down on the sand inside the spiky circle.

"Wake me when the moon is at its zenith," she directed.

He did not reply nor look toward her. Her last impression, as she sank into slumber, was of his muscular figure, immobile as a statue hewn out of bronze, outlined against the low-hanging stars.

2. *By the Blaze of the Fire Jewels*

Valeria awoke with a start, to the realization that a grey dawn was stealing over the plain.

She sat up, rubbing her eyes. Conan squatted beside the cactus, cutting off the thick pears and dexterously twitching out the spikes.

"You didn't awake me," she accused. "You let me sleep all night!"

"You were tired," he answered. "Your posterior must have been sore, too, after that long ride. You pirates aren't used to horseback."

"What about yourself?" she retorted.

"I was a *kozak* before I was a pirate," he answered. "They live in the saddle. I snatch naps like a panther watching beside the trail for a deer to come by. My ears keep watch while my eyes sleep."

And indeed the giant barbarian seemed as much refreshed as if he had slept the whole night on a golden bed. Having removed the thorns, and peeled off the tough skin, he handed the girl a thick, juicy cactus leaf.

"Sink your teeth in that pear. It's food and drink to a desert man. I was a chief of the Zuagirs once — desert men who live by plundering the caravans."

"Is there anything you haven't done?" inquired the girl, half in derision and half in fascination.

"I've never been king of a Hyborian kingdom," he grinned, taking an enormous mouthful of cactus. "But I've dreamed of being even that. I may be too, someday. Why shouldn't I?"

She shook her head in wonder at his calm audacity, and fell to devouring her pear. She found it not unpleasing to the palate, and full of cool and thirst-satisfying juice. Finishing his meal, Conan wiped his hands in the sand, rose, ran his fingers through his thick black mane, hitched at his sword belt and said:

"Well, let's go. If the people in that city are going to cut our throats they may as well do it now, before the heat of the day begins."

His grim humor was unconscious, but Valeria reflected that it might be prophetic. She too hitched her sword-belt as she rose. Her terrors of the night were past. The roaring dragons of the distant forest were like a dim dream. There was a swagger in her stride as she moved off beside the Cimmerian. Whatever perils lay ahead of them, their foes would be men. And Valeria of the Red Brotherhood had never seen the face of the man she feared.

Conan glanced down at her as she strode along beside him with her swinging stride that matched his own.

"You walk more like a hillman than a sailor," he said. "You must be an Aquilonian. The suns of Darfar never burnt your white skin brown. Many a princess would envy you."

"I am from Aquilonia," she replied. His compliments no longer irritated her. His evident admiration pleased her. For another man to have kept her watch while she slept would have angered her; she had always fiercely resented any man's attempting to shield or protect her because of her sex. But she found a secret pleasure in the fact that this man had done so. And he had not taken advantage of her fright and the weakness resulting from it. After all, she reflected, her companion was no common man.

The sun rose up behind the city, turning the towers to a sinister crimson.

"Black last night against the moon," grunted Conan, his eyes clouding with the abysmal superstition of the barbarian. "Blood-red as a threat of blood against the sun this dawn. I do not like this city."

But they went on, and as they went Conan pointed out the fact that no road ran to the city from the north.

"No cattle have trampled the plain on this side of the city," said he. "No plowshare has touched the earth for years, maybe centuries. But look: once this plain was cultivated."

Valeria saw the ancient irrigation ditches he indicated, half-filled in places, and overgrown with cactus. She frowned with perplexity as her eyes swept over the plain that stretched on all sides of the city to the forest edge, which marched in a vast, dim ring. Vision did not extend beyond that ring.

She looked uneasily at the city. No helmets or spearheads gleamed on battlements, no trumpets sounded, no challenge rang from the towers. A silence as absolute as that of the forest brooded over the walls and minarets.

The sun was high above the eastern horizon when they stood before the great gate in the northern wall, in the shadow of the lofty rampart. Rust flecked the iron bracings of the mighty bronze portal. Spider webs glistened thickly on hinge and sill and bolted panel.

"It hasn't been opened for years!" exclaimed Valeria.

"A dead city," grunted Conan. "That's why the ditches were broken and the plain untouched."

"But who built it? Who dwelt here? Where did they go? Why did they abandon it?"

"Who can say? Maybe an exiled clan of Stygians built it. Maybe not. It doesn't look like Stygian architecture. Maybe the people were wiped out by enemies, or a plague exterminated them."

"In that case their treasures may still be gathering

dust and cobwebs in there," suggested Valeria, the acquisitive instincts of her profession waking in her; prodded, too, by feminine curiosity. "Can we open the gate? Let's go in and explore a bit."

Conan eyed the heavy portal dubiously, but placed his massive shoulder against it and thrust with all the power of his muscular calves and thighs. With a rasping screech of rusty hinges the gate moved ponderously inward, and Conan straightened and drew his sword. Valeria stared over his shoulder, and made a sound indicative of surprize.

They were not looking into an open street or court as one would have expected. The opened gate, or door, gave directly into a long, broad hall which ran away and away until its vista grew indistinct in the distance. It was of heroic proportions, and the floor of a curious red stone, cut in square tiles, that seemed to smolder as if with the reflection of flames. The walls were of a shiny green material.

"Jade, or I'm a Shemite!" swore Conan.

"Not in such quantity!" protested Valeria.

"I've looted enough from the Khitan caravans to know what I'm talking about," he asserted. "That's jade!"

The vaulted ceiling was of lapis lazuli, adorned with clusters of great green stones that gleamed with a poisonous radiance.

"Green fire-stones," growled Conan. "That's what the people of Punt call them. They're supposed to be the petrified eyes of those prehistoric snakes the ancients called Golden Serpents. They glow like a cat's eyes in the dark. At night this hall would be lighted by them, but it would be a hellishly weird illumination. Let's look around. We might find a cache of jewels."

"Shut the door," advised Valeria. "I'd hate to have to outrun a dragon down this hall."

Conan grinned, and replied: "I don't believe the dragons ever leave the forest."

But he complied, and pointed out the broken bolt on the inner side.

"I thought I heard something snap when I shoved against it. That bolt's freshly broken. Rust has eaten nearly through it. If the people ran away, why should it have been bolted on the inside?"

"They undoubtedly left by another door," suggested Valeria.

She wondered how many centuries had passed since the light of outer day had filtered into that great hall through the open door. Sunlight was finding its way somehow into the hall, and they quickly saw the source. High up in the vaulted ceiling skylights were set in slot-like openings — translucent sheets of some crystalline substance. In the splotches of shadow between them, the green jewels winked like the eyes of angry cats. Beneath their feet the dully lurid floor smoldered with changing hues and colors of flame. It was like treading the floors of Hell with evil stars blinking overhead.

Three balustraded galleries ran along on each side

of the hall, one above the other.

"A four-storied house," grunted Conan, "and this hall extends to the roof. It's long as a street. I seem to see a door at the other end."

Valeria shrugged her white shoulders.

"Your eyes are better than mine, then, though I'm accounted sharp eyed among the sea-rovers."

They turned into an open door at random, and traversed a series of empty chambers, floored like the hall, and with walls of the same green jade, or of marble or ivory or chalcedony, adorned with friezes of bronze, gold, or silver. In the ceilings the green fire-gems were set, and their light was as ghostly and illusive as Conan had predicted. Under the witch-fire glow the intruders moved like specters.

Some of the chambers lacked this illumination, and their doorways showed black as the mouth of the Pit. These Conan and Valeria avoided, keeping always to the lighted chambers.

Cobwebs hung in the corners, but there was no perceptible accumulation of dust on the floor, or on the tables and seats of marble, jade, or carnelian which occupied the chambers. Here and there were rugs of that silk known as Khitan which is practically indestructible. Nowhere did they find any windows, or doors opening into streets or courts. Each door merely opened into another chamber or hall.

"Why don't we come to a street?" grumbled Valeria. "This palace or whatever we're in must be as big as the king of Turan's seraglio."

"They must not have perished of plague," sad Conan, meditating upon the mystery of the empty city. "Otherwise we'd find skeletons. Maybe it became haunted, and everybody got up and left. Maybe —"

"Maybe, hell!" broke in Valeria rudely. "We'll never know. Look at these friezes. They portray men. What race do they belong to?"

Conan scanned them and shook his head.

"I never saw people exactly like them. But there's the smack of the East about them — Vendhya, maybe, or Kosala."

"Were you a king in Kosala?" she asked, masking her keen curiosity with derision.

"No. But I was a war chief of the Afghulis who live in the Himelian mountains above the borders of Vendhya. These people favor the Kosalans. But why should Kosalans be building a city this far to the west?"

The figures portrayed were those of slender, olive-skinned men and women, with finely chiseled, exotic features. They wore filmy robes and many delicate jeweled ornaments, and were depicted mostly in attitudes of feasting, dancing, or lovemaking.

"Easterners, all right," grunted Conan, "but from where I don't know. They must have lived a disgustingly peaceful life, though, or they'd have scenes of wars and fights. Let's go up those stairs."

It was an ivory spiral that wound up from the chamber in which they were standing. They mounted three flights and came into a broad chamber on the fourth floor, which seemed to be the highest tier in the building. Skylights in the ceiling illuminated the room, in which light the fire-gems winked pallidly. Glancing through the doors they saw, except on one side, a series of similarly lighted chambers. This other door opened upon a balustraded gallery that overhung a hall much smaller than the one they had recently explored on the lower floor.

"Hell!" Valeria sat down disgustedly on a jade bench. "The people who deserted this city must have taken all their treasures with them. I'm tired of wandering through these bare rooms at random."

"All these upper chambers seem to be lighted," said Conan. "I wish we could find a window that overlooked the city. Let's have a look through that door over there."

"You have a look," advised Valeria. "I'm going to sit here and rest my feet."

Conan disappeared through the door opposite that one opening upon the gallery, and Valeria leaned back with her hands clasped behind her head, and thrust her booted legs out in front of her. These silent rooms and halls with their gleaming green clusters of ornaments and burning crimson floors were beginning to depress her. She wished they could find their way out of the maze into which they had wandered and emerge into a street. She wondered idly what furtive, dark feet had glided over those flaming floors in past centuries, how many deeds of cruelty and mystery those winking ceiling-gems had blazed down upon.

It was a faint noise that brought her out of her reflections. She was on her feet with her sword in her hand before she realized what had disturbed her. Conan had not returned, and she knew it was not he that she had heard.

The sound had come from somewhere beyond the door that opened on to the gallery. Soundlessly in her soft leather boots she glided through it, crept across the balcony and peered down between the heavy balustrades.

A man was stealing along the hall.

The sight of a human being in this supposedly deserted city was a startling shock. Crouching down behind the stone balusters, with every nerve tingling, Valeria glared down at the stealthy figure.

The man in no way resembled the figures depicted on the friezes. He was slightly above middle height, very dark, though not Negroid. He was naked but for a scanty silk clout that only partly covered his muscular hips, and a leather girdle, a hand's breadth broad, about his lean waist. His long black hair hung in lank strands about his shoulders, giving him a wild appearance. He was gaunt, but knots and cords of muscles stood out on his arms and legs, without that fleshy padding that presents a pleasing symmetry of contour. He was built with an economy that was almost repellent.

Yet it was not so much his physical appearance as

his attitude that impressed the woman who watched him. He slunk along, stooped in a semi-crouch, his head turning from side to side. He grasped a wide-tipped blade in his right hand and she saw it shake with the intensity of the emotion that gripped him. He was afraid, trembling in the grip of some dire terror. When he turned his head she caught the blaze of wild eyes among the lank strands of black hair.

He did not see her. On tiptoe he glided across the hall and vanished through an open door. A moment later she heard a choking cry, and then silence fell again.

Consumed with curiosity, Valeria glided along the gallery until she came to a door above the one through which the man had passed. It opened into another, smaller gallery that encircled a large chamber.

This chamber was on the third floor, and its ceiling was not so high as that of the hall. It was lighted only by the fire-stones, and their weird green glow left the spaces under the balcony in shadows.

Valeria's eyes widened. The man she had seen was still in the chamber.

He lay face down on a dark crimson carpet in the middle of the room. His body was limp, his arms spread wide. His curved sword lay near him.

She wondered why he should lie there so motionless. Then her eyes narrowed as she stared down at the rug on which he lay. Beneath and about him the fabric showed a slightly different color, a deeper, brighter crimson.

Shivering slightly, she crouched down closer behind the balustrade, intently scanning the shadows under the overhanging gallery. They gave up no secret.

Suddenly another figure entered the grim drama. He was a man similar to the first, and he came in by a door opposite that which gave upon the hall.

His eyes glared at the sight of the man on the floor, and he spoke something in a staccato voice that sounded like "Chicmec!" The other did not move.

The man stepped quickly across the floor, bent, gripped the fallen man's shoulder and turned him over. A choking cry escaped him as the head fell back limply, disclosing a throat that had been severed from ear to ear.

The man let the corpse fall back upon the blood-stained carpet, and sprang to his feet, shaking like a windblown leaf. His face was an ashy mask of fear. But with one knee flexed for flight, he froze suddenly, became as immobile as an image, staring across the chamber with dilated eyes.

In the shadows beneath the balcony a ghostly light began to glow and grow, a light that was not part of the fire-stone gleam. Valeria felt her hair stir as she watched it; for, dimly visible in the throbbing radiance, there floated a human skull, and it was from this skull — human yet appallingly misshapen — that the spectral light seemed to emanate. It hung there like a disembodied head, conjured out of night and the shadows, growing more and more distinct; human, and yet not human as she knew humanity.

The man stood motionless, an embodiment of paralyzed horror, staring fixedly at the apparition. The thing moved out from the wall and a grotesque shadows moved with it. Slowly the shadow became visible as a manlike figure whose naked torso and limbs shone whitely, with the hue of bleached bones. The bare skull on its shoulders grinned eyelessly, in the midst of its unholy nimbus, and the man confronting it seemed unable to take his eyes from it. He stood still, his sword dangling from nerveless fingers, on his face the expression of a man bound by the spells of a mesmerist.

Valeria realized that it was not fear alone that paralyzed him. Some hellish quality of that throbbing glow had robbed him of his power to think and act. She herself, safely above the scene, felt the subtle impact of a nameless emanation that was a threat to sanity.

The horror swept toward its victim and he moved at last, but only to drop his sword and sink to his knees, covering his eyes with his hands. Dumbly he awaited the stroke of the blade that now gleamed in the apparition's hand as it reared above him like Death triumphant over mankind.

Valeria acted according to the first impulse of her wayward nature. With one tigerish movement she was over the balustrade and dropping to the floor behind the awful shape. It wheeled at the thud of her soft boots on the floor, but even as it turned, her keen blade lashed down, and a fierce exultation swept her as she felt the edge cleave solid flesh and mortal bone.

The apparition cried out gurglingly and went down, severed through the shoulder, breastbone and spine, and as it fell the burning skull rolled clear, revealing a lank mop of black hair and a dark face twisted in the convulsions of death. Beneath the horrific masquerade there was a human being, a man similar to the one kneeling supinely on the floor.

The latter looked up at the sound of the blow and the cry, and now he glared in wild-eyed amazement at the white-skinned woman who stood over the corpse with a dripping sword in her hand.

He staggered up, yammering as if the sight had almost unseated his reason. She was amazed to realize that she understood him. He was gibbering in the Stygian tongue, though in a dialect unfamiliar to her.

"Who are you? Whence come you? What do you in Xuchotl?" Then rushing on, without waiting for her to reply: "But you are a friend — goddess or devil, it makes no difference! You have slain the Burning Skull! It was but a man beneath it, after all! We deemed it a demon *they* conjured up out of the catacombs! *Listen!*"

He stopped short in his ravings and stiffened, straining his ears with painful intensity. The girl heard nothing.

"We must hasten!" he whispered. "*They* are west of the Great Hall! They may be all around us here! They may be creeping upon us even now!"

He seized her wrist in a convulsive grasp she found hard to break.

"Whom do you mean by 'they?'" she demanded.

He stared at her uncomprehendingly for an instant, as if he found her ignorance hard to understand.

"They?" he stammered vaguely. "Why — why, the people of Xotalanc! The clan of the man you slew. They who dwell by the eastern gate."

"You mean to say this city is inhabited?" she exclaimed.

"Aye! Aye!" He was writhing in the impatience of apprehension. "Come away! Come quick! We must return to Tecuhltli!"

"Where is that?" she demanded.

"The quarter by the western gate!" He had her wrist again and was pulling her toward the door through which he had first come. Great beads of perspiration dripped from his dark forehead, and his eyes blazed with terror.

"Wait a minute!" she growled, flinging off his hand. "Keep your hands off me, or I'll split your skull. What's all this about? Who are you? Where would you take me?"

He took a firm grip on himself, casting glances to all sides, and began speaking so fast his words tripped over each other.

"My name is Techotl. I am of Techultli. I and this man who lies with his throat cut came into the Halls of Silence to try and ambush some of the Xotalancas. But we became separated and I returned here to find him with his gullet slit. The Burning Skull did it, I know, just as he would have slain me had you not killed him. But perhaps he was not alone. Others may be stealing from Xotalanc! The gods themselves blench at the fate of those they take alive!"

At the thought he shook as with a ague and his dark skin grew ashy. Valeria frowned puzzledly at him. She sensed intelligence behind this rigmarole, but it was meaningless to her.

She turned toward the skull, which still glowed and pulsed on the floor, and was reaching a booted toe tentatively toward it, when the man who called himself Techotl sprang forward with a cry.

"Do not touch it! Do not even look at it! Madness and death lurk in it. The wizards of Xotalanc understand its secret — they found it in the catacombs, where lie the bones of terrible kings who ruled in Xuchotl in the black centuries of the past. To gaze upon it freezes the blood and withers the brain of a man who understands not its mystery. To touch it causes madness and destruction."

She scowled at him uncertainly. He was not a reassuring figure, with his lean, muscle-knotted frame, and snaky locks. In his eyes, behind the glow of terror, lurked a weird light she had never seen in the eyes of a man wholly sane. Yet he seemed sincere in his protestations.

"Come!" he begged, reaching for her hand, and then recoiling as he remembered her warning. "You are a stranger. How you came here I do not know, but if you were a goddess or a demon, come to aid Tecuhltli, you would know all the things you have asked me. You must be from beyond the great forest, whence our ancestors came. But you are our friend, or you would not have slain my enemy. Come quickly, before the Xotalancas find us and slay us!"

From his repellent, impassioned face she glanced to the sinister skull, smoldering and glowing on the floor near the dead man. It was like a skull seen in a dream, undeniably human, yet with disturbing distortions and malformations of contour and outline. In life the wearer of that skull must have presented an alien and monstrous aspect. Life? It seemed to possess some sort of life of its own. Its jaws yawned at her and snapped together. Its radiance grew brighter, more vivid, yet the impression of nightmare grew too; it was a dream; all life was a dream — it was Techotl's urgent voice which snapped Valeria back from the dim gulfs whither she was drifting.

"Do not look at the skull! Do not look at the skull!" It was a far cry from across unreckoned voids.

Valeria shook herself like a lion shaking his mane. Her vision cleared. Techotl was chattering: "In life it housed the awful brain of a king of magicians! It holds still the life and fire of magic drawn from outer spaces!"

With a curse Valeria leaped, lithe as a panther, and the skull crashed to flaming bits under her swinging sword. Somewhere in the room, or in the void, or in the dim reaches of her consciousness, an inhuman voice cried out in pain and rage.

Techotl's hand was plucking at her arm and he was gibbering: "You have broken it! You have destroyed it! Not all the black arts of Xotalanc can rebuild it! Come away! Come away quickly, now!"

"But I can't go," she protested. "I have a friend somewhere nearby —"

The flare of his eyes cut her short as he stared past her with an expression grown ghastly. She wheeled just as four men rushed through as many doors, converging on the pair in the center of the chamber.

They were like the others she had seen, the same knotted muscles bulging on otherwise gaunt limbs, the same lank blue-black hair, the same mad glare in their wild eyes. They were armed and clad like Techotl, but on the breast of each was painted a white skull.

There were no challenges or war-cries. Like blood-mad tigers the men of Xotalanc sprang at the throats of their enemies. Techotl met them with the fury of desperation, ducked the swipe of a wide-headed blade, and grappled with the wielder, and bore him to the floor where they rolled and wrestled in murderous silence.

The other three swarmed on Valeria, their weird eyes red as the eyes of mad dogs.

She killed the first who came within reach before he could strike a blow, her long straight blade splitting his skull even as his own sword lifted for a stroke. She sidestepped a thrust, even as she parried a slash. Her eyes danced and her lips smiled without mercy. Again she was Valeria of the Red Brotherhood, and the hum of her steel was like a bridal song in her ears.

Her sword darted past a blade that sought to parry, and sheathed six inches of its point in a leather-guarded midriff. The man gasped agonizedly and went to his knees, but his tall mate lunged in, in ferocious silence, raining blow on blow so furiously that Valeria had no opportunity to counter. She stepped back coolly, parrying the strokes and watching for her chance to thrust home. He could not long keep up that flailing whirlwind. His arm would tire, his wind would fail; he would weaken, falter, and then her blade would slide smoothly into his heart. A sidelong glance showed her Techotl kneeling on the breast of his antagonist and striving to break the other's hold on his wrist and to drive home a dagger.

Sweat beaded the forehead of the man facing her, and his eyes were like burning coals. Smite as he would, he could not break past nor beat down her guard. His breath came in gusty gulps, his blows began to fall erratically. She stepped back to draw him out — and felt her thighs locked in an iron grip. She had forgotten the wounded man on the floor.

Crouching on his knees, he held her with both arms locked about her legs, and his mate croaked in triumph and began working his way around to come at her from the left side. Valeria wrenched and tore savagely, but in vain. She could free herself of this clinging menace with a downward flick of her sword, but in that instant the curved blade of the tall warrior would crash through her skull. The wounded man began to worry at her bare thigh with his teeth like a wild beast.

She reached down with her left hand and gripped his long hair, forcing his head back so that his white teeth and rolling eyes gleamed up at her. The tall Xotalanc cried out fiercely and leaped in, smiting with all the fury of his arm. Awkwardly she parried the stroke, and it beat the flat of her blade down on her head so that she saw sparks flash before her eyes, and staggered. Up went the sword again, with a low, beast-like cry of triumph — and then a giant form loomed behind the Xotalanc and steel flashed like a jet of blue lightning. The cry of the warrior broke short and he went down like an ox beneath the pole-ax, his brains gushing from his skull that had been split to the throat.

"Conan!" gasped Valeria. In a gust of passion she turned on the Xotalanc whose long hair she still gripped in her left hand. "Dog of Hell!" Her blade swished as it cut the air in an upswinging arc with a blur in the middle, and the headless body slumped down, spurting blood. She hurled the severed head across the room.

"What the devil's going on here?" Conan bestrode the corpse of the man he had killed, broadsword in hand, glaring about him in amazement.

Techotl was rising from the twitching figure of the last Xotalanc, shaking red drops from his dagger. He was bleeding from the stab deep in the thigh. He stared at Conan with dilated eyes.

"What is all this?" Conan demanded again, not yet recovered from the stunning surprize of finding Valeria engaged in a savage battle with these fantastic figures in a city he had thought empty and uninhabited. Returning from an aimless exploration of the upper chambers to find Valeria missing from the room where he had left her, he had followed the sounds of strife that burst on his dumfounded ears.

"Five dead dogs!" exclaimed Techotl, his flaming eyes reflecting a ghastly exultation. "Five slain! Five crimson nails for the black pillar! The gods of blood be thanked!"

He lifted quivering hands on high, and then, with the face of a fiend, he spat on the corpses and stamped on their faces, dancing in his ghoulish glee. His recent allies eyed him in amazement, and Conan asked, in the Aquilonian tongue: "Who is this madman?"

Valeria shrugged her shoulders.

"He says his name's Techotl. From his babblings I

gather that his people live at one end of this crazy city, and these others at the other end. Maybe we'd better go with him. He seems friendly, and it's easy to see that the other clan isn't."

Techotl had ceased his dancing and was listening again, his head tilted sidewise, dog-like, triumph struggling with fear in his repellent countenance.

"Come away, now!" he whispered. "We have done enough! Five dead dogs! My people will welcome you! They will honor you! But come! It is far to Tecuhltli. At any moment the Xotalancs may come on us in numbers too great even for your swords."

"Lead the way," grunted Conan.

Techotl instantly mounted a stair leading up to the gallery, beckoning them to follow him, which they did, moving rapidly to keep on his heels. Having reached the gallery, he plunged into a door that opened toward the west, and hurried through chamber after chamber, each lighted by skylights or green fire-jewels.

"What sort of place can this be?" muttered Valeria under her breath.

"Crom knows!" answered Conan. "I've seen *his* kind before, though. They live on the shores of Lake Zuad, near the border of Kush. They're a sort of mongrel Stygians, mixed with another race that wandered into Stygia from the east some centuries ago and were absorbed by them. They're called Tlazitlans. I'm willing to bet it wasn't they who built this city, though."

Techotl's fear did not seem to diminish as they drew away from the chamber where the dead men lay. He kept twisting his head on his shoulder to listen for sounds of pursuit, and stared with burning intensity into every doorway they passed.

Valeria shivered in spite of herself. She feared no man. But the weird floor beneath her feet, the uncanny jewels over her head, dividing the lurking shadows among them, the stealth and terror of their guide, impressed her with a nameless apprehension, a sensation of lurking, inhuman peril.

"They may be between us and Tecuhltli!" he whispered once. "We must beware lest they be lying in wait!"

"Why don't we get out of this infernal palace, and take to the streets?" demanded Valeria.

"There are no streets in Xuchotl," he answered. "No squares nor open courts. The whole city is built like one giant palace under one great roof. The nearest approach to a street is the Great Hall which traverses the city from the north gate to the south gate. The only doors opening into the outer world are the city gates, through which no living man has passed for fifty years."

"How long have you dwelt here?" asked Conan.

"I was born in the castle of Tecuhltli thirty-five years ago. I have never set foot outside the city. For the love of the gods, let us go silently! These halls may be full of lurking devils. Olmec shall tell you all when we reach Tecuhltli."

So in silence they glided on with the green fire-stones blinking overhead and the flaming floors smoldering under their feet, and it seemed to Valeria as if they fled through Hell, guided by a dark-faced, lank-haired goblin.

Yet it was Conan who halted them as they were crossing an unusually wide chamber. His wilderness-bred ears were keener even than the ears of Techotl, whetted though these were by a lifetime of warfare in this silent corridors.

"You think some of your enemies may be ahead of us, lying in ambush?"

"They prowl through these rooms at all hours," answered Techotl, "as do we. The halls and chambers between Tecuhltli and Xotalanc are a disputed region, owned by no man. We call it the Halls of Silence. Why do you ask?"

"Because men are in the chambers ahead of us," answered Conan. "I heard steel clink against stone."

Again a shaking seized Techotl, and he clenched his teeth to keep them from chattering.

"Perhaps they are your friends," suggested Valeria.

"We dare not chance it," he panted, and moved with frenzied activity. He turned aside and glided through a doorway on the left which led into a chamber from which an ivory staircase wound down into darkness.

"This leads to an unlighted corridor below us!" he hissed, great beads of perspiration standing out on his brow. "They may be lurking there, too. It may all be a trick to draw us into it. But we must take the chance that they have laid their ambush in the rooms above. Come swiftly now!"

Softly as phantoms they descended the stair and came to the mouth of a corridor black as night. They crouched there for a moment, listening, and then melted into it. As they moved along, Valeria's flesh crawled between her shoulders in momentary expectation of a sword-thrust in the dark. But for Conan's iron fingers gripping her arm she had no physical cognizance of her companions. Neither made as much noise as a cat would have made. The darkness was absolute. One hand, outstretched, touched a wall, and occasionally she felt a door under her fingers. The hallway seemed interminable.

Suddenly they were galvanized by a sound behind them. Valeria's flesh crawled anew, for she recognized it as the soft opening of a door. Men had come into the corridor behind them. Even with the thought she stumbled over something that felt like a human skull. It rolled across the floor with an appalling clatter.

"Run!" yelped Techotl, a note of hysteria in his voice, and was away down the corridor like a flying ghost.

Again Valeria felt Conan's hand bearing her up and sweeping her along as they raced after their guide. Conan could see in the dark no better than she, but he possessed a sort of instinct that made his course unerring. Without his support and guidance she would have fallen or stumbled against the wall. Down the corridor they sped, while the swift patter of flying feet drew closer and closer, and then suddenly Techotl panted: "Here is the stair! After me, quick! Oh, quick!"

His hand came out of the dark and caught Valeria's wrist as she stumbled blindly on the steps. She felt herself half-dragged, half-lifted up the winding stair, while Conan released her and turned on the steps, his ears and instincts telling him their foes were hard at their backs. *And the sounds were not all those of human feet.*

Something came writhing up the steps, something that slithered and rustled and brought a chill in the air with it. Conan lashed down with his great sword and felt the blade shear through something that might have been flesh and bone, and cut deep into the stair beneath. Something touched his foot that chilled like the touch of frost, and then the darkness beneath him was disturbed by a frightful thrashing and lashing, and a man cried out in agony.

The next moment Conan was racing up the winding staircase, and through a door that stood open at the head.

Valeria and Techotl were already through, and Techotl slammed the door and shot a bolt across it — the first Conan had seen since they had left the outer gate.

Then he turned and ran across the well-lighted

chamber into which they had come, and as they passed through the farther door, Conan glanced back and saw the door groaning and straining under heavy pressure violently applied from the other side.

Though Techotl did not abate either his speed or his caution, he seemed more confident now. He had the air of a man who had come into familiar territory, within call of friends.

But Conan renewed his terror by asking: "What was that thing I fought on the stairs?"

"The men of Xotalanc," answered Techotl, without looking back. "I told you the halls were full of them."

"This wasn't a man," grunted Conan. "It was something that crawled, and it was as cold as ice to the touch. I think I cut it asunder. It fell back on the men who were following us, and must have killed one of them in its death throes."

Techotl's head jerked back, his face ashy again. Convulsively he quickened his pace.

"It was the Crawler! A monster *they* have brought out of the catacombs to aid them! What it is, we do not know, but we have found our people hideously slain by it. In Set's name, hasten! If they put it on our trail, it will follow us to the very doors of Tecuhltli!"

"I doubt it," grunted Conan. "That was a shrewd cut I dealt it on the stair."

"Hasten! Hasten!" groaned Techotl.

They ran through a series of green-lit chambers,

traversed a broad hall, and halted before a giant bronze door.

Techotl said: "This is Tecuhltli!"

3. The People of the Feud

Techotl smote on the bronze door with his clenched hand, and then turned sidewise, so that he could watch back along the hall.

"Men have been smitten down before this door, when they thought they were safe," he said.

"Why don't they open the door?" asked Conan.

"They are looking at us through the Eye," answered Techotl. "They are puzzled at the sight of you." He lifted his voice and called: "Open the door, Xecelan! It is I, Techotl, with friends from the great world beyond the forest! — They will open," he assured his allies.

"They'd better do it in a hurry, then," said Conan grimly. "I hear something crawling along the floor beyond the hall."

Techotl went ashy again and attacked the door with his fists, screaming: "Open, you fools, open! The Crawler is at our heels!"

Even as he beat and shouted, the great bronze door swung noiselessly back, revealing a heavy chain across the entrance, over which spearheads bristled and fierce countenances regarded them intently for an instant. Then the chain was dropped and Techotl grasped the arms of his friends in a nervous frenzy and fairly dragged them over the threshold. A glance over his shoulder just as the door was closing showed Conan the long dim vista of the hall, and dimly framed at the other end an ophidian shape that writhed slowly and painfully into view, flowing in a dull-hued length from a chamber door, its hideous bloodstained head wagging drunkenly. Then the closing door shut off the view.

Inside the square chamber into which they had come heavy bolts were drawn across the door, and the chain locked into place. The door was made to stand the battering of a siege. Four men stood on guard, of the same lank-haired, dark-skinned breed as Techotl, with spears in their hands and swords at their hips. In the wall near the door there was a complicated contrivance of mirrors which Conan guessed was the Eye Techotl had mentioned, so arranged that a narrow, crystal-paned slot in the wall could be looked through from within without being discernible from without. The four guardsmen stared at the strangers with wonder, but asked no question, nor did Techotl vouchsafe any information. He moved with easy confidence now, as if he had shed his cloak of indecision and fear the instant he crossed the threshold.

"Come!" he urged his new-found friends, but Conan glanced toward the door.

"What about those fellows who were following us? Won't they try to storm that door?"

Techotl shook his head.

"They know they cannot break down the Door of the Eagle. They will flee back to Xotalanc, with their crawling fiend. Come! I will take you to the rulers of Tecuhltli."

One of the four guards opened the door opposite the one by which they had entered, and they passed through into a hallway which, like most of the rooms on that level, was lighted by both the slot-like sky-lights and the clusters of winking fire-gems. But unlike the other rooms they had traversed, this hall showed evidences of occupation. Velvet tapestries adorned the glossy jade walls, rich rugs were on the crimson floors, and the ivory seats, benches and divans were littered with satin cushions.

The hall ended in an ornate door, before which stood no guard. Without ceremony Techotl thrust the door open and ushered his friends into a broad chamber, where some thirty dark-skinned men and women lounged on satin-covered couches sprang up with exclamations of amazement.

The men, all except one, were of the same type as Techotl, and the women were equally dark and strange-eyed, though not unbeautiful in a weird dark way. They wore sandals, golden breastplates, and scanty silk skirts supported by gem-crusted girdles, and their black manes, cut square at their naked shoulders, were bound with silver circlets.

On a wide ivory seat on a jade dais sat a man and a woman who differed subtly from the others. He was a giant, with an enormous sweep of breast and the shoulders of a bull. Unlike the others, he was bearded, with a thick, blue-black beard which fell almost to his broad girdle. He wore a robe of purple silk which reflected changing sheens of color with his every movement, and one wide sleeve, drawn back to his elbow, revealed a forearm massive with corded muscles. The band which confined his blue-black locks was set with glittering jewels.

The woman beside him sprang to her feet with a startled exclamation as the strangers entered, and her eyes, passing over Conan, fixed themselves with burning intensity on Valeria. She was tall and lithe, by far the most beautiful woman in the room. She was clad more scantily even than the others; for instead of a skirt she wore merely a broad strip of gilt-worked purple cloth fastened to the middle of her girdle which fell below her knees. Another strip at the back of her girdle completed that part of her costume, which she wore with a cynical indifference. Her breast-plates and the circlet about her temples were adorned with gems. In her eyes alone of all the dark-skinned people there lurked no brooding gleam of madness. She spoke no word after her first exclamation; she stood tensely, her hands clenched, staring at Valeria.

The man on the ivory seat had not risen.

"Prince Olmec," spoke Techotl, bowing low, with arms outspread and the palms of his hands turned upward, "I bring allies from the world beyond the forest. In the Chamber of Tezcoti the Burning Skull slew Chicmec, my companion —"

"The Burning Skull!" It was a shuddering whisper of fear from the people of Tecuhltli.

"Aye! Then came I, and found Chicmec lying with his throat cut. Before I could flee, the Burning Skull came upon me, and when I looked upon it my blood became as ice and the marrow of my bones melted. I could neither fight nor run. I could only await the stroke. Then came this white-skinned woman and struck him down with her sword; and lo, it was only a dog of Xotalanc with white paint upon his skin and the living skull of an ancient wizard upon his head! Now that skull lies in many pieces, and the dog who wore it is a dead man!"

An indescribably fierce exultation edged the last sentence, and was echoed in the low, savage exclamations from the crowding listeners.

"But wait!" exclaimed Techotl. "There is more! While I talked with the woman, four Xotalancs came upon us! One I slew — there is the stab in my thigh to prove how desperate was the fight. Two the woman killed. But we were hard pressed when this man came into the fray and split the skull of the fourth! Aye! Five crimson nails there are to be driven into the pillar of vengeance!"

He pointed to a black column of ebony which stood behind the dais. Hundreds of red dots scarred its polished surface — the bright scarlet heads of heavy copper nails driven into the black wood.

"Five red nails for five Xotalanca lives!" exulted

Techotl, and the horrible exultation in the faces of the listeners made them inhuman.

"Who are these people?" asked Olmec, and his voice was like the low, deep rumble of a distant bull. None of the people of Xuchotl spoke loudly. It was as if they had absorbed into their souls the silence of the empty halls and deserted chambers.

"I am Conan, a Cimmerian," answered the barbarian briefly. "This woman is Valeria of the Red Brotherhood, an Aquilonian pirate. We are deserters from an army on the Darfar border, far to the north, and are trying to reach the coast."

The woman on the dais spoke loudly, her words tripping in her haste.

"You can never reach the coast! There is no escape from Xuchotl! You will spend the rest of your lives in this city!"

"What do you mean," growled Conan, clapping his hand to his hilt and stepping about so as to face both the dais and the rest of the room. "Are you telling us we're prisoners?"

"She did not mean that," interposed Olmec. "We are your friends. We would not restrain you against your will. But I fear other circumstances will make it impossible for you to leave Xuchotl."

His eyes flickered to Valeria, and he lowered them quickly.

"This woman is Tascela," he said. "She is a princess of Tecuhltli. But let food and drink be brought our guests. Doubtless they are hungry, and weary from their long travels."

He indicated an ivory table, and after an exchange of glances, the adventurers seated themselves. The Cimmerian was suspicious. His fierce blue eyes roved about the chamber, and he kept his sword close to his hand. But an invitation to eat and drink never found him backward. His eyes kept wandering to Tascela, but the princess had eyes only for his white-skinned companion.

Techotl, who had bound a strip of silk about his wounded thigh, placed himself at the table to attend to the wants of his friends, seeming to consider it a privilege and honor to see after their needs. He inspected the food and drink the others brought in gold vessels and dishes, and tasted each before he placed it before his guests. While they ate, Olmec sat in silence on his ivory seat, watching them from under his broad black brows. Tascela sat beside him, chin cupped in her hands and her elbows resting on her knees. Her dark, enigmatic eyes, burning with a mysterious light, never left Valeria's supple figure. Behind her seat a sullen handsome girl waved an ostrich-plume fan with a slow rhythm.

The food was fruit of an exotic kind unfamiliar to the wanderers, but very palatable, and the drink was a light crimson wine that carried a heady tang.

"You have come from afar," said Olmec at last. "I have read the books of our fathers. Aquilonia lies beyone the lands of the Stygians and the Shemites, beyond Argos and Zingara; and Cimmeria lies beyond Aquilonia."

"We have each a roving foot," answered Conan carelessly.

"How you won through the forest is a wonder to me," quoth Olmec. "In bygone days a thousand fighting men scarcely were able to carve a road through its perils."

"We encountered a bench-legged monstrosity about the size of a mastodon," said Conan casually, holding out his wine goblet which Techutl filled with evident pleasure. "But when we'd killed it we had no further trouble."

The wine vessel slipped from Techotl's hand to crash on the floor. His dusky skin went ashy. Olmec started to his feet, an image of stunned amazement, and a low gasp of awe or terror breathed up from the others. Some slipped to their knees as if their legs would not support them. Only Tascela seemed not to have heard. Conan glared about him bewilderedly.

"What's the matter? What are you gaping about?"

"You — you slew the dragon-god?"

"God? I killed a dragon. Why not? It was trying to gobble us up."

"But dragons are immortal!" exclaimed Olmec. "They slay each other, but no man ever killed a dragon! The thousand fighting-men of our ancestors who fought their way to Xuchotl could not prevail against them! Their swords broke like twigs against their scales!"

"If your ancestors had thought to dip their spears in the poisonous juice of Derketa's Apples," quoth Conan, with his mouth full, "and jab them in the eyes or mouth or somewhere like that, they'd have seen that dragons are no more immortal than any other chunk of beef. The carcass lies at the edge of the trees, just within the forest. If you don't believe me, go and look for yourself."

Olmec shook his head, not in disbelief but in wonder.

"It was because of the dragons that our ancestors took refuge in Xuchotl," said he. "They dared not pass through the plain and plunge into the forest beyond. Scores of them were seized and devoured by the monsters before they could reach the city."

"Then your ancestors didn't build Xuchotl?" asked Valeria.

"It was ancient when they first came into the land. How long it had stood here, not even its degenerate inhabitants knew."

"Your people came from Lake Zuad?" questioned Conan.

"Aye. More than half a century ago a tribe of the Tlazitlans rebelled against the Stygian king, and, being defeated in battle, fled southward. For many weeks they wandered over grasslands, desert and hills, and at last they came into the great forest, a thousand fighting-men with their women and children.

"It was in the forest that the dragons fell upon

them and tore many to pieces; so the people fled in a frenzy of fear before them, and at last came into the plain and saw the city of Xuchotl in the midst of it.

"They camped before the city, not daring to leave the plain, for the night was made hideous with the noise of the battling monsters through the forest. They made war incessantly upon one another. Yet they came not into the plain.

"The people of the city shut their gates and shot arrows at our people from the walls. The Tlazitlans were imprisoned on the plain, as if the ring of the forest had been a great wall; for to venture into the woods would have been madness.

"That night there came secretly to their camp a slave from the city, one of our own blood, who with a band of exploring soldiers had wandered into the forest long before, when he was a young man. The dragons had devoured all his companions, but he had been taken into the city to dwell in servitude. His name was Tolkemec." A flame lighted the dark eyes at mention of the name, and some of the people muttered obscenely and spat. "He promised to open the gates to the warriors. He asked only that all captives taken be delivered into his hands.

"At dawn he opened the gates. The warriors swarmed in and the halls of Xuchotl ran red. Only a few hundred folk dwelt there, decaying remnants of a once great race. Tolkemec said they came from the east, long ago, from Old Kosala, when the ancestors of those who now dwell in Kosala came up from the south and drove forth the original inhabitants of the land. They wandered far westward and finally found this forest-girdled plain, inhabited then by a tribe of black people.

"These they enslaved and set to building a city. From the hills to the east they brought jade and marble and lapis lazuli, and gold, silver, and copper. Herds of elephants provided them with ivory. When their city was completed, they slew all the black slaves. And their magicians made a terrible magic to guard the city; for by their necromantic arts they rec-reated the dragons which had once dwelt in this lost land, and whose monstrous bones they found in the forest. Those bones they clothed in flesh and life, and the living beasts walked the earth as they walked it when Time was young. But the wizards wove a spell that kept them in the forest and they came not into the plain.

"So for many centuries the people of Xuchotl dwelt in their city, cultivating the fertile plain, until their wise men learned how to grow fruit within the city — fruit which is not planted in soil, but obtains its nourishment out of the air — and then they let the irrigation ditches run dry, and dwelt more and more in luxurious sloth, until decay seized them. They were a dying race when our ancestors broke through the forest and came into the plain. Their wizards had died, and the people had forgot their ancient necro-mancy. They could fight neither by sorcery nor the sword.

"Well, our fathers slew the people of Xuchotl, all except a hundred which were given living into the hands of Tolkemec, who had been their slave; and for many days and nights the halls re-echoed to their screams under the agony of his tortures.

"So the Tlazitlans dwelt here, for a while in peace, ruled by the brothers Tecuhltli and Xotalanc, and by Tolkemec. Tolkemec took a girl of the tribe to wife, and because he had opened the gates, and because he knew many of the arts of the Xuchotlans, he shared the rule of the tribe with the brothers who had led the rebellion and the flight.

"For a few years, then, they dwelt at peace within the city, doing little but eating, drinking, and making love, and raising children. There was no necessity to till the plain, for Tolkemec taught them how to cultivate the air-devouring fruits. Besides, the slaying of the Xuchotlans broke the spell that held the dragons in the forest, and they came nightly and bellowed about the gates of the city. The plain ran red with the blood of their eternal warfare, and it was then that —" He bit his tongue in the midst of the sentence, then presently continued, but Valeria and Conan felt that he had checked an admission he had considered unwise.

"Five years they dwelt in peace. Then" — Olmec's eyes rested briefly on the silent woman at his side — "Xotalanc took a woman to wife, a woman whom both Tecuhltli and old Tolkemec desired. In his madness, Tecuhltli stole her from her husband.

Aye, she went willingly enough. Tolkemec, to spite Xotalanc, aided Tecuhltli. Xotalanc demanded that she be given back to him, and the council of the tribe decided that the matter should be left to the woman. She chose to remain with Tecuhltli. In wrath Xotalanc sought to take her back by force, and the retainers of the brothers came to blows in the Great Hall.

"There was much bitterness. Blood was shed on both sides. The quarrel became a feud, the feud an open war. From the welter three factions emerged — Tecuhltli, Xotalanc, and Tolkemec. Already, in the days of peace, they had divided the city between them. Tecuhltli dwelt in the western quarter of the city, Xotalanc in the eastern, and Tolkemec with his family by the southern gate.

"Anger and resentment and jealousy blossomed into bloodshed and rape and murder. Once the sword was drawn there was no turning back; for blood called for blood, and vengeance followed swift on the heels of atrocity. Tecuhltli fought with Xotalanc, and Tolkemec aided first one and then the other, betraying each faction as it fitted his purposes. Tecuhltli and his people withdrew into the quarter of the western gate, where we now sit. Xuchotl is built in the shape of an oval. Tecuhltli, which took its name from its prince, occupies the western end of the oval. The people blocked up all doors connecting the quarter with the rest of the city, except one on each floor, which could be defended easily. They went into the pits below the city and built a wall cutting off the western end of the catacombs, where lie the bodies of the ancient Xuchotlans, and of those Tlazitlans slain in the feud. They dwelt as in a besieged castle, making sorties and forays on their enemies.

"The people of Xotalanc likewise fortified the eastern quarter of the city, and Tolkemec did likewise with the quarter by the southern gate. The central part of the city was left bare and uninhabited. Those empty halls and chambers became a battleground, and a region of brooding terror.

"Tolkemec warred on both clans. He was a fiend in the form of a human, worse than Xotalanc. He knew many secrets of the city he never told the others. From the crypts of the catacombs he plundered the dead of their grisly secrets — secrets of ancient kings and wizards, long forgotten by the degenerate Xuchotlans our ancestors slew. But all his magic did not aid him the night we of Tecuhltli stormed his castle and butchered all his people. Tolkemec we tortured for many days."

His voice sank to a caressing slur, and a faraway look grew in his eyes, as if he looked back over the years to a scene which caused him intense pleasure.

"Aye, we kept the life in him until he screamed for death as for a bride. At last we took him living from the torture chamber and cast him into a dungeon for the rats to gnaw as he died. From that dungeon, somehow, he managed to escape, and dragged himself into the catacombs. There without doubt he died, for the only way out of the catacombs beneath Tecuhltli is through Tecuhltli, and he never emerged by that way. His bones were never found and the superstitious among our people swear that his ghost haunts the crypts to this day, wailing among the bones of the dead. Twelve years ago we butchered the people of Tolkemec, but the feud raged on between Tecuhltli and Xotalanc, as it will rage until the last man, the last woman is dead.

"It was fifty years ago that Tecuhltli stole the wife of Xotalanc. Half a century the feud has endured. I was born in it. All in this chamber, except Tascela, were born in it. We expect to die in it.

"We are a dying race, even as were those Xuchotlans our ancestors slew. When the feud began there were hundreds in each faction. Now we of Tecuhltli number only these you see before you, and the men who guard the four doors: forty in all. How many Xotalancas there are we do not know, but I doubt if they are much more numerous than we. For fifteen years no children have been born to us, and we have seen none among the Xotalancas.

"We are dying, but before we die we will slay as many of the men of Xotalanc as the gods permit."

And with his weird eyes blazing, Olmec spoke long of that grisly feud, fought out in silent chambers and dim halls under the blaze of the green fire-jewels, on floors smoldering with the flames of Hell and splashed with deeper crimson from severed veins. In that long butchery a whole generation had perished.

Xotalanc was dead, long ago, slain in a grim battle on an ivory stair. Tecuhltli was dead, flayed alive by the maddened Xotalancas who had captured him.

Without emotion Olmec told of hideous battles fought in black corridors, of ambushes on twisting stairs, and red butcheries. With a redder, more abysmal gleam in his deep dark eyes he told of men and women flayed alive, mutilated and dismembered, of captives howling under tortures so ghastly that even the barbarous Cimmerian grunted. No wonder Techotl had trembled with the terror of capture. Yet he had gone forth to slay if he could, driven by hate that was stronger than his fear. Olmec spoke further, of dark and mysterious matters, of black magic and wizardry conjured out of the black night of the catacombs, of weird creatures invoked out of darkness for horrible allies. In these things the Xotalancas had the advantage, for it was in the eastern catacombs where lay the bones of the greatest wizards of the ancient Xuchotlans, with their immemorial secrets.

Valeria listened with morbid fascination. The feud had become a terrible elemental power driving the people of Xuchotl inexorably on to doom and extinction. It filled their whole lives. They were born in it, and they expected to die in it. They never left their barricaded castle except to steal forth into the Halls of Silence that lay between the opposing fortresses, to slay and be slain. Sometimes the raiders returned with frantic captives, or with grim tokens of victory in fight. Sometimes they did not return at all,

or returned only as severed limbs cast down before
the bolted bronze doors. It was a ghastly, unreal
nightmare existence these people lived, shut off from
the rest of the world, caught together like rabid rats
in the same trap, butchering one another through the
years, crouching and creeping through the sunless
corridors to maim and torture and murder.

While Olmec talked, Valeria felt the blazing eyes
of Tascela fixed upon her. The princess seemed not to
hear what Olmec was saying. Her expression, as he
narrated victories or defeats, did not mirror the wild
rage or fiendish exultation that alternated on the
faces of the other Tecuhltli. The feud that was an
obsession to her clansmen seemed meaningless to
her. Valeria found her indifferent callousness more
repugnant than Olmec's naked ferocity.

"And we can never leave the city," said Olmec.
"For fifty years no one has left it except those —"
Again he checked himself.

"Even without the peril of the dragons," he continued, "we who were born and raised in the city
would not dare leave it. We have never set foot outside the walls. We are not accustomed to the open
sky and the naked sun. No; we were born in Xuchotl,
and in Xuchotl we shall die."

"Well," said Conan, "with your leave we'll take
our chances with the dragons. This feud is none of
our business. If you'll show us to the west gate we'll
be on our way."

Tascela's hands clenched, and she started to

speak, but Olmec interrupted her: "It is nearly night-fall. If you wander forth into the plain by night, you will certainly fall prey to the dragons."

"We crossed it last night, and slept in the open without seeing any," returned Conan.

Tascela smiled mirthlessly. "You dare not leave Xuchotl!"

Conan glared at her with instinctive antagonism; she was not looking at him, but at the woman opposite him.

"I think they dare," stated Olmec. "But look you, Conan and Valeria, the gods must have sent you to us, to cast victory into the laps of the Tecuhltli! You are professional fighters — why not fight for us? We have wealth in abundance — precious jewels are as common in Xuchotl as cobblestones are in the cities of the world. Some the Xuchotlans brought with them from Kosala. Some, like the fire-stones, they found in the hills to the east. Aid us to wipe out the Xotalancas, and we will give you all the jewels you can carry."

"And will you help us destroy the dragons?" asked Valeria. "With bows and poisoned arrows thirty men could slay all the dragons in the forest."

"Aye!" replied Olmec promptly. "We have forgotten the use of the bow, in years of hand-to-hand fighting, but we can learn again."

"What do you say?" Valeria inquired of Conan.

"We're both penniless vagabonds," he grinned hardily. "I'd as soon kill Xotalancas as anybody."

"Then you agree?" exclaimed Olmec, while Techotl fairly hugged himself with delight.

"Aye. And now suppose you show us chambers where we can sleep, so we can be fresh tomorrow for the beginning of the slaying."

Olmec nodded, and waved a hand, and Techotl and a woman led the adventurers into a corridor which led through a door off to the left of the jade dais. A glance back showed Valeria Olmec sitting on his throne, chin on knotted fist, staring after them. His eyes burned with a weird flame. Tascela leaned back in her seat, whispering to the sullen-faced maid, Yasala, who leaned over her shoulder, her ear to the princess's moving lips.

The hallway was not so broad as most they had traversed, but it was long. Presently the woman halted, opened a door, and drew aside for Valeria to enter.

"Wait a minute," growled Conan. "Where do I sleep?"

Techotl pointed to a chamber across the hallway, but one door farther down. Conan hesitated, and seemed inclined to raise an objection, but Valeria smiled spitefully at him and shut the door in his face. He muttered something uncomplimentary about women in general, and strode off down the corridor after Techotl.

In the ornate chamber where he was to sleep, he glanced up at the slot-like skylights. Some were wide enough to admit the body of a slender man, supposing the glass were broken.

"Why don't the Xotalancas come over the roofs and shatter those skylights?" he asked.

"They cannot be broken," answered Techotl. "Besides, the roofs would be hard to clamber over. They are mostly spires and domes and steep ridges."

He volunteered more information about the "castle" of Tecuhltli. Like the rest of the city it contained four stories, or tiers of chambers, with towers jutting up from the roof. Each tier was named; indeed, the people of Xuchotl had a name for each chamber, hall, and stair in the city, as people of more normal cities designate streets and quarters. In Tecuhltli the floors were named The Eagle's Tier, The Ape's Tier, The Tiger's Tier and The Serpent's Tier, in the order as enumerated, The Eagle's Tier being the highest, or fourth, floor.

"Who is Tascela?" asked Conan. "Olmec's wife?"

Techotl shuddered and glanced furtively about him before answering.

"No. She is — Tascela! She was the wife of Xotalanc — the woman Tecuhltli stole, to start the feud."

"What are you talking about?" demanded Conan. "That woman is beautiful and young. Are you trying to tell me that she was a wife fifty years ago?"

"Aye! I swear it! She was a full-grown woman when the Tlazitlans journeyed from Lake Zuad. It was because the king of Stygia desired her for a concubine that Xotalanc and his brother rebelled and

fled into the wilderness. She is a witch, who possesses
the secret of perpetual youth."

"What's that?" asked Conan.

Techotl shuddered again.

"Ask me not! I dare not speak. It is too grisly,
even for Xuchotl!"

And touching his finger to his lips, he glided from
the chamber.

4. Scent of Black Lotus

Valeria unbuckled her sword-belt and laid it with the
sheathed weapon on the couch where she meant to
sleep. She noted that the doors were supplied with
bolts, and asked where they led.

"Those lead to adjoining chambers," answered
the woman, indicating the doors on right and left.
"That one" — pointing to a copper-bound door
opposite that which opened into the corridor —
"leads to a corridor which runs to a stair that de-
scends into the catacombs. Do not fear; naught can
harm you here."

"Who spoke of fear?" snapped Valeria. "I just
like to know what sort of harbor I'm dropping an-
chor in. No, I don't want you to sleep at the foot of
my couch. I'm not accustomed to being waited on —
not by women, anyway. You have my leave to go."

Alone in the room, the pirate shot the bolts on all
the doors, kicked off her boots and stretched luxuri-
ously out on the couch. She imagined Conan simi-

larly situated across the corridor, but her feminine vanity prompted her to visualize him as scowling and muttering with chagrin as he cast himself on his solitary couch, and she grinned with gleeful malice as she prepared herself for slumber.

Outside, night had fallen. In the halls of Xuchotl the green fire-jewels blazed like the eyes of prehistoric cats. Somewhere among the dark towers, a night wind moaned like a restless spirit. Through the dim passages, stealthy figures began stealing, like disembodied shadows.

Valeria awoke suddenly on her couch. In the dusky emerald glow of the fire-gems she saw a shadowy figure bending over her. For a bemused instant the apparition seemed part of the dream she had been dreaming. She had seemed to lie on the couch in the chamber as she was actually lying, while over her pulsed and throbbed a gigantic black blossom so enormous that it hid the ceiling. Its exotic perfume pervaded her being, inducing a delicious, sensuous languor that was something more and less than sleep. She was sinking into scented billows of insensible bliss, when something touched her face. So super-sensitive were her drugged senses, that the light touch was like a dislocating impact, jolting her rudely into full wakefulness. Then it was that she saw, not a gargantuan blossom, but a dark-skinned woman standing above her.

With the realization came anger and instant action. The woman turned lithely, but before she could run Valeria was on her feet and had caught her arm. She fought like a wildcat for an instant, and then subsided as she felt herself crushed by the superior strength of her captor. The pirate wrenched the woman around to face her, caught her chin with her free hand and forced her captive to meet her gaze. It was the sullen Yasala, Tascela's maid.

"What the devil were you doing bending over me? What's that in your hand?"

The woman made no reply, but sought to cast away the object. Valeria twisted her arm around in front of her, and the thing fell to the floor — a great black exotic blossom on a jade-green stem, large as a woman's head, to be sure, but tiny beside the exaggerated vision she had seen.

"The black lotus!" said Valeria between her teeth. "The blossom whose scent brings deep sleep. You were trying to drug me! If you hadn't accidentally touched my face with the petals, you'd have — why did you do it? What's your game?"

Yasala maintained a sulky silence, and with an oath Valeria whirled her around, forced her to her knees and twisted her arm up behind her back.

"Tell me, or I'll tear your arm out of its socket!"

Yasala squirmed in anguish as her arm was forced excruciatingly up between her shoulder blades, but a violent shaking of her head was the only answer she made.

"Slut!" Valeria cast her from her to sprawl on the floor. The pirate glared at the prostrate figure with blazing eyes. Fear and the memory of Tascela's burning eyes stirred in her, rousing all her tigerish instincts of self-preservation. These people were decadent; any sort of perversity might be expected to be encountered among them. But Valeria sensed here something that moved behind the scenes, some secret terror fouler than common degeneracy. Fear and revulsion of this weird city swept her. These people were neither sane nor normal; she began to doubt if they were even human. Madness smoldered in the eyes of them all — all except the cruel, cryptic eyes of Tascela, which held secrets and mysteries more abysmal than madness.

She lifted her head and listened intently. The halls of Xuchotl were as silent as if it were in reality a dead city. The green jewels bathed the chamber in a nightmare glow, in which the eyes of the woman on the floor glittered eerily up at her. A thrill of panic throbbed through Valeria, driving the last vestige of mercy from her fierce soul.

"Why did you try to drug me?" she muttered, grasping the woman's black hair, and forcing her head back to glare into her sullen, long-lashed eyes. "Did Tascela send you?"

No answer. Valeria cursed venomously and slapped the woman first on one cheek and then the other. The blows resounded through the room, but Yasala made no outcry.

"Why don't you scream?" demanded Valeria savagely. "Do you fear someone will hear you? Whom do you fear? Tascela? Olmec? Conan?"

Yasala made no reply. She crouched, watching her captor with eyes baleful as those of a basilisk. Stubborn silence always fans anger. Valeria turned and tore a handful of cords from a nearby hanging.

"You sulky slut!" she said between her teeth. "I'm going to strip you stark naked and tie you across that couch and whip you until you tell me what you were doing here, and who sent you!"

Yasala made no verbal protest, nor did she offer any resistance, as Valeria carried out the first part of her threat with a fury that her captive's obstinacy only sharpened. Then for a space there was no sound in the chamber except the whistle and crackle of hard-woven silken cords on naked flesh. Yasala could not move her fast-bound hands or feet. Her body writhed and quivered under the chastisement, her head swayed from side to side in rhythm with the blows. Her teeth were sunk into her lower lip and a trickle of blood began as the punishment continued. But she did not cry out.

The pliant cords made no great sound as they encountered the quivering body of the captive; only a sharp crackling snap, but each cord left a red streak across Yasala's dark flesh. Valeria inflicted the punishment with all the strength of her war-hardened arm, with all the mercilessness acquired during a life where pain and torment were daily happenings, and with all the cynical ingenuity which only a woman displays toward a woman. Yasala suffered more, physically and mentally, than she would have suffered under a lash wielded by a man, however strong.

It was the application of this feminine cynicism which at last tamed Yasala.

A low whimper escaped from her lips, and Valeria paused, arm lifted, and raked back a damp yellow lock. "Well, are you going to talk?" she demanded. "I can keep this up all night, if necessary."

"Mercy!" whispered the woman. "I will tell."

Valeria cut the cords from her wrists and ankles, and pulled her to her feet. Yasala sank down on the couch, half-reclining on one bare hip, supporting herself on her arm, and writhing at the contact of her smarting flesh with the couch. She was trembling in every limb.

"Wine!" she begged, dry-lipped, indicating with a quivering hand a gold vessel on an ivory table. "Let me drink. I am weak with pain. Then I will tell you all."

Valeria picked up the vessel, and Yasala rose unsteadily to receive it. She took it, raised it toward her lips — then dashed the contents full into the Aquilonian's face. Valeria reeled backward, shaking and clawing the stinging liquid out of her eyes. Through a smarting mist she saw Yasala dart across the room, fling back a bolt, throw open the copper-bound door and run down the hall. The pirate was after her instantly, sword out and murder in her heart.

But Yasala had the start, and she ran with the nervous agility of a woman who has just been whipped to the point of hysterical frenzy. She rounded a corner in the corridor, yards ahead of Valeria, and when the pirate turned it, she saw only an empty hall, and at the other end a door that gaped blackly. A damp moldy scent reeked up from it, and Valeria shivered. That must be the door that led to the catacombs. Yasala had taken refuge among the dead.

Valeria advanced to the door and looked down a flight of stone steps that vanished quickly into utter blackness. Evidently it was a shaft that led straight to the pits below the city, without opening upon any of the lower floors. She shivered slightly at the thought of the thousands of corpses lying in their stone crypts down there, wrapped in their moldering cloths. She had no intention of groping her way down those stone steps. Yasala doubtless knew every turn and twist of the subterranean tunnels.

She was turning back, baffled and furious, when a sobbing cry welled up from the blackness. It seemed to come from a great depth, but human words were faintly distinguishable, and the voice was that of a woman. "Oh, help! Help, in Set's name! Ahhh!" It trailed away, and Valeria thought she caught the echo of a ghostly tittering.

Valeria felt her skin crawl. What had happened to Yasala down there in the thick blackness? There was no doubt that it had been she who had cried out. But what peril could have befallen her? Was a Xotalanca lurking down there? Olmec had assured them that the catacombs below Tecuhltli were walled off from the rest, too securely for their enemies to break through. Besides, that tittering had not sounded like a human being at all.

Valeria hurried back down the corridor, not stopping to close the door that opened on the stair. Regaining her chamber, she closed the door and shot the bolt behind her. She pulled on her boots and buckled her sword-belt about her. She was determined to make her way to Conan's room and urge him, if he still lived, to join her in an attempt to fight their way out of that city of devils.

But even as she reached the door that opened into the corridor, a long-drawn scream of agony rang through the halls, followed by the stamp of running feet and the loud clangor of swords.

5. *Twenty Red Nails*

Two warriors lounged in the guardroom on the floor known as the Tier of the Eagle. Their attitude was casual, though habitually alert. An attack on the great bronze door from without was always a possibility, but for many years no such assault had been attempted on either side.

"The strangers are strong allies," said one. "Olmec will move against the enemy tomorrow, I believe."

He spoke as a soldier in a war might have spoken. In the miniature world of Xuchotl each handful of feudists was an army, and the empty halls between the castles was the country over which they campaigned.

The other meditated for a space.

"Suppose with their aid we destroy Xotalanc," he said. "What then, Xatmec?"

"Why," returned Xatmec, "we will drive red nails for them all. The captives we will burn and flay and quarter."

"But afterward?" pursued the other. "After we have slain them all? Will it not seem strange to have no foe to fight? All my life I have fought and hated the Xotalancas. With the feud ended, what is left?"

Xatmec shrugged his shoulders. His thoughts had never gone beyond the destruction of their foes. They could not go beyond that.

Suddenly both men stiffened at a noise outside the door.

"To the door, Xatmec!" hissed the last speaker. "I shall look through the Eye —"

Xatmec, sword in hand, leaned against the bronze door, straining his ear to hear through the metal. His mate looked into the mirror. He started convulsively. Men were clustered thickly outside the door; grim, dark-faced men with swords gripped in their teeth — *and their fingers thrust into their ears*. One who wore a feathered headdress had a set of pipes which he set to his lips, and even as the Tecuhltli started to shout a warning, the pipes began to skirl.

The cry died in the guard's throat as the thin, weird piping penetrated the metal door and smote on his ears. Xatmec leaned frozen against the door, as if paralyzed in that position. His face was that of a wooden image, his expression one of horrified listening. The other guard, farther removed from the source of the sound, yet sensed the horror of what was taking place, the grisly threat that lay in that demoniac fifing. He felt the weird strains plucking like unseen fingers at the tissues of his brain, filling him with alien emotions and impulses of madness. But with a soul-tearing effort he broke the spell, and shrieked a warning in a voice he did not recognize as his own.

But even as he cried out, the music changed to an unbearable shrilling that was like a knife in the eardrums. Xatmec screamed in sudden agony, and all the sanity went out of his face like a flame blown out in a wind. Like a madman he ripped loose the chain, tore open the door and rushed out into the hall, sword lifted before his mate could stop him. A dozen blades struck him down, and over his mangled body the Xotalancas surged into the guardroom, with a long-drawn, blood-mad yell that sent the unwonted echoes reverberating.

His brain reeling from the shock of it all, the remaining guard leaped to meet them with goring spear. The horror of the sorcery he had just witnessed was submerged in the stunning realization that the enemy were in Tecuhltli. And as his spearhead ripped through a dark-skinned belly he knew no more, for a swinging sword crushed his skull, even as wild-eyed warriors came pouring in from the chambers behind the guardroom.

It was the yelling of men and the clanging of steel that brought Conan bounding from his couch, wide awake and broadsword in hand. In an instant he had reached the door and flung it open, and was glaring out into the corridor just as Techotl rushed up it, eyes blazing madly.

"The Xotalancas!" he screamed, in a voice hardly human. *"They are within the door!"*

Conan ran down the corridor, even as Valeria emerged from her chamber.

"What the devil is it?" she called.

"Techotl says the Xotalancas are in," he answered hurriedly. "That racket sounds like it."

With the Tecuhltli on their heels they burst into the throne room and were confronted by a scene beyond the most frantic dream of blood and fury. Twenty men and women, their black hair streaming, and the white skulls gleaming on their breasts, were locked in combat with the people of Tecuhltli. The women on both sides fought as madly as the men, and already the room and the hall beyond were strewn with corpses.

Olmec, naked but for a breechclout, was fighting before his throne, and as the adventurers entered, Tascela ran from an inner chamber with a sword in her hand.

Xatmec and his mate were dead, so there was none to tell the Tecuhltli how their foes had found their way into their citadel. Nor was there any to say what had prompted that mad attempt. But the losses of the Xotalancas had been greater, their position more desperate, than the Tecuhltli had known. The maiming of their scaly ally, the destruction of the Burning Skull, and the news, gasped by a dying man, that mysterious white-skin allies had joined their enemies, had driven them to the frenzy of desperation and the wild determination to die dealing death to their ancient foes.

The Tecuhltli, recovering from the first stunning shock of the surprize that had swept them back into the throne room and littered the floor with their corpses, fought back with an equally desperate fury, while the door-guards from the lower floors came racing to hurl themselves into the fray. It was the death-fight of rabid wolves, blind, panting, merciless. Back and forth it surged, from door to dais, blades whickering and striking into flesh, blood spurting, feet stamping the crimson floor where redder pools were forming. Ivory tables crashed over, seats were splintered, velvet hangings torn down were stained red. It was the bloody climax of a bloody half-century, and every man there sensed it.

But the conclusion was inevitable. The Tecuhltli outnumbered the invaders almost two to one, and they were heartened by that fact and by the entrance into the mêlée of their light-skinned allies.

These crashed into the fray with the devastating effect of a hurricane plowing through a grove of saplings. In sheer strength no three Tlazitlans were a match for Conan, and in spite of his weight he was quicker on his feet than any of them. He moved through the whirling, eddying mass with the surety and destructiveness of a gray wolf amidst a pack of alley curs, and he strode over a wake of crumpled figures.

Valeria fought beside him, her lips smiling and her eyes blazing. She was stronger than the average man, and far quicker and more ferocious. Her sword was like a living thing in her hand. Where Conan beat down opposition by the sheer weight and power of his blows, breaking spears, splitting skulls and cleaving bosoms to the breastbone, Valeria brought into action a finesse of swordplay that dazzled and bewildered her antagonists before it slew them. Again and again a warrior, heaving high his heavy blade, found her point in his jugular before he could strike. Conan, towering above the field, strode through the welter smiting right and left, but Valeria moved like an illusive phantom, constantly shifting, and thrusting and slashing as she shifted. Swords missed her again and again as the wielders flailed the empty air and died with her point in their hearts or throats, and her mocking laughter in their ears.

Neither sex nor condition was considered by the maddened combatants. The five women of the Xotalancas were down with their throats cut before Conan and Valeria entered the fray, and when a man or woman went down under the stamping feet, there was always a knife ready for the helpless throat, or a sandaled foot eager to crush the prostrate skull.

From wall to wall, from door to door rolled the waves of combat, spilling over into adjoining chambers. And presently only Tecuhltli and their white-skinned allies stood upright in the great throne room. The survivors stared bleakly and blankly at each other, like survivors after Judgement Day or the destruction of the world. On legs wide-braced, hands gripping notched and dripping swords, blood trickling down their arms, they stared at one another across the mangled corpses of friends and foes. They had no breath left to shout, but a bestial mad howling rose from their lips. It was not a human cry of triumph. It was the howling of a rabid wolf-pack stalking among the bodies of its victims.

Conan caught Valeria's arm and turned her about.

"You've got a stab in the calf of your leg," he growled.

She glanced down, for the first time aware of a stinging in the muscles of her leg. Some dying man on the floor had fleshed his dagger with his last effort.

"You look like a butcher yourself," she laughed.

He shook a red shower from his hands.

"Not mine. Oh, a scratch here and there. Nothing to bother about. But that calf ought to be bandaged."

Olmec came through the litter, looking like a ghoul with his naked massive shoulders splashed with blood, and his black beard dabbled in crimson. His eyes were red, like the reflection of flame on black water.

"We have won!" he croaked dazedly. "The feud is ended! The dogs of Xotalanc lie dead! Oh, for a captive to flay alive! Yet it is good to look upon their dead faces. Twenty dead dogs! Twenty red nails for the black column!"

"You'd best see to your wounded," grunted Conan, turning away from him. "Here, girl, let me see that leg."

"Wait a minute!" she shook him off impatiently. The fire of fighting still burned brightly in her soul. "How do we know these are all of them? These might have come on a raid of their own."

"They would not split the clan on a foray like this," said Olmec, shaking his head, and regaining some of his ordinary intelligence. Without his purple robe the man seemed less like a prince than some repellent beast of prey. "I will stake my head upon it that we have slain them all. There were less of them than I dreamed, and they must have been desperate. But how came they in Tecuhltli?"

Tascela came forward, wiping her sword on her naked thigh, and holding in her other hand an object she had taken from the body of the feathered leader of the Xotalancas.

"The pipes of madness," she said. "A warrior tells me that Xatmec opened the door to the Xotalancas and was cut down as they stormed into the guardroom. This warrior came to the guardroom from the inner hall just in time to see it happen and to hear the last of a weird strain of music which froze his very soul. Tolkemec used to talk of these pipes, which the Xuchotlans swore were hidden somewhere in the catacombs with the bones of the ancient wizard who used them in his lifetime. Somehow the dogs of Xotalanc found them and learned their secret."

"Somebody ought to go to Xotalanc and see if any remain alive," said Conan. "I'll go if somebody will guide me."

Olmec glanced at the remnants of his people. There were only twenty left alive, and of these several lay groaning on the floor. Tascela was the only one of the Tecuhltli who had escaped without a wound. The princess was untouched, though she had fought as savagely as any.

"Who will go with Conan to Xotalanc?" asked Olmec.

Techotl limped forward. The wound in his thigh had started bleeding afresh, and he had another gash across his ribs.

"I will go!"

"No, you won't," vetoed Conan. "And you're not going either, Valeria. In a little while that leg will be getting stiff."

"I will go," volunteered a warrior, who was knotting a bandage about a slashed forearm.

"Very well, Yanath. Go with the Cimmerian. And

you, too, Topal." Olmec indicated another man whose
injuries were slight. "But first aid to lift the badly
wounded on these couches where we may bandage
their hurts."

This was done quickly. As they stooped to pick up
a woman who had been stunned by a war-club,
Olmec's beard brushed Topal's ear. Conan thought
the prince muttered something to the warrior, but he
could not be sure. A few moments later he was
leading his companions down the hall.

Conan glanced back as he went out the door, at
that shambles where the dead lay on the smoldering
floor, bloodstained dark limbs knotted in attitudes of
fierce muscular effort, dark faces frozen in masks of
hate, glassy eyes glaring up at the green fire-jewels
which bathed the ghastly scene in a dusky emerald
witch-light. Among the dead the living moved aim-
lessly, like people moving in a trance. Conan heard
Olmec call a woman and direct her to bandage Valeria's leg. The pirate followed the woman into an
adjoining chamber, already beginning to limp slightly.

Warily the two Tecuhltli led Conan along the hall
beyond the bronze door, and through chamber after
chamber shimmering in the green fire. They saw no
one, heard no sound. After they crossed the Great
Hall which bisected the city from north to south,
their caution was increased by the realization of their
nearness to enemy territory. But chambers and halls
lay empty to their wary gaze, and they came at last
along a broad dim hallway and halted before a

bronze door similar to the Eagle Door of Tecuhltli. Gingerly they tried it, and it opened silently under their fingers. Awed, they started into the green-lit chambers beyond. For fifty years no Tecuhltli had entered those halls save as a prisoner going to a hideous doom. To go to Xotalanc had been the ultimate horror that could befall a man of the western castle. The terror of it had stalked through their dreams since earliest childhood. To Yanath and Topol that bronze door was like the portal of Hell.

They cringed back, unreasoning horror in their eyes, and Conan pushed past them and strode into Xotalanc.

Timidly they followed him. As each man set foot over the threshold he stared and glared wildly about him. But only their quick, hurried breathing disturbed the silence.

They had come into a square guardroom, like that behind the Eagle Door of Tecuhltli, and, similarly, a hall ran away from it to a broad chamber that was a counterpart of Olmec's throne room.

Conan glanced down the hall with its rugs and divans and hangings, and stood listening intently. He heard no noise, and the rooms had an empty feel. He did not believe there were any Xotalancas left alive in Xuchotl.

"Come on," he muttered, and started down the hall.

He had not gone far when he was aware that only Yanath was following him. He wheeled back to see

Topal standing in an attitude of horror, one arm out as if to fend off some threatening peril, his distended eyes fixed with hypnotic intensity on something protruding from behind a divan.

"What the devil?" Then Conan saw what Topal was staring at, and he felt a faint twitching of the skin between his giant shoulders. A monstrous head protruded from behind the divan, a reptilian head, broad as the head of a crocodile, with down-curving fangs that projected over the lower jaw. But there was an unnatural limpness about the thing, and the hideous eyes were glazed.

Conan peered behind the couch. It was a great serpent which lay there limp in death, but such a serpent as he had never seen in his wanderings. The reek and chill of the deep black earth were about it, and its color was an indeterminable hue which changed with each new angle from which he surveyed it. A great wound in the neck showed what had caused its death.

"It is the Crawler!" whispered Yanath.

"It's the thing I slashed on the stair," grunted Conan. "After it trailed us to the Eagle Door, it dragged itself here to die. How could the Xotalancas control such a brute?"

The Tecuhltli shivered and shook their heads.

"They brought it up from the black tunnels *below* the catacombs. They discovered secrets unknown to Tecuhltli."

"Well, it's dead, and if they'd had any more of them, they'd have brought them along when they came to Tecuhltli. Come on."

They crowded close at his heels as he strode down the hall and thrust on the silver-worked door at the other end.

"If we don't find anybody on this floor," he said, "we'll descend into the lower floors. We'll explore Xotalanc from the roof to the catacombs. If Xotalanc is like Tecuhltli, all the rooms and halls in this tier will be lighted — what the devil!"

They had come into the broad throne chamber, so similar to that one in Tecuhltli. There were the same jade dais and ivory seat, the same divans, rugs and hangings on the walls. No black, red-scarred column stood behind the throne-dais, but evidences of the grim feud were not lacking.

Ranged along the wall behind the dais were rows of glass-covered shelves. And on those shelves hundreds of human heads, perfectly preserved, stared at the startled watchers with emotionless eyes, as they had stared for only the gods knew how many months and years.

Topal muttered a curse, but Yanath stood silent, the mad light growing in his wide eyes. Conan frowned, knowing that Tlazitlan sanity was hung on a hair-trigger.

Suddenly Yanath pointed to the ghastly relics with a twitching finger.

"There is my brother's head!" he murmured. "And there is my father's younger brother! And there beyond them is my sister's eldest son!"

Suddenly he began to weep, dry-eyed, with harsh, loud sobs that shook his frame. He did not take his eyes from the heads. His sobs grew shriller, changed to frightful, high-pitched laughter, and that in turn became an unbearable screaming. Yanath was stark mad.

Conan laid a hand on his shoulder, and as if the touch had released all the frenzy in his soul, Yanath screamed and whirled, striking at the Cimmerian with his sword. Conan parried the blow, and Topal tried to catch Yanath's arm. But the madman avoided him and with froth flying from his lips, he drove his sword deep into Topal's body. Topal sank down with a groan, and Yanath whirled for an instant like a crazy dervish; then he ran at the shelves and began hacking at the glass with his sword, screeching blasphemously.

Conan sprang at him from behind, trying to catch him unaware and disarm him, but the madman wheeled and lunged at him, screaming like a lost soul. Realizing that the warrior was hopelessly insane, the Cimmerian sidestepped, and as the maniac went past, he swung a cut that severed the shoulder-bone and breast, and dropped the man dead beside his dying victim.

Conan bent over Topal, seeing that the man was at his last gasp. It was useless to seek to stanch the blood gushing from the horrible wound.

"You're done for, Topal," grunted Conan. "Any word you want to send to your people?"

"Bend closer," gasped Topal, and Conan complied — and an instant later caught the man's wrist as Topal struck at his breast with a dagger.

"Crom!" swore Conan. "Are you mad, too?"

"Olmec ordered it!" gasped the dying man. "I know not why. As we lifted the wounded upon the couches he whispered to me, bidding me to slay you as we returned to Tecuhltli —" And with the name of his clan on his lips, Topal died.

Conan scowled down at him in puzzlement. This whole affair had an aspect of lunacy. Was Olmec mad, too? Were all the Tecuhltli madder than he had realized? With a shrug of his shoulders he strode down the hall and out of the bronze door, leaving the dead Tecuhltli lying before the staring dead eyes of their kinsmen's heads.

Conan needed no guide back through the labyrinth they had traversed. His primitive instinct of direction led him unerringly along the route they had come. He traversed it as warily as he had before, his sword in his hand, and his eyes fiercely searching each shadowed nook and corner; for it was his former allies he feared now, not the ghosts of the slain Xotalancas.

He had crossed the Great Hall and entered the chambers beyond when he heard something moving ahead of him — something which gasped and panted, and moved with a strange, floundering, scrambling noise. A moment later Conan saw a man crawling over the flaming floor toward him — a man whose progress left a broad bloody smear on the smoldering surface. It was Techotl and his eyes were already glazing; from a deep gash in his breast blood gushed steadily between the fingers of his clutching hand. With the other he clawed and hitched himself along.

"Conan," he cried chokingly, "Conan! Olmec has taken the yellow-haired woman!"

"So that's why he told Topal to kill me!" murmured Conan, dropping to his knee beside the man, who his experienced eye told him was dying. "Olmec isn't as mad as I thought."

Techotl's groping fingers plucked at Conan's arm. In the cold, loveless, and altogether hideous life of the Tecuhltli his admiration and affection for the invaders from the outer world formed a warm, human oasis, constituted a tie that connected him with a more natural humanity that was totally lacking in his fellows, whose only emotions were hate, lust, and the urge of sadistic cruelty.

"I sought to oppose him," gurgled Techotl, blood bubbling frothily to his lips. "But he struck me down. He thought he had slain me, but I crawled away. Ah, Set, how far I have crawled in my own blood! Beware, Conan! Olmec may have set an ambush for your return! Slay Olmec! He is a beast. Take Valeria and flee! Fear not to traverse the forest. Olmec and Tascela lied about the dragons. They slew each other years ago, all save the strongest. For a dozen years there has been only one dragon. If you have slain him, there is naught in the forest to harm

you. He was the god Olmec worshipped; and Olmec
fed human sacrifices to him, the very old and the very
young, bound and hurled from the wall. Hasten!
Olmec has taken Valeria to the Chamber of the —"

His head slumped down and he was dead before it
came to rest on the floor.

Conan sprang up, his eyes like live coals. So that
was Olmec's game, having first used the strangers to
destroy his foes! He should have known that something of the sort would be going on in that black-
bearded degenerate's mind.

The Cimmerian started toward Tecuhltli with
reckless speed. Rapidly he reckoned the numbers of
his former allies. Only twenty-one, counting Olmec,
had survived that fiendish battle in the throne room.
Three had died since, which left seventeen enemies
with which to reckon. In his rage Conan felt capable
of accounting for the whole clan single-handed.

But the innate craft of the wilderness rose to guide
his berserk rage. He remembered Techotl's warning
of an ambush. It was quite probable that the prince
would make such provisions, on the chance that
Topal might have failed to carry out his order. Olmec
would be expecting him to return by the same route
he had followed in going to Xotalanc.

Conan glanced up at a skylight under which he
was passing and caught the blurred glimmer of stars.
They had not yet begun to pale for dawn. The events
of the night had been crowded into a comparatively
short space of time.

He turned aside from his direct course and descended a winding staircase to the floor below. He did not know where the door was to be found that let into the castle on that level, but he knew he could find it. How he was to force the locks he did not know; he believed that the doors of Tecuhltli would all be locked and bolted, if for no other reason than the habits of half a century. But there was nothing else but to attempt it.

Sword in hand, he hurried noiselessly on through a maze of green-lit or shadowy rooms and halls. He knew he must be near Tecuhltli, when a sound brought him up short. He recognized it for what it was — a human being trying to cry out through a stifling gag. It came from somewhere ahead of him, and to the left. In those deathly-still chambers a small sound carried a long way.

Conan turned aside and went seeking after the sound, which continued to be repeated. Presently he was glaring through a doorway upon a weird scene. In the room into which he was looking a low rack-like frame of iron lay on the floor, and a giant figure was bound prostrate upon it. His head rested on a bed of iron spikes, which were already crimson-pointed with blood where they had pierced his scalp. A peculiar harness-like contrivance was fastened about his head, though in such a manner that the leather band did not protect his scalp from the spikes. This harness was connected by a slender chain to the mechanism that upheld a huge iron ball which was suspended above the captive's hairy breast. As long as the man could force himself to remain motionless the iron ball hung in its place. But when the pain of the iron points caused him to lift his head, the ball lurched downward a few inches. Presently his aching neck muscles would no longer support his head in its unnatural position and it would fall back on the spikes again. It was obvious that eventually the ball would crush him to a pulp, slowly and inexorably. The victim was gagged, and above the gag his great black ox-eyes rolled wildly toward the man in the doorway, who stood in silent amazement. The man on the rack was Olmec, prince of Tecuhltli.

6. *The Eyes of Tascela*

"Why did you bring me into this chamber to bandage my leg?" demanded Valeria. "Couldn't you have done it just as well in the throne room?"

She sat on a couch with her wounded leg extended upon it, and the Tecuhltli woman had just bound it with silk bandages. Valeria's red-stained sword lay on the couch beside her.

She frowned as she spoke. The woman had done her task silently and efficiently, but Valeria liked neither the lingering, caressing touch of her slim fingers nor the expression in her eyes.

"They have taken the rest of the wounded into the other chambers," answered the woman in the soft

speech of the Tecuhltli women, which somehow did
not suggest either softness or gentleness in the speak-
ers. A little while before, Valeria had seen this same
woman stab a Xotalanca woman through the breast
and stamp the eyeballs out of a wounded Xotalanca
man.

"They will be carrying the corpses of the dead
down into the catacombs," she added, "lest the
ghosts escape into the chambers and dwell there."

"Do you believe in ghosts?" asked Valeria.

"I know the ghost of Tolkemec dwells in the catacombs," she answered with a shiver. "Once I saw it,
as I crouched in a crypt among the bones of a dead
queen. It passed by in the form of an ancient man
with flowing white beard and locks, and luminous
eyes that blazed in the darkness. It was Tolkemec; I
saw him living when I was a child and he was being
tortured."

Her voice sank to a fearful whisper: "Olmec
laughs, but I *know* Tolkemec's ghost dwells in the
catacombs! They say it is rats which gnaw the flesh
from the bones of the newly dead — but ghosts eat
flesh. Who knows but that —"

She glanced up quickly as a shadow fell across the
couch. Valeria looked up to see Olmec gazing down
at her. The prince had cleansed his hands, torso, and
beard of the blood that had splashed them; but he
had not donned his robe, and his great dark-skinned
hairless body and limbs renewed the impression of
strength bestial in its nature. His deep black eyes

burned with a more elemental light, and there was the suggestion of a twitching in the fingers that tugged at his thick blue-black beard.

He stared fixedly at the woman, and she rose and glided from the chamber. As she passed through the door she cast a look over her shoulder at Valeria, a glance full of cynical derision and obscene mockery.

"She has done a clumsy job," criticized the prince, coming to the divan and bending over the bandage. "Let me see —"

With a quickness amazing in one of his bulk he snatched her sword and threw it across the chamber. His next move was to catch her in his giant arms.

Quick and unexpected as the move was, she almost matched it; for even as he grabbed her, her dirk was in her hand and she stabbed murderously at his throat. More by luck than skill he caught her wrist, and then began a savage wrestling-match. She fought him with fists, feet, knees, teeth, and nails, with all the strength of her magnificent body and all the knowledge of hand-to-hand fighting she had acquired in her years of roving and fighting on sea and land. It availed her nothing against his brute strength. She lost her dirk in the first moment of contact, and thereafter found herself powerless to inflict any appreciable pain on her giant attacker.

The blaze in his weird black eyes did not alter, and their expression filled her with fury, fanned by the sardonic smile that seemed carved upon his bearded lips. Those eyes and that smile contained all the cruel

cynicism that seethes below the surface of a sophisti-
cated and degenerate race, and for the first time in
her life Valeria experienced fear of a man. It was like
struggling against some huge elemental force; his
iron arms thwarted her efforts with an ease that sent
panic racing through her limbs. He seemed imper-
vious to any pain she could inflict. Only once, when
she sank her white teeth savagely into his wrist so
that the blood started, did he react. And that was to
buffet her brutally upon the side of the head with his
open hand, so that stars flashed before her eyes and
her head rolled on her shoulders.

Her shirt had been torn open in the struggle, and
with cynical cruelty he rasped his thick beard across
her bare breasts, bringing the blood to suffuse the
fair skin, and fetching a cry of pain and outraged fury
from her. Her convulsive resistance was useless; she
was crushed down on a couch, disarmed and panting, her eyes blazing up at him like the eyes of a
trapped tigress.

A moment later he was hurrying from the chamber, carrying her in his arms. She made no resistance,
but the smoldering of her eyes showed that she was
unconquered in spirit, at least. She had not cried out.
She knew that Conan was not within call, and it did
not occur to her that any in Tecuhltli would oppose
their prince. But she noticed that Olmec went stealthily, with his head on one side as if listening for sounds
of pursuit, and he did not return to the throne chamber. He carried her through a door that stood opposite

that through which he had entered, crossed another
room and began stealing down a hall. As she became
convinced that he feared some opposition to the ab-
duction, she threw back her head and screamed at the
top of her lusty voice.

She was rewarded by a slap that half-stunned her,
and Olmec quickened his pace to a shambling run.

But her cry had been echoed, and twisting her
head about, Valeria, through the tears and stars that
partly blinded her, saw Techotl limping after them.

Olmec turned with a snarl, shifting the woman to
an uncomfortable and certainly undignified position
under one huge arm, where he held her writhing and
kicking vainly, like a child.

"Olmec!" protested Techotl. "You cannot be such
a dog as to do this thing! She is Conan's woman! She
helped us slay the Xotalancas, and —"

Without a word Olmec balled his free hand into a
huge fist and stretched the wounded warrior senseless at his feet. Stooping, and hindered not at all by
the struggles and imprecations of his captive, he
drew Techotl's sword from its sheath and stabbed the
warrior in the breast. Then casting aside the weapon
he fled on along the corridor. He did not see a
woman's dark face peer cautiously after him from
behind a hanging. It vanished, and presently Techotl
groaned and stirred, rose dazedly and staggered
drunkenly away, calling Conan's name.

Olmec hurried on down the corridor, and descended a winding ivory staircase. He crossed several

corridors and halted at last in a broad chamber
whose doors were veiled with heavy tapestries, with
one exception — a heavy bronze door similar to the
Door of the Eagle on the upper floor.

He was moved to rumble, pointing to it: "That is
one of the outer doors of Tecuhltli. For the first time
in fifty years it is unguarded. We need not guard it
now, for Xotalanc is no more."

"Thanks to Conan and me, you bloody rogue!"
sneered Valeria, trembling with fury and the shame
of physical coercion. "You trecherous dog! Conan
will cut your throat for this!"

Olmec did not bother to voice his belief that
Conan's own gullet had already been severed according to his whispered command. He was too
utterly cynical to be at all interested in her thoughts
or opinions. His flame-lit eyes devoured her, dwelling burningly on the generous expanses of clear
white flesh exposed where her shirt and breeches had
been torn in the struggle.

"Forget Conan," he said thickly. "Olmec is lord
of Xuchotl. Xotalanc is no more. There will be no
more fighting. We shall spend our lives in drinking
and lovemaking. First let us drink!"

He seated himself on an ivory table and pulled her
down on his knees, like a dark-skinned satyr with a
white nymph in his arms. Ignoring her un-nymphlike
profanity, he held her helpless with one great arm
about her waist while the other reached across the
table and secured a vessel of wine.

"Drink!" he commanded, forcing it to her lips, as she writhed her head away.

The liquor slopped over, stinging her lips, splashing down on her naked breasts.

"Your guest does not like your wine, Olmec," spoke a cool, sardonic voice.

Olmec stiffened; fear grew in his flaming eyes. Slowly he swung his great head about and stared at Tascela who posed negligently in the curtained doorway, one hand on her smooth hip. Valeria twisted herself about in his iron grip, and when she met the burning eyes of Tascela, a chill tingled along her supple spine. New experiences were flooding Valeria's proud soul that night. Recently she had learned to fear a man; now she knew what it was to fear a woman.

Olmec sat motionless, a gray pallor growing under his swarthy skin. Tascela brought her other hand from behind her and displayed a small gold vessel.

"I feared she would not like your wine, Olmec," purred the princess, "so I brought some of mine, some I brought with me long ago from the shores of Lake Zuad — do you understand, Olmec?"

Beads of sweat stood out suddenly on Olmec's brow. His muscles relaxed, and Valeria broke away and put the table between them. But though reason told her to dart from the room, some fascination she could not understand held her rigid, watching the scene.

Tascela came toward the seated prince with a swaying, undulating walk that was mockery in itself.

Her voice was soft, slurringly caressing, but he eyes gleamed. Her slim fingers stroked his beard lightly.

"You are selfish, Olmec," she crooned, smiling. "You would keep our handsome guest to yourself, though you knew I wished to entertain her. You are much at fault, Olmec!"

The mask dropped for an instant; he eyes flashed, her face was contorted and with an appalling show of strength her hand locked convulsively in his beard and tore out a great handful. This evidence of unnatural strength was no more terrifying than the momentary baring of the hellish fury that raged under her bland exterior.

Olmec lurched up with a roar, and stood swaying like a bear, his mighty hands clenching and unclenching.

"Slut!" His booming voice filled the room. "Witch! She-devil! Tecuhltli should have slain you fifty years ago! Begone! I have endured too much from you! This white-skinned wench is mine! Get hence before I slay you!"

The princess laughed and dashed the blood-stained strands into his face. Her laughter was less merciful than the ring of flint on steel.

"Once you spoke otherwise, Olmec," she taunted. "Once, in your youth, you spoke words of love. Aye, you were my lover once, years ago, and because you loved me, you slept in my arms beneath the enchanted lotus — and thereby put into my hands the chains that enslaved you. You know you cannot withstand me. You know I have but to gaze into your eyes, with the mystic power a priest of Stygia taught me, long ago, and you are powerless. You remember the night beneath the black lotus that waved above us, stirred by no worldly breeze; you scent again the unearthly perfumes that stole and rose like a cloud about you to enslave you. You cannot fight against me. You are my slave as you were that night — as you shall be so long as you live, Olmec of Xuchotl!"

Her voice had sunk to a murmur like the rippling of a stream running through starlit darkness. She leaned close to the prince and spread her long tapering fingers upon his giant breast. His eyes glared, his great hands fell limply to his sides.

With a smile of cruel malice, Tascela lifted the vessel and placed it to his lips.

"Drink!"

Mechanically the prince obeyed. And instantly the glaze passed from his eyes and they were flooded with fury, comprehension and an awful fear. His mouth gaped, but no sound issued. For an instant he reeled on buckling knees, and then fell in a sodden heap on the floor.

His fall jolted Valeria out of her paralysis. She turned and sprang toward the door, but with a movement that would have shamed a leaping panther, Tascela was before her. Valeria struck at her with her clenched fist, and all the power of her supple body behind the blow. It would have stretched a man senseless on the floor. But with a lithe twist of her torso, Tascela avoided the blow and caught the pirate's wrist. The next instant Valeria's left hand was imprisoned, and holding her wrists together with one hand, Tasacela calmly bound them with a cord she drew from her girdle. Valeria thought she had tasted the ultimate in humiliation already that night, but her shame at being manhandled by Olmec was nothing to the sensations that now shook her supple frame. Valeria had always been inclined to despise the other members of her sex; and it was overwhelming to encounter another woman who could handle her like a child. She scarcely resisted at all when Tascela forced her into a chair and drawing her bound wrists down between her knees, fastened them to the chair.

Casually stepping over Olmec, Tascela walked to the bronze door and shot the bolt and threw it open, revealing a hallway without.

"Opening upon this hall," she remarked, speaking to her feminine captive for the first time, "there is a chamber which in old times was used as a torture room. When we retired into Tecuhltli, we brought most of the apparatus with us, but there was one piece too heavy to move. It is still in working order. I think it will be quite convenient now."

An understanding flame of terror rose in Olmec's eyes. Tascela strode back to him, bent and gripped him by the hair.

"He is only paralyzed temporarily," she remarked

conversationally. "He can hear, think, and feel — aye, he can feel very well indeed!"

With which sinister observation she started toward the door, dragging the giant bulk with an ease that made the pirate's eyes dilate. She passed into the hall and moved down it without hesitation, presently disappearing with her captive into a chamber that opened into it, and whence shortly thereafter issued the clank of iron.

Valeria swore softly and tugged vainly, with her legs braced against the chair. The cords that confined her were apparently unbreakable.

Tascela presently returned alone; behind her a muffled groaning issued from the chamber. She closed the door but did not bolt it. Tascela was beyond the grip of habit, as she was beyond the touch of other human instincts and emotions.

Valeria sat dumbly, watching the woman in whose slim hands, the pirate realized, her destiny now rested.

Tascela grasped her yellow locks and forced back her head, looking impersonally down into her face. But the glitter in her dark eyes was not impersonal.

"I have chosen you for a great honor," she said. "You shall restore the youth of Tascela. Oh, you stare at that! My appearance is that of youth, but through my veins creeps the sluggish chill of approaching age, as I have felt it a thousand times before. I am old, so old I do not remember my childhood. But I was a girl once, and a priest of Stygia loved me, and gave me the secret of immortality and youth everlasting. He died, then — some said by poison. But I dwelt in my palace by the shores of Lake Zuad and the passing years touched me not. So at last a king of Stygia desired me, and my people rebelled and brought me to this land. Olmec called me a princess. I am not of royal blood. I am greater than a princess. I am Tascela, whose youth your own glorious youth shall restore."

Valeria's tongue clove to the roof of her mouth. She sensed here a mystery darker than the degeneracy she had anticipated.

The taller woman unbound the Aquilonian's wrists and pulled her to her feet. It was not fear of the dominant strength that lurked in the princess' limbs that made Valeria a helpless, quivering captive in her hands. It was the burning, hypnotic, terrible eyes of Tascela.

7. *He Comes from the Dark*

"Well, I'm a Kushite!"

Conan glared down at the man on the iron rack.

"What the devil are *you* doing on that thing?"

Incoherent sounds issued from behind the gag and Conan bent and tore it away, evoking a bellow of fear from the captive; for his action caused the iron ball to lurch down until it nearly touched the broad breast.

"Be careful, for Set's sake!" begged Olmec.

"What for?" demanded Conan. "Do you think I care what happens to you? I only wish I had time to stay here and watch that chunk of iron grind your guts out. But I'm in a hurry. Where's Valeria?"

"Loose me!" urged Olmec. "I will tell you all!"

"Tell me first."

"Never!" The prince's heavy jaws set stubbornly.

"All right." Conan seated himself on a nearby bench. "I'll find her myself, after you've been reduced to a jelly. I believe I can speed up that process by twisting my sword-point around in your ear," he added, extending the weapon experimentally.

"Wait!" Words came in a rush from the captive's ashy lips. "Tascela took her from me. I've never been anything but a puppet in Tascela's hands."

"Tascela?" snorted Conan, and spat. "Why, the filthy —"

"No, no!" panted Olmec. "It's worse than you think. Tascela is old — centuries old. She renews her life and her youth by the sacrifice of beautiful young women. That's one thing that has reduced the clan to its present state. She will draw the essence of Valeria's life into her own body, and bloom with fresh vigor and beauty."

"Are the doors locked?" asked Conan, thumbing his sword edge.

"Aye! But I know a way to get into Tecuhltli. Only Tascela and I know, and she thinks me helpless and you slain. Free me and I swear I will help you rescue Valeria. Without my help you cannot win into

Tecuhltli; for even if you tortured me into revealing
the secret, you couldn't work it. Let me go, and we
will steal on Tascela and kill her before she can work
magic — before she can fix her eyes on us. A knife
thrown from behind will do the work. I should have
killed her thus long ago, but I feared that without her
to aid us the Xotalancas would overcome us. She
needed my help, too; that's the only reason she let me
live this long. Now neither needs the other, and one
must die. I swear that when we have slain the witch,
you and Valeria shall go free without harm. My
people will obey me when Tascela is dead."

Conan stooped and cut the ropes that held the
prince, and Olmec slid cautiously from under the
great ball and rose, shaking his head like a bull and
muttering imprecations as he fingered his lacerated
scalp. Standing shoulder to shoulder the two men presented a formidable picture of primitive power. Olmec
was as tall as Conan, and heavier; but there was something repellent about the Tlazitlan, something
abysmal and monstrous that contrasted unfavorably
with the clean-cut, compact hardness of the Cimmerian. Conan had discarded the remnants of his tattered, blood-soaked shirt, and stood with his
remarkable muscular development impressively revealed. His great shoulders were as broad as those of
Olmec, and more cleanly outlined, and his huge breast
arched with a more impressive sweep to a hard waist
that lacked the paunchy thickness of Olmec's
midsection. He might have been an image of primal

strength cut out of bronze. Olmec was darker, but not from the burning of the sun. If Conan was a figure out of the dawn of Time, Olmec was a shambling, somber shape from the darkness of Time's pre-dawn.

"Lead on," demanded Conan. "And keep ahead of me. I don't trust you any farther than I can throw a bull by the tail."

Olmec turned and stalked on ahead of him, one hand twitching slightly as it plucked at his matted beard.

Olmec did not lead Conan back to the bronze door, which the prince naturally supposed Tascela had locked, but to a certain chamber on the border of Tecuhltli.

"This secret has been guarded for half a century," he said. "Not even our own clan knew of it, and the Xotalancas never learned. Tecuhltli himself built this secret entrance, afterwards slaying the slaves who did the work; for he feared that he might find himself locked out of his own kingdom some day because of the spite of Tascela, whose passion for him soon changed to hate. But she discovered the secret, and barred the hidden door against him one day as he fled back from an unsuccessful raid, and the Xotalancas took him and flayed him. But once, spying upon her, I saw her enter Tecuhltli by this route, and so learned the secret."

He pressed upon a gold ornament in the wall, and a panel swung inward, disclosing an ivory stair leading upward.

"This stair is built within the wall," said Olmec. "It leads up to a tower upon the roof, and thence other stairs wind down to the various chambers. Hasten!"

"After you, comrade!" retorted Conan satirically, swaying his broadsword as he spoke, and Olmec shrugged his shoulders and stepped onto the staircase. Conan instantly followed him, and the door shut behind them. Far above a cluster of fire-jewels made the staircase a well of dusky dragon-light.

They mounted until Conan estimated that they were above the level of the fourth floor, and then came out into a cylindrical tower, in the domed roof of which was set the bunch of fire-jewels that lighted the stair. Through gold-barred windows, set with unbreakable crystal panes, the first windows he had seen in Xuchotl, Conan got a glimpse of high ridges, domes and more towers, looming darkly against the stars. He was looking across the roofs of Xuchotl.

Olmec did not look through the windows. He hurried down one of the several stairs that wound down from the tower, and when they had descended a few feet, this stair changed into a narrow corridor that wound tortuously on for some distance. It ceased at a steep flight of steps leading downward. There Olmec paused.

Up from below, muffled, but unmistakable, welled a woman's scream, edged with fright, fury, and shame. And Conan recognized Valeria's voice.

In the swift rage roused by that cry, and the amazement of wondering what peril could wring such a shriek from Valeria's reckless lips, Conan forgot Olmec. He pushed past the prince and started down the stair. Awakening instinct brought him about again, just as Olmec struck with his great mallet-like fist. The blow, fierce and silent, was aimed at the base of Conan's brain. But the Cimmerian wheeled in time to receive the buffet on the side of his neck instead. The impact would have snapped the vertebrae of a lesser man. As it was, Conan swayed backward, but even as he reeled he dropped his sword, useless at such close quarters, and grasped Olmec's extended arm, dragging the prince with him as he fell. Headlong they went down the steps together, in a revolving whirl of limbs and heads and bodies. And as they went Conan's iron fingers found and locked in Olmec's bull-throat.

The barbarian's neck and shoulder felt numb from the sledge-like impact of Olmec's huge fist, which had carried all the strength of the massive forearm, thick triceps and great shoulder. But this did not affect his ferocity to any appreciable extent. Like a bulldog he hung on grimly, shaken and battered and beaten against the steps as they rolled, until at last they struck an ivory panel-door at the bottom with such an impact that they splintered it its full length and crashed through its ruins. But Olmec was already dead, for those iron fingers had crushed out his life and broken his neck as they fell.

Conan rose, shaking the splinters from his great shoulders, blinking blood and dust out of his eyes.

He was in the great throne room. There were fifteen people in that room besides himself. The first person he saw was Valeria. A curious black altar stood before the throne-dais. Ranged about it, seven black candles in golden candlesticks sent up oozing spirals of thick green smoke, disturbingly scented. These spirals united in a cloud near the ceiling, forming a smoky arch above the altar. On that altar lay Valeria, stark naked, her white flesh gleaming in shocking contrast to the glistening ebon stone. She was not bound. She lay at full length, her arms stretched out above her head to their fullest extent. At the head of the altar knelt a young man, holding her wrists firmly. A young woman knelt at the other end of the altar, grasping her ankles. Between them she could neither rise nor move.

Eleven men and women of Tecuhltli knelt dumbly in a semicircle, watching the scene with hot, lustful eyes.

On the ivory throne-seat Tascela lolled. Bronze bowls of incense rolled their spirals about her; the wisps of smoke curled about her naked limbs like caressing fingers. She could not sit still; she squirmed and shifted about with sensuous abandon, as if finding pleasure in the contact of the smooth ivory with her sleek flesh.

The crash of the door as it broke beneath the impact of the hurtling bodies caused no change in the scene. The kneeling men and women merely glanced incuriously at the corpse of their prince and at the man who rose from the ruins of the door, then swung their eyes greedily back to the writhing white shape on the black altar. Tascela looked insolently at him, and sprawled back on her seat, laughing mockingly.

"Slut!" Conan saw red. His hands clenched into iron hammers as he started for her. With his first step something clanged loudly and steel bit savagely into his leg. He stumbled and almost fell, checked in his headlong stride. The jaws of an iron trap had closed on his leg, with teeth that sank deep and held. Only the ridged muscles of his calf saved the bone from being splintered. The accursed thing had sprung out of the smoldering floor without warning. He saw the slots now, in the floor where the jaws had lain, perfectly camouflaged.

"Fool!" laughed Tascela. "Did you think I would not guard against your possible return? Every door in this chamber is guarded by such traps. Stand there and watch now, while I fulfill the destiny of your handsome friend! Then I will decide your own."

Conan's hand instinctively sought his belt, only to encounter an empty scabbard. His sword was on the stair behind him. His poniard was lying back in the forest, where the dragon had torn it from his jaw. The steel teeth in his leg were like burning coals, but the pain was not as savage as the fury that seethed in his soul. He was trapped, like a wolf. If he had had his sword he would have hewn off his leg and crawled across the floor to slay Tascela. Valeria's eyes rolled toward him with mute appeal, and his own helplessness sent red waves of madness surging through his brain.

Dropping on the knee of his free leg, he strove to get his fingers between the jaws of the trap, to tear them apart by sheer strength. Blood started from beneath his fingernails, but the jaws fitted close about his leg in a circle whose segments jointed perfectly, contracted until there was no space between his mangled flesh and the fanged iron. The sight of Valeria's naked body added flame to the fire of his rage.

Tascela ignored him. Rising languidly from her seat she swept the ranks of her subjects with a searching glance, and asked: "Where are Xamec, Zlanath and Tachic?"

"They did not return from the catacombs, princess," answered a man. "Like the rest of us, they bore bodies of the slain into the crypts, but they have not returned. Perhaps the ghost of Tolkemec took them."

"Be silent, fool!" she ordered harshly. "The ghost is a myth."

She came down from her dais, playing with a thin gold-hilted dagger. Her eyes burned like nothing on the hither side of Hell. She paused beside the altar and spoke in the tense stillness.

"Your life shall make me young, white woman!" she said. "I shall lean upon your bosom and place my lips over yours, and slowly — ah, slowly! — sink this blade through your heart, so that your life, fleeing your stiffening body, shall enter mine, making me bloom again with youth and with life everlasting!"

Slowly, like a serpent arching toward its victim, she bent down through the writhing smoke, closer and closer over the now motionless woman who stared up into her glowing dark eyes — eyes that grew larger and deeper, blazing like black moons in the swirling smoke.

The kneeling people gripped their hands and held their breath, tense for the bloody climax, and the only sound was Conan's fierce panting as he strove to tear his leg from the trap.

All eyes were glued on the altar and the white figure there; the crash of a thunderbolt could hardly have broken the spell, yet it was only a low cry that shattered the fixity of the scene and bought all whirling about — a low cry, yet one to make the hair stand up stiffly on the scalp. They looked, and they saw.

Framed in the door to the left of the dais stood a nightmare figure. It was a man, with a tangle of white hair and a matted white beard that fell over his breast. Rags only partly covered his gaunt frame, revealing half-naked limbs strangely unnatural in appearance. The skin was not like that of a normal human. There was a suggestion of *scaliness* about it, as if the owner had dwelt long under conditions almost antithetical to those conditions under which human life ordinarily thrives. And there was nothing at all human about the eyes that blazed from the tangle of white hair. They were great gleaming disks that started unwinkingly, luminous, whitish, and without a hint of normal emotion or sanity. The mouth gaped, but no coherent words issued — only a high-pitched tittering.

"Tolkemec!" whispered Tascela, livid, while the others crouched in speechless horror. "No myth, then, no ghost! Set! You have dwelt for twelve years in darkness! Twelve years among the bones of the dead! What grisly food did you find? What mad travesty of life did you live, in the stark blackness of that eternal night? I see now why Xamec and Zlanath and Tachic did not return from the catacombs — and never will return. But why have you waited so long to strike? Were you seeking something, in the pits? Some secret weapon you knew was hidden there? And have you found it at last?"

That hideous tittering was Tolkemec's only reply, as he bounded into the room with a long leap that carried him over the secret trap before the door — by chance, or by some faint recollection of the ways of Xuchotl. He was not mad, as a man is mad. He had dwelt apart from humanity so long that he was no longer human. Only an unbroken thread of memory embodied in hate and the urge for vengeance had connected him with the humanity from which he had been cut off, and held him lurking near the people he hated. Only that thin string had kept him from racing and prancing off forever into the black corridors and realms of the subterranean world he had discovered, long ago.

"You sought something hidden!" whispered Tascela, cringing back. "And you have found it! You remember the feud! After all these years of blackness, you remember!"

For in the lean hand of Tolkemec now waved a curious jade-hued wand, on the end of which glowed a knob of crimson shaped like a pomegranate. She sprang aside as he thrust it out like a spear, and a beam of crimson fire lanced from the pomegranate. It missed Tascela, but the woman holding Valeria's ankles was in the way. It smote between her shoulders. There was a sharp crackling sound and the ray of fire flashed from her bosom and struck the black altar, with a snapping of blue sparks. The woman toppled sidewise, shriveling and withering like a mummy even as she fell.

Valeria rolled from the altar on the other side, and started for the opposite wall on all fours. For Hell had burst loose in the throne room of dead Olmec.

The man who had held Valeria's hands was the next to die. He turned to run, but before he had taken half a dozen steps, Tolkemec, with an agility appalling in such a frame, bounded around to a position that placed the man between him and the altar. Again the red fire-beam flashed and the Tecuhltli rolled lifeless to the floor, as the beam completed its course with a burst of blue sparks against the altar.

Then began the slaughter. Screaming insanely the people rushed about the chamber, caroming from one another, stumbling and falling. And among them Tolkemec capered and pranced, dealing death. They could not escape by the doors; for apparently the metal of the portals served like the metal veined stone altar to complete the circuit for whatever hellish power flashed like thunderbolts from the witch-wand the ancient waved in his hand. When he caught a man or a woman between him and a door or the altar, that one died instantly. He chose no special victim. He took them as they came, with his rags flapping about his wildly gyrating limbs, and the gusty echoes of his tittering sweeping the room above the screams. And bodies fell like falling leaves about the altar and at the doors. One warrior in desperation rushed at him, lifting a dagger, only to fall before he could strike. But the rest were like crazed cattle, with no thought for resistance, and no chance of escape.

The last Tecuhltli except Tascela had fallen when the princess reached the Cimmerian and the girl who had taken refuge beside him. Tascela bent and touched the floor, pressing a design upon it. Instantly the iron jaws released the bleeding limb and sank back into the floor.

"Slay him if you can!" she panted, and pressed a heavy knife into his hand. "I have no magic to withstand him!"

With a grunt he sprang before the woman, not heeding his lacerated leg in the heat of the fighting-lust. Tolkemec was coming toward him, his weird eyes ablaze, but he hesitated at the gleam of the knife in Conan's hand. Then began a grim game, as Tolkemec sought to circle about Conan and get the barbarian between him and the altar or a metal door, while Conan sought to avoid this and drive home his knife. The women watched tensely, holding their breath.

There was no sound except the rustle and scrape of quick-shifting feet. Tolkemec pranced and capered no more. He realized that grimmer game confronted him than the people who had died screaming and fleeing. In the elemental blaze of the barbarian's eyes he read an intent deadly as his own. Back and forth they weaved, and when one moved the other moved as if invisible threads bound them together. But all the time Conan was getting closer and closer to his enemy. Already the coiled muscles of his thighs were beginning to flex for a spring, when Valeria cried out. For a fleeting instant a bronze door was in line with Conan's moving body. The red line leaped, searing Conan's flank as he twisted aside, and even as he shifted he hurled the knife. Old Tolkemec went down, truly slain at last, the hilt vibrating on his breast.

Tascela sprang — not toward Conan, but toward the wand where it shimmered like a live thing on the floor. But as she leaped, so did Valeria, with a dagger snatched from a dead man; and the blade, driven with all the power of the pirate's muscles, impaled the princess of Tecuhltli so that the point stood out between her breasts. Tascela screamed once and fell dead, and Valeria spurned the body with her heel as it fell.

"I had to do that much, for my own self-respect!" panted Valeria, facing Conan across the limp corpse.

"Well, this cleans up the feud," he grunted. "It's been a hell of a night! Where did these people keep their food? I'm hungry."

"You need a bandage on that leg." Valeria ripped a length of silk from a hanging and knotted it about her waist, then tore off some smaller strips which she bound efficiently about the barbarian's lacerated limb.

"I can walk on it," he assured her. "Let's begone. It's dawn, outside this infernal city. I've had enough of Xuchotl. It's well the breed exterminated itself. I don't want any of their accursed jewels. They might be haunted."

"There is enough clean loot in the world for you and me," she said, straightening to stand tall and splendid before him.

The old blaze came back in his eyes, and this time she did not resist as he caught her fiercely in his arms.

"It's a long way to the coast," she said presently, withdrawing her lips from his.

"What matter?" he laughed. "There's nothing we can't conquer. We'll have our feet on a ship's deck before the Stygians open their ports for the trading season. And then we'll show the world what plundering means!"

SOLOMON KANE'S HOMECOMING

Fanciful Tales, **Fall 1936**

The white gulls wheeled above the cliffs, the air was slashed
    with foam,
The long tides moaned along the strand when Solomon Kane
    came home.
He walked in silence strange and dazed through the little Devon
    town,
His gaze, like a ghost's come back to life, roamed up the streets
    and down.

The people followed wonderingly to mark his spectral stare,
And in the tavern silently they thronged about him there.
He heard as a man hears in a dream the worn old rafters creak,
And Solomon lifted his drinking-jack and spoke as a ghost
    might speak:

"There sat Sir Richard Grenville once; in smoke and flame he passed.
"And we were one to fifty-three, but we gave them blast for blast.
"From crimson dawn to crimson dawn, we held the Dons at bay.
"The dead lay littered on our decks, our masts were shot away.

"We beat them back with broken blades, till crimsom ran the tide;
"Death thundered in the cannon smoke when Richard Grenville
    died.
"We should have blown her hull apart and sunk beneath the Main."
The people saw upon his wrist the scars of the racks of Spain.

"Where is Bess?" said Solomon Kane. "Woe that I caused her tears."
"In the quiet churchyard by the sea she has slept these seven
*   years."*
The sea-wind moaned at the window-pane, and Solomon
*   bowed his head.*
"Ashes to ashes and dust to dust, and the fairest fade," he said.

His eyes were mystical deep pools that drowned unearthly things,
And Solomon lifted up his head and spoke of his wanderings.
"Mine eyes have looked on sorcery in dark and naked lands,
"Horror born of the jungle gloom and death on the pathless sands.

"And I have known a deathless queen in a city old as Death,
"Where towering pyramids of skulls her glory witnesseth.
"Her kiss was like an adder's fang, with the sweetness Lilith had,
"And her red-eyed vassals howled for blood in that City of the Mad.

"And I have slain a vampire shape that sucked a black king white,
"And I have roamed through grisly hills where dead men walked
*   at night.*
"And I have seen heads fall like fruit in a slaver's barracoon,
"And I have seen winged demons fly all naked in the moon.

"My feet are weary of wandering and age comes on apace;
"I fain would dwell in Devon now, forever in my place."
The howling of the ocean pack came whistling down the gale,
And Solomon Kane threw up his head like a hound that sniffs
*   the trail.*

A-down the wind like a running pack the hounds of the ocean
*   bayed,*
And Solomon Kane rose up again and girt his Spanish blade.
In his strange cold eyes a vagrant gleam grew wayward and blind
*   and bright,*
And Solomon put the people by and went into the night.

A wild moon rode the wild white clouds, the waves in white
　　crests flowed,
When Solomon Kane went forth again and no man knew his road.
They glimpsed him etched against the moon, where clouds on
　　hilltop thinned;
They heard an eery echoed call that whistled down the wind.

BLACK HOUNDS OF DEATH

Weird Tales, **November 1936**

1. *The Killer in the Dark*

Egyptian darkness! The phrase is too vivid for complete comfort, suggesting not only blackness, but unseen things lurking in that blackness; things that skulk in the deep shadows and shun the light of day; slinking figures that prowl beyond the edge of normal life.

Some such thoughts flitted vaguely through my mind that night as I groped along the narrow trail that wound through the deep pinelands. Such thoughts are likely to keep company with any man who dares invade, in the night, that lonely stretch of densely timbered river-country which the black people call Egypt, for some obscurely racial reason.

There is no blackness this side of Hell's unlighted abyss as absolute as the blackness of the pine woods. The trail was but a half-guessed trace winding between walls of solid ebony. I followed it as much by the instincts of the piney woods dweller as by the guidance of the external senses. I went as hurriedly as I dared, but stealth was mingled with my haste, and my ears were whetted to knife-edge alertness. This caution did not spring from the uncanny speculations roused by the darkness and silence. I had good, material reason to be wary. Ghosts might roam the pinelands with gaping, bloody throats and cannibalistic hunger as the Negroes maintained, but it was no ghost I feared. I listened for the snap of a twig under a great, splay foot, for any sound that would presage murder striking from the black shadows. The creature which, I feared, haunted Egypt was more to be dreaded than any gibbering phantom.

That morning the worst Negro desperado in that part of the state had broken from the clutches of the law, leaving a ghastly toll of dead behind him. Down along the river, bloodhounds were baying through the brush and hard-eyed men with rifles were beating up the thickets.

They were seeking him in the fastnesses near the scattered black settlements, knowing that a Negro seeks his own kind in his extremity. But I knew Tope Braxton better than they did; I knew he deviated from the general type of his race. He was unbelievably primitive, atavistic enough to plunge into uninhabited wilderness and live like a blood-mad gorilla in solitude that would have terrified and daunted a more normal member of his race.

So while the hunt flowed away in another direction, I rode toward Egypt, alone. But it was not altogether to look for Tope Braxton that I plunged into that isolated fastness. My mission was one of warning, rather than search. Deep in the mazy pine labyrinth, a white man and his servant lived alone, and it was the duty of any man to warn them that a red-handed killer might be skulking about their cabin.

I was foolish, perhaps, to be traveling on foot; but men who wear the name of Garfield are not in the habit of turning back on a task once attempted. When my horse unexpectedly went lame, I left him at one of the Negro cabins which fringe the edge of Egypt, and went on afoot. Night overtook me on the path, and I intended remaining until morning with the man I was going to warn — Richard Brent. He was a taciturn recluse, suspicious and peculiar, but he could scarcely refuse to put me up for the night. He was a mysterious figure; why he chose to hide himself in a southern pine forest none knew. He had been living in an old cabin in the heart of Egypt for about six months.

Suddenly, as I forged through the darkness, my speculations regarding the mysterious recluse were cut short, wiped clear out of my mind. I stopped dead, the nerves tingling in the skin on the backs of my hands. A sudden shriek in the dark has that effect, and this scream was edged with agony and terror. It came from somewhere ahead of me. Breathless silence followed that cry, a silence in which the forest seemed to hold its breath and the darkness shut in more blackly still.

Again the scream was repeated, this time closer. Then I heard the pound of bare feet along the trail, and a form hurled itself at me out of the darkness.

My revolver was in my hand, and I instinctively

thrust it out to fend the creature off. The only thing that kept me from pulling the trigger was the noise the object was making — gasping, sobbing noises of fear and pain. It was a man, and direly stricken. He blundered full into me, shrieked again, and fell sprawling, slobbering and yammering.

"Oh, my God, save me! Oh, God have mercy on me!"

"What the devil is it?" I demanded, my hair stirring on my scalp at the poignant agony in the gibbering voice.

The wretch recognized my voice; he clawed at my knees.

"Oh, Mas' Kirby, don' let him tetch me! He's done killed my body, and now he wants my soul! It's me — po' Jim Tike. Don' let him git me!"

I struck a match, and stood staring in amazement, while the match burned down to my fingers. A black man groveled in the dust before me, his eyes rolling up whitely. I knew him well — one of the Negroes who lived in their tiny log cabins along the fringe of Egypt. He was spotted and splashed with blood, and I believed he was mortally wounded. Only abnormal energy rising from frenzied panic could have enabled him to run as far as he had. Blood jetted from torn veins and arteries in breast, shoulder and neck, and the wounds were ghastly to see, great ragged tears, that were never made by bullet or knife. One ear had been torn from his head, and hung loose, with a great piece of flesh from the angle of his jaw and neck, as if some gigantic beast had ripped it out with his fangs.

"What in God's name did this?" I ejaculated as the match went out, and he became merely an indistinct blob in the darkness below me. "A bear?" Even as I spoke I knew that no bear had been seen in Egypt for thirty years.

"*He* done it!" The thick, sobbing mumble welled up through the dark. "De white man dat come by my cabin and ask me to guide him to Mistuh Brent's house. He said he had a tooth-ache, so he had his head bandaged; but de bandages slipped and I seen his face — he killed me for seein' him."

"You mean he set dogs on you?" I demanded, for his wounds were such as I have seen on animals worried by vicious hounds.

"No, suh," whimpered the ebbing voice. "He done it hisself — aaaggghhh!"

The mumble broke in a shriek as he twisted his head, barely visible in the gloom, and stared back the way he had come. Death must have struck him in the midst of that scream, for it broke short at the highest note. He flopped convulsively once, like a dog hit by a truck, and then lay still.

I strained my eyes into the darkness, and made out a vague shape a few yards away in the trail. It was erect and tall as a man; it made no sound.

I opened my mouth to challenge the unknown visitant, but no sound came. An indescribable chill flowed over me, freezing my tongue to my palate. It was fear, primitive and unreasoning, and even while I stood paralyzed I could not understand it, could not guess why that silent, motionless figure, sinister as it was, should rouse such instinctive dread.

Then suddenly the figure moved quickly toward me, and I found my voice. "Who comes there?"

No answer; but the form came on in a rush, and as I groped for a match, it was almost upon me. I struck the match — with a ferocious snarl the figure hurled itself against me, the match was struck from my hand and extinguished, and I felt a sharp pain on the side of my neck. My gun exploded almost involuntarily and without aim, and its flash dazzled me, obscuring rather than revealing the tall man-like figure that struck at me; then with a crashing rush through the trees my assailant was gone, and I staggered alone on the forest trail.

Swearing angrily, I felt for another match. Blood was trickling down my shoulder, soaking through my shirt. When I struck the match and investigated, another chill swept down my spine. My shirt was torn and the flesh beneath slightly cut; the wound was little more than a scratch, but the thing that roused nameless fear in my mind was the fact that *the wound was similar to those on poor Jim Tike.*

2. *"Dead Men with Torn Throats!"*

Jim Tike was dead, lying face down in a pool of his own blood, his red-dabbled limbs sprawling drunkenly. I stared uneasily at the surrounding forest that hid the thing that had killed him. That it was a man I knew; the outline, in the brief light of the match, had been vague, but unmistakably human. But what sort of a weapon could make a wound like the merciless champing of great bestial teeth? I shook my head, recalling the ingenuity of mankind in the creation of implements of slaughter, and considered a more acute problem. Should I risk my life further by continuing upon my course, or should I return to the outer world and bring in men and dogs, to carry out poor Jim Tike's corpse, and hunt down his murderer?

I did not waste much time in indecision. I had set out to perform a task. If a murderous criminal besides Tope Braxton were abroad in the piney woods, there was all the more reason for warning the men in that lonely cabin. As for my own danger, I was already more than halfway to the cabin. It would scarcely be more dangerous to advance than to retreat. If I did turn back, and escape from Egypt alive, before I could rouse a posse, anything might happen in that isolated cabin under the black trees.

So I left Jim Tike's body there in the trail, and went on, gun in hand, and nerves sharpened by the new peril. That visitant had not been Tope Braxton. I had the dead man's word for it that the attacker was a mysterious white man; the glimpse I had had of the figure had confirmed the fact that he was not Tope Braxton. I would have known that squat, apish body even in the dark. This man was tall and spare, and the mere recollection of that gaunt figure made me shiver, unreasoningly.

It is no pleasant experience to walk along a black forest trail with only the stars glinting through the dense branches, and the knowledge that a ruthless murderer is lurking near, perhaps within arm's length in the concealing darkness. The recollection of the butchered black man burned vividly in my brain. Sweat beaded my face and hands, and I wheeled a score of times, glaring into the blackness where my ears had caught the rustle of leaves or the breaking of a twig — how could I know whether the sounds were but the natural noises of the forest, or the stealthy movements of the killer?

Once I stopped, with an eery crawling of my skin, as far away, through the black trees, I glimpsed a faint, lurid glow. It was not stationary; it moved, but it was too far away for me to make out the source. With my hair prickling unpleasantly I waited, for I knew not what; but presently the mysterious glow vanished, and so keyed up I was to unnatural happenings, that it was only then that I realized the light might well have been made by a man walking with a pine-knot torch. I hurried on, cursing myself for my fears, the more baffling because they were so nebulous. Peril was no stranger to me in that land of feud and violence where century-old hates still smoldered down the generations. Threat of bullet or knife openly or from ambush had never shaken my nerves before; but I knew now that I was afraid — afraid of something I could not understand, or explain.

I sighed with relief when I saw Richard Brent's light gleaming through the pines, but I did not relax my vigilance. Many a man, danger-dogged, has been struck down at the very threshold of safety. Knocking on the door, I stood sidewise, peering into the shadows that ringed the tiny clearing and seemed to repel the faint light from the shuttered windows.

"Who's there?" came a deep harsh voice from within. "Is that you, Ashley?"

"No; it's me — Kirby Garfield. Open the door."

The upper half of the door swung inward, and Richard Brent's head and shoulders were framed in the opening. The light behind him left most of his face in shadow, but could not obscure the harsh gaunt lines of his features nor the gleam of the bleak gray eyes.

"What do you want, at this time of night?" he demanded, with his usual bruqueness.

I replied shortly, for I did not like the man; courtesy in our part of the country is an obligation no gentleman thinks of shirking.

"I came to tell you that it's very likely that a dangerous Negro is prowling in your vicinity. Tope Braxton killed Constable Joe Sorley and a Negro trusty, and broke out of jail this morning. I think he took refuge in Egypt. I thought you ought to be warned."

"Well, you've warned me," he snapped, in his short-clipped Eastern accent. "Why don't you be off?"

"Because I have no intention of going back

through those woods tonight," I answered angrily. "I came in here to warn you, not because of any love of you, but simply because you're a white man. The least you can do is to let me put up in your cabin until morning. All I ask is a pallet on the floor; you don't even have to feed me."

That last was an insult I could not withhold, in my resentment; at least in the piney woods it is considered an insult. But Richard Brent ignored my thrust at his penuriousness and discourtesy. He scowled at me. I could not see his hands.

"Did you see Ashley anywhere along the trail?" he asked finally.

Ashley was his servant, a saturnine figure as taciturn as his master, who drove into the distant river village once a month for supplies.

"No; he might have been in town, and left after I did."

"I guess I'll have to let you in," he muttered, grudgingly.

"Well, hurry up," I requested. "I've got a gash in my shoulder I want to wash and dress. Tope Braxton isn't the only killer abroad tonight."

At that he halted in his fumbling at the lower door, and his expression changed.

"What do you mean?"

"There's a dead nigger a mile or so up the trail. The man who killed him tried to kill me. He may be after you, for all I know. The nigger he killed was guiding him here."

Richard Brent started violently, and his face went livid.

"Who — what do you mean?" His voice cracked, unexpectedly falsetto. "What man?"

"I don't know. A fellow who manages to rip his victims like a hound —"

"A hound!" The words burst out in a scream. The change in Brent was hideous. His eyes seemed starting from his head; his hair stood up stiffly on his scalp, and his skin was the hue of ashes. His lips drew back from his teeth in a grin of sheer terror.

He gagged and then found voice.

"Get out!" he choked. "I see it, now! I know why you wanted to get into my house! You bloody devil! *He* sent you! You're his spy! *Go!*" The last was a scream and his hands rose above the lower half of the door at last. I stared into the gaping muzzles of a sawed-off shotgun. "Go, before I kill you!"

I stepped back off the stoop, my skin crawling at the thought of a close-range blast from that murderous implement of destruction. The black muzzles and the livid, convulsed face behind them promised sudden demolition.

"You cursed fool!" I growled, courting disaster in my anger. "Be careful with that thing. I'm going. I'd rather take a chance with a murderer than a madman."

Brent made no reply; panting and shivering like a man smitten with ague, he crouched over his shotgun and watched me as I turned and strode across the clearing. Where the trees began I could have wheeled and shot him down without much danger, for my .45 would out-range his shortened scatter-gun. But I had come there to warn the fool, not to kill him.

The upper door slammed as I strode in under the trees, and the stream of light was cut abruptly off. I drew my gun and plunged into the shadowy trail, my ears whetted again for sounds under the black branches.

My thoughts reverted to Richard Brent. It was surely no friend who had sought guidance to his cabin! The man's frantic fear had bordered on insanity. I wondered if it had been to escape this man that Brent had exiled himself in this lonely stretch of pinelands and river. Surely it had been to escape *something* that he had come; for he never concealed his hatred of the country nor his contempt for the native people, white and black. But I had never believed that he was a criminal, hiding from the law.

The light fell away behind me, vanished among the black trees. A curious, chill, sinking feeling obsessed me, as if the disappearance of that light, hostile as was its source, had severed the only link that connected this nightmarish adventure with the world of sanity and humanity. Grimly taking hold of my nerves, I strode on up the trail. But I had not gone far when again I halted.

This time it was the unmistakable sound of horses running; the rumble of wheels mingled with the pounding of hoofs. Who would be coming along that nighted trail in a rig but Ashley? But instantly I realized that the team was headed in the other direction. The sound receded rapidly, and soon became only a distant blur of noise.

I quickened my pace, much puzzled, and presently I heard hurried, stumbling footsteps ahead of me, and a quick, breathless panting that seemed indicative of panic. I distinguished the footsteps of two people, though I could see nothing in the intense darkness. At that point the branches interlaced over the trail, forming a black arch through which not even the stars gleamed.

"Ho, there!" I called cautiously. "Who are you?"

Instantly the sounds ceased abruptly, and I could picture two shadowy figures standing tensely still, with bated breath.

"Who's there?" I repeated. "Don't be afraid. It's me — Kirby Garfield."

"Stand where you are!" came a hard voice I recognized as Ashley's. "You sound like Garfield — but I want to be sure. If you move you'll get a slug through you."

There was a scratching sound and a tiny flame leaped up. A human hand was etched in its glow, and behind it the square, hard face of Ashley peering in my direction. A pistol in his other hand caught the glint of the fire; and on that arm rested another hand — a slim, white hand, with a jewel sparkling on one finger. Dimly I made out the slender figure of a woman; her face was like a pale blossom in the gloom.

"Yes, it's you, all right," Ashley grunted. "What are you doing here?"

"I came to warn Brent about Tope Braxton," I answered shortly; I do not relish being called on to account for my actions to anybody. "You've heard about it, naturally. If I'd known you were in town, it would have saved me a trip. What are you-all doing on foot?"

"Our horses ran away a short distance back," he answered. "There was a dead Negro in the trail. But that's not what frightened the horses. When we got out to investigate, they snorted and wheeled and bolted with the rig. We had to come on on foot. It's been a pretty nasty experience. From the looks of the Negro I judge a pack of wolves killed him, and the scent frightened the horses. We've been expecting an attack any minute."

"Wolves don't hunt in packs and drag down human beings in these woods. It was a man that killed Jim Tike."

In the waning glow of the match Ashley stood staring at me in amazement, and then I saw the astonishment ebb from his countenance and horror grow there. Slowly his color ebbed, leaving his bronzed face as ashy as that of his master had been. The match went out, and we stood silent.

"Well," I said impatiently, "speak up, man! Who's the lady with you?"

"She's Mr. Brent's niece." The answer came tonelessly through dry lips.

"I am Gloria Brent!" she exclaimed in a voice whose cultured accent was not lost in the fear that caused it to tremble. "Uncle Richard wired for me to come to him at once —"

"I've seen the wire," Ashley muttered. "You showed it to me. But I don't know how he sent it. He hasn't been to the village, to my knowledge, in months."

"I came on from New York as fast as I could!" she exclaimed. "I can't understand why the telegram was sent to me, instead of to somebody else in the family —"

"You were always your uncle's favorite, Miss," said Ashley.

"Well, when I got off the boat at the village just before nightfall, I found Ashley, just getting ready to drive home. He was surprized to see me, but of course he brought me on out; and then — that — that dead man —"

She seemed considerably shaken by the experience. It was obvious that she had been raised in a very refined and sheltered atmosphere. If she had been born in the piney woods, as I was, the sight of a dead man, white or black, would not have been an uncommon phenomenon to her.

"The — the dead man —" she stammered, and then she was answered most hideously.

From the black woods beside the trail rose a shriek of blood-curdling laughter. Slavering, mouthing sounds followed it, so strange and garbled that at first I did not recognize them as human words. Their unhuman intonations sent a chill down my spine.

"Dead men!" the inhuman voice chanted. "Dead men with torn throats! There will be dead men among the pines before dawn! Dead men! Fools, you are all dead!"

Ashley and I both fired in the direction of the voice, and in the crashing reverberations of our shots the ghastly chant was drowned. But the weird laugh rang out again, deeper in the woods, and then silence closed down like a black fog, in which I heard the semi-hysterical gasping of the girl. She had released Ashley and was clinging frantically to me. I could feel the quivering of her lithe body against mine. Probably she had merely followed her feminine instinct to seek refuge with the strongest; the light of the match had shown her that I was a bigger man than Ashley.

"Hurry, for God's sake!" Ashley's voice sounded strangled. "It can't be far to the cabin. Hurry! You'll come with us, Mr. Garfield?"

"What was it?" the girl was panting. "Oh, what *was* it?"

"A madman, I think," I answered, tucking her trembling little hand under my left arm. But at the back of my mind was whispering the grisly realization that no madman ever had a voice like that. It sounded — God! — it sounded like some bestial creature speaking with human words, but not with a human tongue!

"Get on the other side of Miss Brent, Ashley," I

directed. "Keep as far from the trees as you can. If anything moves on that side, shoot first and ask questions later. I'll do the same on this side. Now come on!"

He made no reply as he complied; his fright seemed deeper than that of the girl; his breath came in shuddering gasps. The trail seemed endless, the darkness abysmal. Fear stalked along the trail on either hand, and slunk grinning at our backs. My flesh crawled with the thought of a demoniacal clawed and fanged *thing* hurling itself upon my shoulders.

The girl's little feet scarcely touched the ground, as we almost carried her between us. Ashley was almost as tall as I, though not so heavy, and was strongly made.

Ahead of us a light glimmered between the trees at last, and a gusty sigh of relief burst from his lips. He increased his pace until we were almost running.

"The cabin at last, thank God!" he gasped, as we plunged out of the trees.

"Hail your employer, Ashley," I grunted. "He's driven me off with a gun once tonight. I don't want to be shot by the old —" I stopped, remembering the girl.

"Mr. Brent!" shouted Ashley. "Mr. Brent! Open the door quick! It's me — Ashley!"

Instantly light flooded from the door as the upper half was drawn back, and Brent peered out, shotgun in hand, blinking into the darkness.

"Hurry and get in!" Panic still thrummed in his voice. Then: "Who's that standing beside you?" he shouted furiously.

"Mr. Garfield and your niece, Miss Gloria."

"Uncle Richard!" she cried, her voice catching in a sob. Pulling loose from us, she ran forward and threw her lithe body half-over the lower door, throwing her arms around his neck. "Uncle Richard, I'm so afraid! What does this all mean?"

He seemed thunderstruck.

"Gloria!" he repeated. "What in heaven's name are you doing here?"

"Why, you sent for me!" She fumbled out a crumpled yellow telegraph form. "See? You said for me to come at once!"

He went livid again.

"I never sent that, Gloria! Good God, why should I drag you into my particular hell? There's something devilish here. Come in — come in quickly!"

He jerked open the door and pulled her inside, never relinquishing the shotgun. He seemed to fumble in a daze. Ashley shouldered in after her, and exclaimed to me: "Come in, Mr. Garfield! Come in — come in!"

I had made no move to follow them. At the mention of my name, Brent, who seemed to have forgotten my presence, jerked loose from the girl with a choking cry and wheeled, throwing up the shotgun. But this time I was ready for him. My nerves were too much on edge to let me submit to any more bullying. Before he could bring the gun into position, he was looking in the muzzle of my .45.

"Put it down, Brent," I snapped. "Drop it, before I break your arm. I'm fed up on your idiotic suspicions."

He hesitated, glaring wildly, and behind him the girl shrank away. I suppose that in the full flood of the light from the doorway I was not a figure to inspire confidence in a young girl, with my frame which is built for strength and not looks, and my dark face, scarred by many a brutal river battle.

"He's our friend, Mr. Brent," interposed Ashley. "He helped us, in the woods."

"He's a devil!" raved Brent, clinging to his gun, though not trying to lift it. "He came here to murder us! He lied when he said he came to warn us against a black man. What man would be fool enough to come into Egypt at night, just to warn a stranger? My God, has he got you both fooled? I tell you, *he wears the brand of the hound!*"

"Then you know *he's* here!" cried Ashley.

"Yes; this fiend told me, trying to worm his way into the house. God, Ashley, *he's* tracked us down, in spite of all our cleverness. We have trapped ourselves! In a city, we might buy protection; but here, in this accursed forest, who will hear our cries or come to our aid when the fiend closes in upon us? What fools — what fools we were to think to hide from *him* in this wilderness!"

"I heard him laugh," shuddered Ashley. "He taunted us from the bushes in his beast's voice. I saw the man he killed — ripped and mangled as if by the fangs of Satan himself. What — what are we to do?"

"What can we do except lock ourselves in and fight to the last?" shrieked Brent. His nerves were in frightful shape.

"Please tell me what it is all about?" pleaded the trembling girl.

With a terrible despairing laugh Brent threw out his arm, gesturing toward the black woods beyond the faint light. "A devil in human form is lurking out there!" he exclaimed. "He has tracked me across the world, and has cornered me at last! Do you remember Adam Grimm?"

"The man who went with you to Mongolia five years ago? But he died, you said. You came back without him."

"I thought he was dead," muttered Brent. "Listen, I will tell you. Among the black mountains of Inner Mongolia, where no white man had ever penetrated, our expedition was attacked by fanatical devil-worshippers — the black monks of Erlik who dwell in the forgotten and accursed city of Yahlgan. Our guides and servants were killed, and all our stock driven off but one small camel.

"Grimm and I stood them off all day, firing from behind the rocks when they tried to rush us. That night we planned to make a break for it, on the camel that remained to us. But it was evident to me that the beast could not carry us both to safety. One man might have a chance. When darkness fell, I struck

Grimm from behind with my gun butt, knocking him senseless. Then I mounted the camel and fled —"

He did not heed the look of sick amazement and abhorrence growing in the girl's lovely face. Her wide eyes were fixed on her uncle as if she were seeing the real man for the first time, and was stricken by what she saw. He plunged on, too obsessed and engulfed by fear to care or heed what she thought of him. The sight of a soul stripped of its conventional veneer and surface pretense is not always pleasant.

"I broke through the lines of the besiegers and escaped in the night. Grimm, naturally, fell into the hands of the devil-worshippers, and for years I supposed that he was dead. They had the reputation of slaying, by torture, every alien that they captured. Years passed, and I had almost forgotten the episode. Then, seven months ago, I learned that he was alive — was, indeed, back in America, thirsting for my life. The monks had not killed him; through their damnable arts they had *altered* him. The man is no longer wholly human, but his whole soul is bent on my destruction. To appeal to the police would have been useless; he would have tricked them and wreaked his vengeance in spite of them. I fled from him up and down across the country for more than a month, like a hunted animal, and finally, when I thought I had thrown him off the track, I took refuge in this God-forsaken wilderness, among these barbarians, of whom that man Kirby Garfield is a typical example."

"*You* can talk of barbarians!" she flamed, and her

scorn would have cut the soul of any man who was not so totally engrossed in his own fears.

She turned to me. "Mr. Garfield, please come in. You must not try to traverse this forest at night, with that fiend at large."

"No!" shrieked Brent. "Get back from that door, you little fool! Ashley, hold your tongue. I tell you, he is one of Adam Grimm's creatures! He shall not set foot in this cabin!"

She looked at me, pale, helpless and forlorn, and I pitied her as I despised Richard Brent; she looked so small and bewildered.

"I wouldn't sleep in your cabin if all the wolves of Hell were howling outside," I snarled at Brent. "I'm going, and if you shoot me in the back, I'll kill you before I die. I wouldn't have come back at all, but the young lady needed my protection. She needs it now, but it's your privilege to deny her that. Miss Brent," I said, "if you wish, I'll come back tomorrow with a buckboard and carry you to the village. You'd better go back to New York."

"Ashley will take her to the village," roared Brent, "Damn you, *will* you go?"

With a sneer that brought the blood purpling his countenance, I turned squarely upon him and strode off. The door banged behind me, and I heard his falsetto voice mingled with the tearful accents of his niece. Poor girl, it must have been like a nightmare to her: to have been snatched out of her sheltered urban life and dropped down in a country strange and primitive to her, among people whose ways seemed incredibly savage and violent, and into a bloody episode of wrong and menace and vengeance. The deep pinelands of the Southwest seem strange and alien enough at any time to the average Eastern city-dweller; and added to their gloomy mystery and primordial wildness was this grim phantom out of an unsuspected past, like the figment of a nightmare.

I turned squarely about, stood motionless in the black trail, staring back at the pinpoint of light which still winked through the trees. Peril hovered over the cabin in that tiny clearing, and it was no part of a white man to leave that girl with the protection of none but her half-lunatic uncle and his servant. Ashley looked like a fighter. But Brent was an unpredictable quantity. I believed he was tinged with madness. His insane rages and equally insane suspicions seemed to indicate as much. I had no sympathy for him. A man who would sacrifice his friend to save his own life deserves death.

But evidently Grimm was mad. His slaughter of Jim Tike suggested homicidal insanity. Poor Jim Tike had never wronged him. I would have killed Grimm for that murder, alone, if I had had the opportunity. And I did not intend that the girl should suffer for the sins of her uncle. If Brent had not sent that telegram, as he swore, then it looked much as if she had been summoned for a sinister purpose. Who but Grimm himself would have summoned her, to share the doom he planned for Richard Brent?

Turning, I strode back down the trail. If I could not enter the cabin, I could at least lurk in the shadows ready at hand if my help was needed. A few moments later I was under the fringe of trees that ringed the clearing.

Light still shone through the cracks in the shutters, and at one place a portion of the windowpane was visible. And even as I looked, this pane was shattered, as if something had been hurled through it. Instantly the night was split by a sheet of flame that burst in a blinding flash out of the doors and windows and chimney of the cabin. For one infinitesimal instant I saw the cabin limned blackly against the tongues of flame that flashed from it. With the flash came the thought that the cabin had been blown up — but no sound accompanied the explosion.

Even while the blaze was still in my eyes, another explosion filled the universe with blinding sparks, and this one was accompanied by a thunderous reverberation. Consciousness was blotted out too suddenly for me to know that I had been struck on the head from behind, terrifically and without warning.

3. *Black Hands*

A flickering light was the first thing that impressed itself upon my awakening faculties. I blinked, shook my head, came suddenly fully awake. I was lying on my back in a small glade, walled by towering black trees which fitfully reflected the uncertain light that emanated from a torch stuck upright in the earth near me. My head throbbed, and blood clotted my scalp; my hands were fastened together before me by a pair of handcuffs. My clothes were torn and my skin scratched as if I had been dragged brutally through the brush.

A huge black shape squatted over me — a black man of medium height but of gigantic breadth and thickness, clad only in ragged, muddy breeches — Tope Braxton. He held a gun in each hand, and alternately aimed first one and then the other at me, squinting along the barrel. One pistol was mine; the other had once belonged to the constable that Braxton had brained.

I lay silent for a moment, studying the play of the torchlight on the great black torso. His huge body gleamed shiny ebony or dull bronze as the light flickered. He was like a shape from the abyss whence mankind crawled ages ago. His primitive ferocity was reflected in the bulging knots of muscles that corded his long, massive apish arms, his huge sloping shoulders; above all the bullet-shaped head that jutted forward on a column-like neck. The wide, flat nostrils, murky eyes, thick lips that writhed back from tusk-like teeth — all proclaimed the man's kinship with the primordial.

"Where the devil do you fit into this nightmare?" I demanded.

He showed his teeth in an ape-like grin.

"I thought it was time you was comin' to, Kirby Garfield," he grinned. "I wanted you to come to 'fo' I kill you, so you know *who* kill you. Den I go back and watch Mistuh Grimm kill de ol' man and de gal."

"What do you mean, you black devil?" I demanded harshly. "Grimm? What do you know about Grimm?"

"I meet him in de deep woods, after he kill Jim Tike. I heah a gun fire and come with a torch to see who — thought maybe somebody after me. I meet Mistuh Grimm."

"So you were the man I saw with the torch," I grunted.

"Mistuh Grimm smaht man. He say if I help him kill some folks, he help me git away. He take and throw bomb into de cabin; dat bomb don't kill dem folks, just paralyze 'em. I watchin' de trail, and hit you when you come back. Dat man Ashley ain't plumb paralyze, so Mistuh Grimm, he take and bite out he throat like he done Jim Tike."

"What do you mean, bite out his throat?" I demanded.

"Mistuh Grimm ain't a human bein'. He stan' up and walk like a man, but he part hound, or wolf."

"You mean a werewolf?" I asked, my scalp prickling.

He grinned. "Yeah, dat's it. Dey had 'em in de old country." Then he changed his mood. "I done talk long enough. Gwine blow yo' brains out now!"

His thick lips froze in a killer's mirthless grin as he squinted along the barrel of the pistol in his right hand. My whole body went tense, as I sought desperately for a loophole to save my life. My legs were not tied, but my hands were manacled, and a single movement would bring hot lead crashing through my brain. In my desperation I plumbed the depths of black folklore for a dim, all but forgotten superstition.

"These handcuffs belonged to Joe Sorley, didn't they?" I demanded.

"Uh huh," he grinned, without ceasing to squint along the sights. "I took 'em 'long with his gun after I beat his head in with window-bar. I thought I might need 'em."

"Well," I said, "if you kill me while I'm wearing them, you're eternally damned! Don't you know that if you kill a man who's wearing a cross, his ghost will haunt you forever after?"

He jerked the gun down suddenly, and his grin was replaced by a snarl.

"What you mean, white man?"

"Just what I say. There's a cross scratched on the inside of one of these cuffs. I've seen it a thousand times. Now go ahead and shoot, and I'll haunt you into Hell."

"Which cuff?" he snarled, lifting a gun-butt threateningly.

"Find out for yourself," I sneered. "Go ahead;

why don't you shoot? I hope you've had plenty of sleep lately, because I'll see to it that you never sleep again. In the night, under the trees, you'll see my face leering at you. You'll hear my voice in the wind that moans through the cypress branches. When you close your eyes in the dark, you'll feel my fingers at your throat."

"Shut up!" he roared, brandishing his pistols. His black skin was tinged with an ashy hue.

"Shut me up — if you dare!" I struggled up to a sitting position, and then fell back cursing. "Damn you, my leg's broken!"

At that the ashy tinge faded from his ebon skin, and purpose rose in his reddish eyes.

"So yo' leg's busted!" He bared his glistening teeth in a beastly grin. "Thought you fell mighty hard, and then I dragged you a right smart piece."

Laying both pistols on the ground, well out of my reach, he rose and leaned over me, dragging a key out of his breeches pocket. His confidence was justified; for was I not unarmed, helpless with a broken leg? I did not need the manacles. Bending over me he turned the key in the old-fashioned handcuffs and tore them off. And like twin striking snakes my hands shot to his black throat, locked fiercely and dragged him down on top of me.

I had always wondered what would be the outcome of a battle between me and Tope Braxton. One can hardly go about picking fights with black men. But now a fierce joy surged in me, a grim gratification that the question of our relative prowess was to be settled once and for all, with life for the winner and death for the loser.

Even as I gripped him, Braxton realized that I had tricked him into freeing me — that I was no more crippled than he was. Instantly he exploded into a hurricane of ferocity that would have dismembered a lesser man than I. We rolled on the pine-needles, rending and tearing.

Were I penning an elegant romance, I should tell how I vanquished Tope Braxton by a combination of higher intelligence, boxing skill and deft science that defeated his brute strength. But I must stick to facts in this chronicle.

Intelligence played little part in that battle. It would have helped me no more than it would help a man in the actual grip of a gorilla. As for artificial skill, Tope would have torn the average boxer or wrestler limb from limb. Man-developed science alone could not have withstood the blinding speed, tigerish ferocity and bone-crushing strength that lurked in Tope Braxton's terrible thews.

It was like fighting a wild beast, and I met him at his own game. I fought Tope Braxton as the rivermen fight, as savages fight, as bull apes fight. Breast to breast, muscle straining against muscle, iron fist crushing against hard skull, knee driven to groin, teeth slashing sinewy flesh, gouging, tearing, smashing. We both forgot the pistols on the ground; we must have rolled over them half a dozen times. Each of us was aware of only one desire, one blind crimson urge to kill with naked hands, to rend and tear and maul and trample until the other was a motionless mass of bloody flesh and splintered bone.

I do not know how long we fought; time faded into a blood-shot eternity. His fingers were like iron talons that tore the flesh and bruised the bone beneath. My head was swimming from its impacts against the hard ground, and from the pain in my side I knew at least one rib was broken. My whole body was a solid ache and burn of twisted joints and wrenched thews. My garments hung in ribbons, drenched by the blood that sluiced from an ear that had been ripped loose from my head. But if I was taking terrible punishment, I was dealing it too.

The torch had been knocked down and kicked aside, but it still smoldered fitfully, lending a lurid dim light to that primordial scene. Its light was not so red as the murder-lust that clouded my dimming eyes.

In a red haze I saw his white teeth gleaming in a grin of agonized effort, his eyes rolling whitely from a mask of blood. I had mauled his face out of all human resemblance; from eyes to waist his black hide was laced with crimson. Sweat slimed us, and our fingers slipped as they gripped. Writhing half-free from his rending clutch, I drove every straining knot of muscle in my body behind my fist that smashed like a mallet against his jaw. There was a crack of bone, an involuntary groan; blood spurted and the broken jaw dropped down. A bloody froth covered the loose lips. Then for the first time those black, tearing fingers faltered; I felt the great body that strained against mine yield and sag. And with a wild-beast sob of gratified ferocity ebbing from my pulped lips, my fingers at last met in his throat.

Down on his back he went, with me on his breast. His failing hands clawed at my wrists, weakly and more weakly. And I strangled him, slowly, with no trick of jujitsu or wrestling, but with sheer brute strength, bending his head back and back between its shoulders until the thick neck snapped like a rotten branch.

In that drunkenness of battle, I did not know when he died, did not know that it was death that had at last melted the iron thews of the body beneath me. Reeling up numbly, I dazedly stamped on his breast and head until the bones gave way under my heels, before I realized that Tope Braxton was dead.

Then I would have fallen and lapsed into insensibility, but for the dizzy realization that my work was not yet ended. Groping with numb hands I found the pistols, and reeled away through the pines, in the direction in which my forest-bred instinct told me the cabin of Richard Brent stood. With each step my tough recuperative powers asserted themselves.

Tope had not dragged me far. Following his jungle instincts, he had merely hauled me off the trail into the deeper woods. A few steps brought me to the trail, and I saw again the light of the cabin gleaming through the pines. Braxton had not been lying then, about the nature of that bomb. At least the soundless explosion had not destroyed the cabin, for it stood as I had seen it last, apparently undamaged. Light poured, as before, from the shuttered windows, but from it came a high-pitched inhuman laughter that froze the blood in my veins. It was the same laughter that had mocked us beside the shadowed trail.

4. *The Hound of Satan*

Crouching in the shadows, I circled the little clearing to reach a side of the cabin which was without a window. In the thick darkness, with no gleam of light to reveal me, I glided out from the trees and approached the building. Near the wall I stumbled over something bulky and yielding, and almost went to my knees, my heart shooting into my throat with the fear of the noise betraying me. But the ghastly laughter still belled horribly from inside the cabin, mingled with the whimpering of a human voice.

It was Ashley I had stumbled over, or rather his body. He lay on his back, staring sightlessly upward, his head lolling back on the red ruin of his neck. His throat had been torn out; from chin to collar it was a great, gaping, ragged wound. His garments were slimy with blood.

Slightly sickened, in spite of my experience with violent deaths, I glided to the cabin wall and sought without success for a crevice between the logs. The laughter had ceased in the cabin and that frightful, unhuman voice was ringing out, making the nerves quiver in the backs of my hands. With the same difficulty that I had experienced before, I made out the words.

" — And so they did not kill me, the black monks of Erlik. They preferred a jest — a delicious jest, from their point of view. Merely to kill me would be too kind; they thought it more humorous to play with me awhile, as cats do with a mouse, and then send me back into the world with a mark I could never erase — the brand of the hound. That's what they call it. And they did their job well, indeed. None knows better than they how to *alter* a man. Black magic? Bah! Those devils are the greatest scientists in the world. What little the Western world knows about science has leaked out in little trickles from those black mountains.

"Those devils could conquer the world, if they wanted to. They know things that no modern even dares to guess. They know more about plastic surgery, for instance, than all the scientists of the world put together. They understand glands, as no European or American understands them; they know how to retard or exercise them, so as to produce certain results — God, what results! Look at me! Look, damn you, and go mad!"

I glided about the cabin until I reached a window, and peered through a crack in the shutter.

Richard Brent lay on a divan in a room incongruously richly furnished for that primitive setting. He was bound hand and foot; his face was livid and scarcely human. In his starting eyes was the look of a man who has at last come face to face with ultimate horror. Across the room from him the girl, Gloria, was spread-eagled on a table, held helpless with cords on her wrists and ankles. She was stark naked, her clothing lying in scattered confusion on the floor as if they had been brutally ripped from her. Her head was twisted about as she stared in wide-eyed horror at the tall figure which dominated the scene.

He stood with his back toward the window where I crouched, as he faced Richard Brent. To all appearances this figure was human — the figure of a tall, spare man in dark, close-fitting garments, with a sort of cape hanging from his lean, wide shoulders. But at the sight a strange trembling took hold of me, and I recognized at last the dread I had felt since I first glimpsed that gaunt form on the shadowy trail above the body of poor Jim Tike. There was something unnatural about the figure, something not apparent as he stood there with his back to me, yet an unmistakable suggestion of *abnormality;* and my feelings were the dread and loathing that normal men naturally feel toward the abnormal.

"They made me the horror I am today, and then drove me forth," he was yammering in his horrible mouthing voice. "But the *change* was not made in a day, or a month, or a year! They played with me, as devils play with a screaming soul on the white-hot grids of Hell! Time and again I would have died, in spite of them, but I was upheld by the thought of vengeance! Through the long black years, shot red with torture and agony, I dreamed of the day when I would pay the debt I owed to you, Richard Brent, you spawn of Satan's vilest gutter!

"So at last the hunt began. When I reached New York I sent you a photograph of my — my face, and a letter detailing what had happened — and what *would* happen. You fool, did you think you could escape me? Do you think I would have warned you, if I were not sure of my prey? I wanted you to suffer with the knowledge of your doom; to live in terror, to flee and hide like a hunted wolf. You fled and I hunted you, from coast to coast. You did temporarily give me the slip when you came here, but it was inevitable that I should smell you out. When the black monks of Yahlgan gave me *this*" (his hand seemed to stab at his face, and Richard Brent cried out slobberingly), "they also instilled in my nature something of the spirit of the beast they copied.

"To kill you was not enough. I wished to glut my vengeance to the last shuddering ounce. That is why I sent a telegram to your niece, the one person in the world that you cared for. My plans worked out perfectly — with one exception. The bandages I have worn ever since I left Yahlgan were displaced by a branch and I had to kill the fool who was guiding me to your cabin. No man looks upon my face and lives, except Tope Braxton who is more like an ape than a man, anyway. I fell in with him shortly after I was fired at by the man Garfield, and I took him into my confidence, recognizing a valuable ally. He is too brutish to feel the same horror at my appearance that the other Negro felt. He thinks I am a demon of some sort, but so long as I am not hostile toward him, he sees no reason why he should not ally himself with me.

"It was fortunate I took him in, for it was he who struck down Garfield as he was returning. I would have already killed Garfield myself, but he was too strong, too handy with his gun. You might have learned a lesson from these people, Richard Brent. They live hardily and violently, and they are tough and dangerous as timber wolves. But you — you are soft and over-civilized. You will die far too easily. I wish you were as hard as Garfield was. I would like to keep you alive for days, to suffer.

"I gave Garfield a chance to get away, but the fool came back and had to be dealt with. That bomb I threw through the window would have had little effect upon him. It contained one of the chemical secrets I managed to learn in Mongolia, but it is effective only in relation to the bodily strength of the victim. It was enough to knock out a girl and a soft, pampered degenerate like you. But Ashley was able to stagger out of the cabin and would quickly have regained his full powers, if I had not come upon him and put him beyond power of harm."

Brent lifted a moaning cry. There was no intelligence in his eyes, only a ghastly fear. Foam flew from his lips. He was mad — mad as the fearful being that posed and yammered in that room of horror. Only the girl, writhing pitifully on that ebony table, was sane. All else was madness and nightmare. And suddenly complete delirium overcame Adam Grimm, and the laboring monotones shattered in a heart-stopping scream.

"First the girl!" shrieked Adam Grimm — or the thing that had been Adam Grimm. "The girl — to be slain as I have seen women slain in Mongolia — to be skinned alive, slowly — oh, so slowly! She shall bleed to make you suffer, Richard Brent — suffer as I suffered in black Yahlgan! She shall not die until there is no longer an inch of skin left on her body below her neck! Watch me flay your beloved niece, Richard Brent!"

I do not believe Richard Brent comprehended. He was beyond understanding anything. He yammered gibberish, tossing his head from side to side, spattering foam from his livid, working lips. I was lifting a revolver, but just then Adam Grimm whirled, and the sight of his face froze me into paralysis. What unguessed masters of nameless science dwell in the black towers of Yahlgan I dare not dream, but surely black sorcery from the pits of Hell went into the remolding of that countenance.

Ears, forehead and eyes were those of an ordinary man; but the nose, mouth and jaws were such as men have not even imagined in nightmares. I find myself unable to find adequate descriptive phrases. They were hideously elongated, like the muzzle of an animal. There was no chin; upper and lower jaws jutted like the jaws of a hound or a wolf, and the teeth, bared by the snarling bestial lips, were gleaming fangs. How those jaws managed to frame human words I cannot guess.

But the change was deeper than superficial appearance. In his eyes, which blazed like coals of Hell's fire, was a glare that never shone from any human's eyes, sane or mad. When the black devil-monks of Yahlgan altered Adam Grimm's face, they wrought a corresponding change in his soul. He was no longer a human being; he was a veritable were-wolf, as terrible as any in medieval legend.

The thing that had been Adam Grimm rushed toward the girl, a curved skinning-knife gleaming in his hand, and I shook myself out of my daze of horror, and fired through the hole in the shutter. My aim was unerring; I saw the cape jerk to the impact of the slug, and at the crash of the shot the monster staggered and the knife fell from his hand. Then, instantly, he whirled and dashed back across the room toward Richard Brent. With lightning comprehension he realized what had happened, knew he could take only one victim with him, and made his choice instantly.

I do not believe that I can logically be blamed for what happened. I might have smashed that shutter, leaped into the room and grappled with the thing that the monks of Inner Mongolia had made of Adam Grimm. But so swiftly did the monster move that Richard Brent would have died anyway before I could have burst into the room. I did what seemed the only obvious thing — I poured lead through the window into that loping horror as it crossed the room.

That should have halted it, should have crashed it down dead on the floor. But Adam Grimm plunged on, heedless of the slugs ripping into him. His vitality was more than human, more than bestial; there was something demoniac about him, invoked by the black arts that made him what he was. No natural creature could have crossed that room under that raking hail of close-range lead. At that distance I could not miss. He reeled at each impact, but he did not fall until I had smashed home the sixth bullet. Then he crawled on, beast-like, on hands and knees, froth and blood dripping from his grinning jaws. Panic swept me. Frantically I snatched the second gun and emptied it into that body that writhed painfully onward, spattering blood at every movement. But all Hell could not keep Adam Grimm from his prey, and death itself shrank from the ghastly determination in that once-human soul.

With twelve bullets in him, literally shot to pieces, his brains oozing from a great hole in his temple, Adam Grimm reached the man on the divan. The misshapen head dipped; a scream gurgled in Richard Brent's throat as the hideous jaws locked. For a mad instant those two frightful visages seemed to melt together, to my horrified sight — the mad human and the mad inhuman. Then with a wild-beast gesture, Grimm threw up his head, ripping out his enemy's jugular, and blood deluged both figures. Grimm lifted his head, with his dripping fangs and bloody muzzle, and his lips writhed back in a last peal of ghastly laughter that choked in a rush of blood, as he crumpled and lay still.

THE FIRE OF ASSHURBANIPAL

Weird Tales, December 1936

Yar Ali squinted carefully down the blue barrel of his Lee-Enfield, called devoutly on Allah and sent a bullet through the brain of a flying rider.

"Allaho akbar!"

The big Afghan shouted in glee, waving his weapon above his head, "God is great! By Allah, *sahib*, I have sent another one of the dogs to Hell!"

His companion peered cautiously over the rim of the sand-pit they had scooped with their hands. He was a lean and wiry American, Steve Clarney by name.

"Good work, old horse," said this person. "Four left. Look — they're drawing off."

The white-robed horsemen were indeed reining away, clustering together just out of accurate rifle-range, as if in council. There had been seven when they had first swooped down on the comrades, but the fire from the two rifles in the sand-pit had been deadly.

"Look, *sahib* — they abandon the fray!"

Yar Ali stood up boldly and shouted taunts at the departing riders, one of whom whirled and sent a bullet that kicked up sand thirty feet in front of the pit.

"They shoot like the sons of dogs," said Yar Ali in complacent self-esteem. "By Allah, did you see that rogue plunge from his saddle as my lead went home? Up, *sahib*; let us run after them and cut them down!"

Paying no attention to this outrageous proposal — for he knew it was but one of the gestures Afghan nature continually demands — Steve rose, dusted off his breeches and gazing after the riders, now white specks far out on the desert, said musingly: "Those fellows ride as if they had some set purpose in mind — not a bit like men running from a licking."

"Aye," agreed Yar Ali promptly and seeing nothing inconsistent with his present attitude and recent bloodthirsty suggestion, "they ride after more of their kind — they are hawks who give up their prey not quickly. We had best move our position quickly, Steve *sahib*. They will come back — maybe in a few hours, maybe in a few days — it all depends on how far away lies the oasis of their tribe. But they will be back. We have guns and lives — they want both. And behold."

The Afghan levered out the empty shell and slipped a single cartridge into the breech of his rifle.

"My last bullet, *sahib*."

Steve nodded. "I've got three left."

The raiders whom their buffets had knocked from the saddle had been looted by their own comrades. No use searching the bodies which lay in the sand for ammunition. Steve lifted his canteen and shook it.

Not much water remained. He knew that Yar Ali had only a little more than he, though the big Afridi, bred in a barren land, had used and needed less water than did the American; although the latter, judged from a white man's standards, was hard and tough as a wolf. As Steve unscrewed the canteen cap and drank very sparingly, he mentally reviewed the chain of events that had led them to their present position.

Wanderers, soldiers of fortune, thrown together by chance and attracted to each other by mutual admiration, he and Yar Ali had wandered from India up through Turkistan and down through Persia, an oddly assorted but highly capable pair. Driven by the restless urge of inherent wanderlust, their avowed purpose — which they swore to and sometimes believed themselves — was the accumulation of some vague and undiscovered treasure, some pot of gold at the foot of some yet unborn rainbow.

Then in ancient Shiraz they had heard of the Fire of Asshurbanipal. From the lips of an ancient Persian trader, who only half-believed what he repeated to them, they heard the tale that he in turn had heard from the babbling lips of delirium, in his distant youth. He had been a member of a caravan, fifty years before, which, wandering far on the southern shore of the Persian Gulf trading for pearls, had followed the tale of a rare pearl far into the desert.

The pearl, rumored found by a diver and stolen by a shaykh of the interior, they did not find, but they did pick up a Turk who was dying of starvation, thirst and a bullet wound in the thigh. As he died in delirium, he babbled a wild tale of a silent dead city of black stone set in the drifting sands of the desert far to the westward, and of a flaming gem clutched in the bony fingers of a skeleton on an ancient throne.

He had not dared bring it away with him, because of an overpowering brooding horror that haunted the place, and thirst had driven him into the desert again, where Bedouins had pursued and wounded him. Yet he had escaped, riding hard until his horse fell under him. He died without telling how he had reached the mythical city in the first place, but the old trader thought he must have come from the northwest — a deserter from the Turkish army, making a desperate attempt to reach the Gulf.

The men of the caravan had made no attempt to plunge still further into the desert in search of the city; for, said the old trader, they believed it to be the ancient, ancient City of Evil spoken of in the *Necronomicon* of the mad Arab Alhazred — the city of the dead on which an ancient curse rested. Legends named it vaguely: the Arabs called it *Beled-el-Djinn*, the City of Devils, and the Turks, *Kara-Shehr*, the Black City. And the gem was that ancient and accursed jewel belonging to a king of long ago, whom the Grecians called Sardanapalus and the Semitic peoples Asshurbanipal.

Steve had been fascinated by the tale. Admitting to himself that it was doubtless one of the ten thousand cock-and-bull myths mooted about the East, still there was a possibility that he and Yar Ali had stumbled onto a trace of that pot of rainbow gold for which they searched. And Yar Ali had heard hints before of a silent city of the sands; tales had followed the eastbound caravans over the high Persian uplands and across the sands of Turkistan, into the mountain country and beyond — vague tales, whispers of a black city of the djinn, deep in the hazes of a haunted desert.

So, following the trail of the legend, the companions had come from Shiraz to a village on the Arabian shore of the Persian Gulf, and there had heard more from an old man who had been a pearl-diver in his youth. The loquacity of age was on him and he told tales repeated to him by wandering tribesmen who had them in turn from the wild nomads of the deep interior; and again Steve and Yar Ali heard of the still black city with giant beasts carved of stone, and the skeleton sultan who held the blazing gem.

And so, mentally swearing at himself for a fool, Steve had made the plunge, and Yar Ali, secure in the knowledge that all things lay on the lap of Allah, had come with him. Their scanty supply of money had been just sufficient to provide riding-camels and provisions for a bold flying invasion of the unknown. Their only chart had been the vague rumors that placed the supposed location of Kara-Shehr.

There had been days of hard travel, pushing the beasts and conserving water and food. Then, deep in the desert they invaded, they had encountered a blinding sand-wind in which they had lost the camels. After that came long miles of staggering through the sands, battered by a flaming sun, subsisting on rapidly dwindling water from their canteens, and food Yar Ali had in a pouch. No thought of finding the mythical city now. They pushed on blindly, in hope of stumbling upon a spring; they knew that behind them no oases lay within a distance they could hope to cover on foot. It was a desperate chance, but their only one.

Then white-clad hawks had swooped down on them, out of the haze of the skyline, and from a shallow and hastily scooped trench the adventurers had exchanged shots with the wild riders who circled them at top speed. The bullets of the Bedouins had skipped through their makeshift fortifications, knocking dust into their eyes and flicking bits of cloth from their garments, but by good chance neither had been hit.

Their one bit of luck, reflected Clarney, as he cursed himself for a fool. What a mad venture it had been, anyway! To think that two men could so dare the desert and live, much less wrest from its abysmal bosom the secrets of the ages! And that crazy tale of a skeleton hand gripping a flaming jewel in a dead city — bosh! What utter rot! He must have been crazy himself to credit it, the American decided with the clarity of view that suffering and danger bring.

"Well, old horse," said Steve, lifting his rifle, "let's get going. It's a toss-up if we die of thirst or get sniped off by the desert-brothers. Anyway, we're doin' no good here."

"God gives," agreed Yar Ali cheerfully. "The sun sinks westward. Soon the coolness of night will be upon us. Perhaps we shall find water yet, *sahib*. Look, the terrain changes to the south."

Clarney shaded his eyes against the dying sun. Beyond a level, barren expanse of several miles width, the land did indeed become more broken; aborted hills were in evidence. The American slung his rifle over his arm and sighed.

"Heave ahead; we're food for the buzzards anyhow."

The sun sank and the moon rose, flooding the desert with weird silver light. Drifted sand glimmered in long ripples, as if a sea had suddenly been frozen into immobility. Steve, parched fiercely by a thirst he dared not fully quench, cursed beneath his breath. The desert was beautiful beneath the moon, with the beauty of a cold marble lorelei to lure men to destruction. What a mad quest! his weary brain reiterated; the Fire of Asshurbanipal retreated into the mazes of unreality with each dragging step. The desert became not merely a material wasteland, but the gray mists of the lost eons, in whose depths dreamed sunken things.

Clarney stumbled and swore; was he failing already? Yar Ali swung along with the easy, tireless stride of the mountain man, and Steve set his teeth, nerving himself to greater effort. They were entering the broken country at last, and the going became harder. Shallow gullies and narrow ravines knifed the earth with wavering patterns. Most of them were nearly filled with sand, and there was no trace of water.

"This country was once oasis country," commented Yar Ali. "Allah knows how many centuries ago the sand took it, as the sand has taken so many cities in Turkistan."

They swung on like dead men in a gray land of death. The moon grew red and sinister as she sank, and shadowy darkness settled over the desert before they had reached a point where they could see what lay beyond the broken belt. Even the big Afghan's feet began to drag, and Steve kept himself erect only by a savage effort of will. At last they toiled up a sort of ridge, on the southern side of which the land sloped downward.

"We rest," declared Steve. "There's no water in this hellish country. No use in goin' on forever. My legs are stiff as gun-barrels. I couldn't take another step to save my neck. Here's a kind of stunted cliff, about as high as a man's shoulder, facing south. We'll sleep in the lee of it."

"And shall we not keep watch, Steve *sahib*?"

"We don't," answered Steve. "If the Arabs cut our throats while we're asleep, so much the better. We're goners anyhow."

With which optimistic observation Clarney lay down stiffly in the deep sand. But Yar Ali stood,

leaning forward, straining his eyes into the elusive
darkness that turned the star-flecked horizons to
murky wells of shadow.

"Something lies on the skyline to the south," he
muttered uneasily. "A hill? I cannot tell, or even be
sure that I see anything at all."

"You're seeing mirages already," said Steve irritably. "Lie down and sleep."

And so saying Steve slumbered.

The sun in his eyes awoke him. He sat up, yawning, and his first sensation was that of thirst. He
lifted his canteen and wet his lips. One drink left. Yar
Ali still slept. Steve's eyes wandered over the southern horizon and he started. He kicked the recumbent
Afghan.

"Hey, wake up, Ali. I reckon you weren't seeing
things after all. There's your hill — and a queer-
lookin' one, too."

The Afridi woke as a wild thing wakes, instantly
and completely, his hand leaping to his long knife
as he glared about for enemies. His gaze followed
Steve's pointing fingers and his eyes widened.

"By Allah and by Allah!" he swore. "We have
come into a land of djinn! That is no hill — it is a city
of stone in the midst of the sands!"

Steve bounded to his feet like a steel spring released. As he gazed with bated breath, a fierce shout
escaped his lips. At his feet the slope of the ridge ran
down into a wide and level expanse of sand that
stretched away southward. And far away, across

those sands, to his straining sight the "hill" slowly took shape, like a mirage growing from the drifting sands.

He saw great uneven walls, massive battlements; all about crawled the sands like a living, sensate thing, drifted high about the walls, softening the rugged outlines. No wonder that at first glance the whole had appeared like a hill.

"Kara-Shehr!" Clarney exclaimed fiercely. "Beled-el-Djinn! The city of the dead! It wasn't a pipe-dream after all! We've found it — by Heaven, we've found it! Come on! Let's go!"

Yar Ali shook his head uncertainly and muttered something about evil djinn under his breath, but he followed. The sight of the ruins had swept from Steve his thirst and hunger, and the fatigue that a few hours' sleep had not fully overcome. He trudged on swiftly, oblivious to the rising heat, his eyes gleaming with the lust of the explorer. It was not altogether greed for the fabled gem that had prompted Steve Clarney to risk his life in that grim wilderness; deep in his soul lurked the age-old heritage of the white man, the urge to seek out the hidden places of the world, and that urge had been stirred to the depths by the ancient tales.

Now as they crossed the level wastes that separated the broken land from the city, they saw the shattered walls take clearer form and shape, as if they grew out of the morning sky. The city seemed built of huge blocks of black stone, but how high the walls had been there was no telling because of the sand that drifted high about their base; in many places they had fallen away and the sand hid the fragments entirely.

The sun reached her zenith and thirst intruded itself in spite of zeal and enthusiasm, but Steve fiercely mastered his suffering. His lips were parched and swollen, but he would not take that last drink until he had reached the ruined city. Yar Ali wet his lips from his own canteen and tried to share the remainder with his friend. Steve shook his head and plodded on.

In the ferocious heat of the desert afternoon they reached the ruin, and passing through a wide breach in the crumbling wall, gazed on the dead city. Sand choked the ancient streets and lent fantastic form to huge, fallen and half-hidden columns. So crumbled into decay and so covered with sand was the whole that the explorers could make out little of the original plan of the city; now it was but a waste of drifted sand and crumbling stone over which brooded, like an invisible cloud, an aura of unspeakable antiquity.

But directly in front of them ran a broad avenue, the outline of which not even the ravaging sands and winds of time had been able to efface. On either side of the wide way were ranged huge columns, not unusually tall, even allowing for the sand that hid their bases, but incredibly massive. On the top of each column stood a figure carved from solid stone — great, somber images, half-human, half-bestial, partaking of the brooding brutishness of the whole city. Steve cried out in amazement.

"The winged bulls of Nineveh! The bulls with men's heads! By the saints, Ali, the old tales are true! The Assyrians did build this city! The whole tale's true! They must have come here when the Babylonians destroyed Assyria — why, this scene's a dead ringer for pictures I've seen — reconstructed scenes of old Nineveh! And look!"

He pointed down the broad street to the great building which reared at the other end, a colossal, brooding edifice whose columns and walls of solid black stone blocks defied the winds and sands of time. The drifting, obliterating sea washed about its foundations, overflowing into its doorways, but it would require a thousand years to inundate the whole structure.

"An abode of devils!" muttered Yar Ali, uneasily.

"The temple of Baal!" exclaimed Steve. "Come on! I was afraid we'd find all the palaces and temples hidden by the sand and have to dig for the gem."

"Little good it will do us," muttered Yar Ali. "Here we die."

"I reckon so." Steve unscrewed the cap of his canteen. "Let's take our last drink. Anyway, were safe from the Arabs. They'd never dare come here, with their superstitions. We'll drink and then we'll die, I reckon, but first we'll find the jewel. When I pass out, I want to have it in my hand. Maybe a few centuries later some lucky son-of-a-gun will find our skeletons — and the gem. Here's to him, whoever he is!"

With which grim jest Clarney drained his canteen and Yar Ali followed suit. They had played their last ace; the rest lay on the lap of Allah.

They strode up the broad way, and Yar Ali, utterly fearless in the face of human foes, glanced nervously to right and left, half-expecting to see a horned and fantastic face leering at him from behind a column. Steve himself felt the somber antiquity of the place, and almost found himself fearing a rush of bronze war chariots down the forgotten streets, or to hear the sudden menacing flare of bronze trumpets. The silence in dead cities was so much more intense, he reflected, than that on the open desert.

They came to the portals of the great temple. Rows of immense columns flanked the wide doorway, which was ankle-deep in sand, and from which sagged massive bronze frameworks that had once braced mighty doors, whose polished woodwork had rotted away centuries ago. They passed into a mighty hall of misty twilight, whose shadowy stone roof was upheld by columns like the trunks of forest trees. The whole effect of the architecture was one of awesome magnitude and sullen, breathtaking splendor, like a temple built by somber giants for the abode of dark gods.

Yar Ali walked fearfully, as if he expected to awake sleeping gods, and Steve, without the Afridi's superstitions, yet felt the gloomy majesty of the place lay somber hands on his soul.

No trace of a footprint showed in the deep dust

on the floor; half a century had passed since the affrighted and devil-ridden Turk had fled these silent halls. As for the Bedouins, it was easy to see why those superstitious sons of the desert shunned this haunted city — and haunted it was, not by actual ghosts, perhaps, but by the shadows of lost splendors.

As they trod the sands of the hall, which seemed endless, Steve pondered many questions: How did these fugitives from the wrath of frenzied rebels build this city? How did they pass through the country of their foes? — for Babylonia lay between Assyria and the Arabian desert. Yet there had been no other place for them to go; westward lay Syria and the sea, and north and east swarmed the "dangerous Medes", those fierce Aryans whose aid had stiffened the arm of Babylon to smite her foe to the dust.

Possibly, thought Steve, Kara-Shehr — whatever its name had been in those dim days — had been built as an outpost border city before the fall of the Assyrian empire, whither survivals of that overthrow fled. At any rate it was possible that Kara-Shehr had outlasted Nineveh by some centuries — a strange, hermit city, no doubt, cut off from the rest of the world.

Surely, as Yar Ali had said, this was once fertile country, watered by oases; and doubtless in the broken country they had passed over the night before, there had been quarries that furnished the stone for the building of the city.

Then what caused its downfall? Did the encroachment of the sands and the filling up of the springs cause the people to abandon it, or was Kara-Shehr a city of silence before the sands crept over the walls? Did the downfall come from within or without? Did civil war blot out the inhabitants, or were they slaughtered by some powerful foe from the desert? Clarney shook his head in baffled chagrin. The answers to those questions were lost in the maze of forgotten ages.

"Allaho akbar!" They had traversed the great shadowy hall and at its further end they came upon a hideous black stone altar, behind which loomed an ancient god, bestial and horrific. Steve shrugged his shoulders as he recognized the monstrous aspect of the image — aye, that was Baal, on whose black altar in other ages many a screaming, writhing, naked victim had offered up its naked soul. The idol embodied in its utter, abysmal and sullen bestiality the whole soul of this demoniac city. Surely, thought Steve, the builders of Nineveh and Kara-Shehr were cast in another mold from the people of today. Their art and culture were too ponderous, too grimly barren of the lighter aspects of humanity, to be wholly human, as modern man understands humanity. Their architecture was repellent; of high skill, yet so massive, sullen and brutish in effect as to be almost beyond the comprehension of moderns.

The adventurers passed through a narrow door which opened in the end of the hall close to the idol, and came into a series of wide, dim, dusty chambers connected by column-flanked corridors. Along these they strode in the gray ghostly light, and came at last to a wide stair, whose massive stone steps led upward and vanished in the gloom. Here Yar Ali halted.

"We have dared much, *sahib*," he muttered. "Is it wise to dare more?"

Steve, aquiver with eagerness, yet understood the Afghan's mind. "You mean we shouldn't go up those stairs?"

"They have an evil look. To what chambers of silence and horror may they lead? When djinn haunt deserted buildings, they lurk in the upper chambers. At any moment a demon may bite off our heads."

"We're dead men anyhow," grunted Steve. "But I tell you — you go on back through the hall and watch for the Arabs while I go upstairs."

"Watch for a wind on the horizon," responded the Afghan gloomily, shifting his rifle and loosening his long knife in its scabbard. "No Bedouin comes here. Lead on, *sahib*. Thou'rt mad after the manner of all Franks, but I would not leave thee to face the djinn alone."

So the companions mounted the massive stairs, their feet sinking deep into the accumulated dust of centuries at each step. Up and up they went, to an incredible height, until the depths below merged into a vague gloom.

"We walk blind to our doom, *sahib*," muttered Yar Ali. "*Allah il allah* — and Muhammad is his

Prophet! Nevertheless, I feel the presence of slumbering Evil and never again shall I hear the wind blowing up the Khyber Pass."

Steve made no reply. He did not like the breathless silence that brooded over the ancient temple, nor the grisly gray light that filtered from some hidden source.

Now above them the gloom lightened somewhat and they emerged into a vast circular chamber, grayly illuminated by light that filtered in through the high, pierced ceiling. But another radiance lent itself to the illumination. A cry burst from Steve's lips, echoed by Yar Ali.

Standing on the top step of the broad stone stair, they looked directly across the broad chamber, with its dust-covered heavy tile floor and bare black stone walls. From about the center of the chamber, massive steps led up to a stone dais, and on this dais stood a marble throne. About this throne gloved and shimmered an uncanny light, and the awestruck adventurers gasped as they saw its source. On the throne slumped a human skeleton, an almost shapeless mass of moldering bones. A fleshless hand sagged outstretched upon the broad marble throne-arm, and in its grisly clasp there pulsed and throbbed like a living thing, a great crimson stone.

The Fire of Asshurbanipal! Even after they had found the lost city Steve had not really allowed himself to believe that they would find the gem, or that it even existed in reality. Yet he could not doubt the evidence of his eyes, dazzled by that evil, incredible glow. With a fierce shout he sprang across the chamber and up the steps. Yar Ali was at his heels, but when Steve would have seized the gem, the Afghan laid a hand on his arm.

"Wait!" exclaimed the big Muhammadan. "Touch it not yet, *sahib*! A curse lies on ancient things — and surely this is a thing triply accursed! Else why has it lain here untouched in a country of thieves for so many centuries? It is not well to disturb the possessions of the dead."

"Bosh!" snorted the American. "Superstitions! The Bedouins were scared by the tales that have come down to 'em from their ancestors. Being desert-dwellers they mistrust cities anyway, and no doubt this one had an evil reputation in its lifetime. And nobody except Bedouins have seen this place before, except that Turk, who was probably half-demented with suffering.

"These bones may be those of the king mentioned in the legend — the dry desert air preserves such things indefinitely — but I doubt it. May be Assyrian — most likely Arab — some beggar that got the gem and then died on that throne for some reason or other."

The Afghan scarcely heard him. He was gazing in fearful fascination at the great stone, as a hypnotized bird stares into a serpent's eye.

"Look at it, *sahib*!" he whispered. "What is it? No such gem as this was ever cut by mortal hands!

Look how it throbs and pulses like the heart of a cobra!"

Steve was looking, and he was aware of a strange undefined feeling of uneasiness. Well versed in the knowledge of precious stones, he had never seen a stone like this. At first glance he had supposed it to be a monster ruby, as told in the legends. Now he was not sure, and he had a nervous feeling that Yar Ali was right, that this was no natural, normal gem. He could not classify the style in which it was cut, and such was the power of its lurid radiance that he found it difficult to gaze at it closely for any length of time. The whole setting was not one calculated to soothe restless nerves. The deep dust on the floor suggested an unwholesome antiquity; the gray light evoked a sense of unreality, and the heavy black walls towered grimly, hinting at hidden things.

"Let's take the stone and go!" muttered Steve, an unaccustomed panicky dread rising in his bosom.

"Wait!" Yar Ali's eyes were blazing, and he gazed, not at the gem, but at the sullen stone walls. "We are flies in the lair of the spider! *Sahib*, as Allah lives, it is more than the ghosts of old fears that lurk over this city of horror! I feel the presence of peril, as I have felt it before — as I felt it in a jungle cavern where a python lurked unseen in the darkness — as I felt it in the temple of Thuggee where the hidden stranglers of Siva crouched to spring upon us — as I feel it now, tenfold!"

Steve's hair prickled. He knew that Yar Ali was a

grim veteran, not to be stampeded by silly fear or senseless panic; he well remembered the incidents referred to by the Afghan, as he remembered other occasions upon which Yar Ali's oriental telepathic instinct had warned him of danger before that danger was seen or heard.

"What is it, Yar Ali?" he whispered.

The Afghan shook his head, his eyes filled with a weird mysterious light as he listened to the dim occult promptings of his subconsciousness.

"I know not; I know it is close to us, and that it is very ancient and very evil. I think —" Suddenly he halted and wheeled, the eery light vanishing from his eyes to be replaced by a glare of wolflike fear and suspicion.

"Hark, *sahib*!" he snapped. "Ghosts or dead men mount the stair!"

Steve stiffened as the stealthy pad of soft sandals on stone reached his ear.

"By Judas, Ali!" he rapped; "something's out there —"

The ancient walls re-echoed to a chorus of wild yells as a horde of savage figures flooded the chamber. For one dazed insane instant Steve believed wildly that they were being attacked by re-embodied warriors of a vanished age; then the spiteful crack of a bullet past his ear and the acrid smell of powder told him that their foes were material enough. Clarney cursed; in their fancied security they had been caught like rats in a trap by the pursuing Arabs.

Even as the American threw up his rifle, Yar Ali fired point-blank from the hip with deadly effect, hurled his empty rifle into the horde and went down the steps like a hurricane, his three-foot Khyber knife shimmering in his hairy hand. Into his gusto for battle went real relief that his foes were human. A bullet ripped the turban from his head, but an Arab went down with a split skull beneath the hillman's first, shearing stroke.

A tall Bedouin clapped his gun-muzzle to the Afghan's side, but before he could pull the trigger, Clarney's bullet scattered his brains. The very number of the attackers hindered their onslaught on the big Afridi, whose tigerish quickness made shooting as dangerous to themselves as to him. The bulk of them swarmed about him, striking with scimitar and rifle-stock while others charged up the steps after Steve. At that range there was no missing; the American simply thrust his rifle muzzle into a bearded face and blasted it into a ghastly ruin. The others came on, screaming like panthers.

And now as he prepared to expend his last cartridge, Clarney saw two things in one flashing instant — a wild warrior who, with froth on his beard and a heavy scimitar uplifted, was almost upon him, and another who knelt on the floor drawing a careful bead on the plunging Yar Ali. Steve made an instant choice and fired over the shoulder of the charging swordsman, killing the rifleman — and voluntarily offering his own life for his friend's; for the scimitar was swinging at his own head. But even as the Arab swung, grunting with the force of the blow, his sandaled foot slipped on the marble steps and the curved blade, veering erratically from its arc, clashed on Steve's rifle-barrel. In an instant the American clubbed his rifle, and as the Bedouin recovered his balance and again heaved up the scimitar, Clarney struck with all his rangy power, and stock and skull shattered together.

Then a heavy ball smacked into his shoulder, sickening him with the shock.

As he staggered dizzily, a Bedouin whipped a turban-cloth about his feet and jerked viciously. Clarney pitched headlong down the steps, to strike with stunning force. A gun-stock in a brown hand went up to dash out his brains, but an imperious command halted the blow.

"Slay him not, but bind him hand and foot."

As Steve struggled dazedly against many gripping hands, it seemed to him that somewhere he had heard that imperious voice before.

The American's downfall had occurred in a matter of seconds. Even as Steve's second shot had cracked, Yar Ali had half-severed a raider's arm and himself received a numbing blow from a rifle-stock on his left shoulder. His sheepskin coat, worn despite the desert heat, saved his hide from half a dozen slashing knives. A rifle was discharged so close to his face that the powder burnt him fiercely, bringing a bloodthirsty yell from the maddened Afghan. As Yar

Ali swung up his dripping blade the rifleman, ashy-faced, lifted his rifle above his head in both hands to parry the downward blow, whereat the Afridi, with a yelp of ferocious exultation, shifted as a jungle-cat strikes and plunged his long knife into the Arab's belly. But at that instant a rifle-stock, swung with all the hearty ill-will its wielder could evoke, crashed against the giant's head, laying open the scalp and dashing him to his knees.

With the dogged and silent ferocity of his breed, Yar Ali staggered blindly up again, slashing at foes he could scarcely see, but a storm of blows battered him down again, nor did his attackers cease beating him until he lay still. They would have finished him in short order then, but for another peremptory order from their chief; whereupon they bound the senseless knife-man and flung him down alongside Steve, who was fully conscious and aware of the savage hurt of the bullet in his shoulder.

He glared up at the tall Arab who stood looking down at him.

"Well, *sahib*," said this one — and Steve saw he was no Bedouin — "do you not remember me?"

Steve scowled; a bullet-wound is no aid to concentration.

"You look familiar — by Judas! — you are! Nureddin El Mekru!"

"I am honored! The *sahib* remembers!" Nureddin salaamed mockingly. "And you remember, no doubt, the occasion on which you made me a present of — this?"

The dark eyes shadowed with bitter menace and the shaykh indicated a thin white scar on the angle of his jaw.

"I remember," snarled Clarney, whom pain and anger did not tend to make docile. "It was in Somaliland, years ago. You were in the slave-trade then. A wretch of a nigger escaped from you and took refuge with me. You walked into my camp one night in your high-handed way, started a row and in the ensuing scrap you got a butcher-knife across your face. I wish I'd cut your lousy throat."

"You had your chance," answered the Arab. "Now the tables are turned."

"I thought your stamping-ground lay west," growled Clarney; "Yemen and the Somali country."

"I quit the slave-trade long ago," answered the shaykh. "It is an outworn game. I led a band of thieves in Yemen for a time; then again I was forced to change my location. I came here with a few faithful followers, and by Allah, these wild men nearly slit my throat at first. But I overcame their suspicions, and now I lead more men than have followed me in years.

"They whom you fought off yesterday were my men — scouts I had sent out ahead. My oasis lies far to the west. We have ridden for many days, for I was on my way to this very city. When my scouts rode in and told me of two wanderers, I did not alter my course, for I had business first in Beled-el-Djinn. We rode into the city from the west and saw your tracks in the sand. We followed them, and you were blind buffalo who heard not our coming."

Steve snarled. "You wouldn't have caught us so easy, only we thought no Bedouin would dare come into Kara-Shehr."

Nureddin nodded. "But I am no Bedouin. I have traveled far and seen many lands and many races, and I have read many books. I know that fear is smoke, that the dead are dead, and that djinn and ghosts and curses are mists that the wind blows away. It was because of the tales of the red stone that I came into this forsaken desert. But it has taken months to persuade my men to ride with me here.

"But — I am here! And your presence is a delightful surprise. Doubtless you have guessed why I had you taken alive; I have more elaborate entertainment planned for you and that Pathan swine. Now — I take the Fire of Asshurbanipal and we will go."

He turned toward the dais, and one of his men, a bearded one-eyed giant, exclaimed, "Hold, my lord! Ancient evil reigned here before the days of Muhammad! The djinn howl through these halls when the winds blow, and men have seen ghosts dancing on the walls beneath the moon. No man of mortals has dared this black city for a thousand years — save one, half a century ago, who fled shrieking.

"You have come here from Yemen; you do not know the ancient curse on this foul city, and this evil stone, which pulses like the red heart of Satan! We have followed you here against our judgment, because you have proven yourself a strong man, and have said you hold a charm against all evil beings. You said you but wished to look on this mysterious gem, but now we see it is your intention to take it for yourself. Do not offend the djinn!"

"Nay, Nureddin, do not offend the djinn!" chorused the other Bedouins. The shaykh's own hard-bitten ruffians, standing in a compact group somewhat apart from the Bedouins, said nothing; hardened to crimes and deeds of impiety, they were less affected by the superstitions of the desert men, to whom the dread tale of the accursed city had been repeated for centuries. Steve, even while hating Nureddin with concentrated venom, realized the magnetic power of the man, the innate leadership that had enabled him to overcome thus far the fears and traditions of ages.

"The curse is laid on infidels who invade the city," answered Nureddin, "not on the Faithful. See, in this chamber have we overcome our *kafar* foes!"

A white-bearded desert hawk shook his head.

"The curse is more ancient than Muhammad, and recks not of race or creed. Evil men reared this black city in the dawn of the Beginnings of Days. They oppressed our ancestors of the black tents, and warred among themselves; aye, the black walls of this foul city were stained with blood, and echoed to the shouts of unholy revel and the whispers of dark intrigues.

"Thus came the stone to the city: there dwelt a magician at the court of Asshurbanipal, and the black wisdom of ages was not denied to him. To gain honor and power for himself, he dared the horrors of a nameless vast cavern in a dark, untraveled land, and from those fiend-haunted depths he brought that blazing gem, which is carved of the frozen flames of Hell! By reason of his fearful power in black magic, he put a spell on the demon which guarded the ancient gem, and so stole away the stone. And the demon slept in the cavern unknowing.

"So this magician — Xuthltan by name — dwelt in the court of the sultan Asshurbanipal and did magic and forecast events by scanning the lurid deeps of the stone, into which no eyes but his could look unblinded. And men called the stone the Fire of Asshurbanipal, in honor of the king.

"But evil came upon the kingdom and men cried out that it was the curse of the djinn, and the sultan in great fear bade Xuthltan take the gem and cast it into the cavern from which he had taken it, lest worse ill befall them.

"Yet it was not the magician's will to give up the gem wherein he read strange secrets of pre-Adamite days, and he fled to the rebel city of Kara-Shehr, where soon civil war broke out and men strove with one another to possess the gem. Then the king who ruled the city, coveting the stone, seized the magician and put him to death by torture, and in this very room he watched him die; with the gem in his hand the king sat upon the throne — even as he has sat throughout the centuries — even as now he sits!"

The Arab's finger stabbed at the moldering bones on the marble throne, and the wild desert men bleached; even Nureddin's own scoundrels recoiled, catching their breath, but the shaykh showed no sign of perturbation.

"As Xuthltan died," continued the old Bedouin, "he cursed the stone whose magic had not saved him, and he shrieked aloud the fearful words which undid the spell he had put upon the demon in the cavern, and set the monster free. And crying out on the forgotten gods, Cthulhu and Koth and Yog-Sothoth, and all the pre-Adamite Dwellers in the black cities under the sea and the caverns of the earth, he called upon them to take back that which was theirs, and with his dying breath pronounced doom on the false king, and that doom was that the king should sit on his throne holding in his hand the Fire of Asshurbanipal until the thunder of Judgment Day.

"Thereat the great stone cried out as a live thing cries, and the king and his soldiers saw a black cloud spinning up from the floor, and out of the cloud blew a fetid wind, and out of the wind came a grisly shape which stretched forth fearsome paws and laid them on the king, who shriveled and died at their touch. And the soldiers fled screaming, and all the people of the city ran forth wailing into the desert where they perished or gained through the wastes to the far oasis towns. Kara-Shehr lay silent and deserted, the haunt of the lizard and the jackal. And when some of the desert-people ventured into the city they found the king dead on his throne, clutching the blazing gem, but they dared not lay hand upon it, for they knew the demon lurked near to guard it through all the ages — as he lurks near even as we stand here."

The warriors shuddered involuntarily and glanced about, and Nureddin said, "Why did he not come forth when the Franks entered the chamber? Is he deaf, that the sound of the combat has not awakened him?"

"We have not touched the gem," answered the old Bedouin, "nor had the Franks molested it. Men have looked on it and lived; but no mortal may touch it and survive."

Nureddin started to speak, gazed at the stubborn, uneasy faces and realized the futility of argument. His attitude changed abruptly.

"I am master here," he snapped, dropping a hand to his holster. "I have not sweat and bled for this gem to be balked at the last by groundless fears! Stand back, all! Let any man cross me at the peril of his head!"

He faced them, his eyes blazing, and they fell back, cowed by the force of his ruthless personality. He strode boldly up the marble steps, and the Arabs caught their breath, recoiling toward the door; Yar Ali, conscious at last, groaned dismally. God! thought Steve, what a barbaric scene! — bound captives on the dust-heaped floor, wild warriors clustered about, gripping their weapons, the raw acrid scent of blood and burnt powder still fouling the air, corpses strewn in a horrid welter of blood, brains and entrails — and on the dais, the hawk-faced shaykh, oblivious to all except the evil crimson glow in the skeleton fingers that rested on the marble throne.

A tense silence gripped all as Nureddin stretched forth his hand slowly, as if hypnotized by the throbbing crimson light. And in Steve's subconsciousness there shuddered a dim echo, as of something vast and loathsome waking suddenly from an age-long slumber. The American's eyes moved instinctively toward the grim cyclopean walls. The jewel's glow had altered strangely; it burned a deeper, darker red, angry and menacing.

"Heart of all evil," murmured the shaykh, "how many princes died for thee in the Beginnings of Happenings? Surely the blood of kings throbs in thee. The sultans and the princesses and the generals who wore thee, they are dust and are forgotten, but thou blazest with majesty undimmed, fire of the world —"

Nureddin seized the stone. A shuddery wail broke from the Arabs, cut through by a sharp inhuman cry. To Steve it seemed, horribly, that the great jewel had cried out like a living thing! The stone slipped from the shaykh's hand. Nureddin might have dropped it; to Steve it looked as though it leaped convulsively, as a live thing might leap. It rolled from the dais, bounding from step to step, with Nureddin springing after it, cursing as his clutching hand missed it. It struck the floor, veered sharply, and despite the deep dust, rolled like a revolving ball of fire toward the back wall. Nureddin was close upon it — it struck the wall — the shaykh's hand reached for it.

A scream of mortal fear ripped the tense silence. Without warning the solid wall had opened. Out of the black wall that gaped there, a tentacle shot and gripped the shaykh's body as a python girdles its victim, and jerked him headlong into the darkness. And then the wall showed blank and solid once more; only from within sounded a hideous, high-pitched, muffled screaming that chilled the blood of the listeners. Howling wordlessly, the Arabs stampeded, jammed in a battling, screeching mass in the doorway, tore through and raced madly down the wide stairs.

Steve and Yar Ali, lying helplessly, heard the frenzied clamor of their flight fade away into the distance, and gazed in dumb horror at the grim wall. The shrieks had faded into a more horrific silence. Holding their breath, they heard suddenly a sound that froze the blood in their veins — the soft sliding of metal or stone in a groove. At the same time the hidden door began to open, and Steve caught a glimmer in the blackness that might have been the glitter of monstrous eyes. He closed his own eyes; he dared not look upon whatever horror slunk from that hideous black well. He knew that there are strains the human brain cannot stand, and every primitive instinct in his soul cried out to him that this thing was nightmare and lunacy. He sensed that Yar Ali likewise closed his eyes, and the two lay like dead men.

Clarney heard no sound, but he sensed the presence of a horrific evil too grisly for human comprehension — of an Invader from Outer Gulfs and far black reaches of cosmic being. A deadly cold pervaded the chamber, and Steve felt the glare of inhuman eyes sear through his closed lids and freeze his consciousness. If he looked, if he opened his eyes, he knew stark black madness would be his instant lot.

He felt a soul-shakingly foul breath against his face and knew that the monster was bending close above him, but he lay like a man frozen in a nightmare. He clung to one thought: neither he nor Yar Ali had touched the jewel this horror guarded.

Then he no longer smelled the foul odor, the coldness in the air grew appreciably less, and he heard again the secret door slide in its groove. The fiend was returning to its hiding-place. Not all the legions of Hell could have prevented Steve's eyes from opening a trifle. He had only a glimpse as the hidden door slid to — and that one glimpse was enough to drive all consciousness from his brain. Steve Clarney, iron-nerved adventurer, fainted for the only time in his checkered life.

How long he lay there Steve never knew, but it could not have been long, for he was roused by Yar

Ali's whisper, "Lie still, *sahib*, a little shifting of my body and I can reach thy cords with my teeth."

Steve felt the Afghan's powerful teeth at work on his bonds, and as he lay with his face jammed into the thick dust, and his wounded shoulder began to throb agonizingly — he had forgotten it until now — he began to gather the wandering threads of his consciousness, and it all came back to him. How much, he wondered dazedly, had been the nightmares of delirium, born from suffering and the thirst that caked his throat? The fight with the Arabs had been real — the bonds and the wounds showed that — but the grisly doom of the shaykh — the thing that had crept out of the black entrance in the wall — surely that had been a figment of delirium. Nureddin had fallen into a well or pit of some sort — Steve felt his hands were free and he rose to a sitting posture, fumbling for a pocketknife the Arabs had overlooked. He did not look up or about the chamber as he slashed the cords that bound his ankles, and then freed Yar Ali, working awkwardly because his left arm was stiff and useless.

"Where are the Bedouins?" he asked, as the Afghan rose, lifting him to his feet.

"Allah, *sahib*," whispered Yar Ali, "are you mad? Have you forgotten? Let us go quickly before the djinn returns!"

"It was a nightmare," muttered Steve. "Look — the jewel is back on the throne —" His voice died out. Again that red glow throbbed about the ancient throne, reflecting from the moldering skull; again in the outstretched finger-bones pulsed the Fire of Asshurbanipal. But at the foot of the throne lay another object that had not been there before — the severed head of Nureddin el Mekru stared sightlessly up at the gray light filtering through the stone ceiling. The bloodless lips were drawn back from the teeth in a ghastly grin, the staring eyes mirrored an intolerable horror. In the thick dust of the floor three spoors showed — one of the shaykh's where he had followed the red jewel as it rolled to the wall, and above it two other sets of tracks, coming to the throne and returning to the wall — vast, shapeless tracks, as of splayed feet, taloned and gigantic, neither human not animal.

"My God!" choked Steve. "It was true — and the Thing — the Thing I saw —"

Steve remembered the flight from that chamber as a rushing nightmare, in which he and his companion hurtled headlong down an endless stair that was a gray well of fear, raced blindly through dusty silent chambers, past the glowering idol in the mighty hall and into the blazing light of the desert sun, where they fell slavering, fighting for breath.

Again Steve was roused by the Afridi's voice: "*Sahib, sahib,* in the Name of Allah the Compassionate, out luck has turned!"

Steve looked at his companion as a man might look in a trance. The big Afghan's garments were in totters, and blood-soaked. He was stained with dust and caked with blood, and his voice was a croak. But his eyes were alight with hope and he pointed with a trembling finger.

"In the shade of yon ruined wall!" he croaked, striving to moisten his blackened lips. "*Allah il allah*! The horses of the men we killed! With canteens and food-pouches at the saddle-horns! Those dogs fled without halting for the steeds of their comrades!"

New life surged up into Steve's bosom and he rose, staggering.

"Out of here," he mumbled. "Out of here, quick!"

Like dying men they stumbled to the horses, tore them loose and climbed fumblingly into the saddles.

"We'll lead the spare mounts," croaked Steve, and Yar Ali nodded emphatic agreement.

"Belike we shall need them ere we sight the coast."

Though their tortured nerves screamed for the water that swung in canteens at the saddle horns, they turned the mounts aside and, swaying in the saddle, rode like flying corpses down the long sandy street of Kara-Shehr, between the ruined palaces and the crumbling columns, crossed the fallen wall and swept out into the desert. Not once did either glance back toward that black pile of ancient horror, nor did either speak until the ruins faded into the hazy distance. Then and only then did they draw rein and ease their thirst.

"*Allah il allah!*" said Yar Ali piously. "Those dogs have beaten me until it is as though every bone in my body were broken. Dismount, I beg thee, *sahib*, and let me probe for that accursed bullet, and dress thy shoulder to the best of my meager ability."

While this was going on, Yar Ali spoke, avoiding his friend's eye, "You said, *sahib*, you said something about — about seeing? What saw ye, in Allah's name?"

A strong shudder shook the American's steely frame.

"You didn't look when — when the — the Thing put back the jewel in the skeleton's hand and left Nureddin's head on the dais?"

"By Allah, not I!" swore Yar Ali. "My eyes were as closed as if they had been welded together by the molten irons of Satan!"

Steve made no reply until the comrades had once more swung into the saddle and started on their long trek for the coast, which, with spare horses, food, water and weapons, they had a good chance to reach.

"I looked," the American said somberly. "I wish I had not; I know I'll dream about it for the rest of my life. I had only a glance; I couldn't describe it as a man describes an earthly thing. God help me, it wasn't earthly or sane either. Mankind isn't the first owner of the earth; there were Beings here before his coming — and now, survivals of hideously ancient epochs. Maybe spheres of alien dimensions press unseen on this material universe today. Sorcerers have called up sleeping devils before now and controlled them with magic. It is not unreasonable to

suppose an Assyrian magician could invoke an elemental demon out of the earth to avenge him and
guard something that must have come out of Hell in
the first place.

"I'll try to tell you what I glimpsed; then we'll
never speak of it again. It was gigantic and black and
shadowy; it was a hulking monstrosity that walked
upright like a man, but it was like a toad, too, and it
was winged and tentacled. I saw only its back; if I'd
seen the front of it — its face — I'd have undoubtedly
lost my mind. The old Arab was right; God help us, it
was the monster that Xuthltan called up out of the
dark blind caverns of the earth to guard the Fire of
Asshurbanipal!"

DIG ME NO GRAVE

Weird Tales, **February 1937**

The thunder of my old-fashioned door-knocker, re-verberating eerily through the house, roused me from a restless and nightmare-haunted sleep. I looked out the window. In the last light of the sinking moon, the white face of my friend John Conrad looked up at me.

"May I come up, Kirowan?" His voice was shaky and strained.

"Certainly!" I sprang out of bed and pulled on a bathrobe as I heard him enter the front door and ascend the stairs.

A moment later he stood before me, and in the light which I had turned on I saw his hands tremble and noticed the unnatural pallor of his face.

"Old John Grimlan died an hour ago," he said abruptly.

"Indeed? I had not known that he was ill."

"It was a sudden, virulent attack of peculiar nature, a sort of seizure somewhat akin to epilepsy. He had been subject to such spells of late years, you know."

I nodded. I knew something of the old hermit-like man who had lived in his great dark house on the hill; indeed, I had once witnessed one of his strange seizures, and I had been appalled at the writhings, howlings and yammerings of the wretch, who had groveled on the earth like a wounded snake, gibbering terrible curses and black blasphemies until his voice broke in a wordless screaming which spattered his lips with foam. Seeing this, I understood why people in old times looked on such victims as men possessed by demons.

" — some hereditary taint," Conrad was saying. "Old John doubtless fell heir to some ingrown weakness brought on by some loathsome disease, which was his heritage from perhaps a remote ancestor — such things occasionally happen. Or else — well, you know old John himself pried about in the mysterious parts of the earth, and wandered all over the East in his younger days. It is quite possible that he was infected with some obscure malady in his wanderings. There are still many unclassified diseases in Africa and the Orient."

"But," said I, "you have not told me the reason for this sudden visit at this unearthly hour — for I notice that it is past midnight."

My friend seemed rather confused.

"Well, the fact is that John Grimlan died alone, except for myself. He refused to receive any medical aid of any sort, and in the last few moments when it was evident that he was dying, and I was prepared to go for some sort of help in spite of him, he set up such a howling and screaming that I could not refuse his passionate pleas — which were that he should not be left to die alone.

"I have seen men die," added Conrad, wiping the perspiration from his pale brow, "but the death of John Grimlan was the most fearful I have ever seen."

"He suffered a great deal?"

"He appeared to be in much physical agony, but this was mostly submerged by some monstrous mental or psychic suffering. The fear in his distended eyes and his screams transcended any conceivable earthly terror. I tell you, Kirowan, Grimlan's fright was greater and deeper than the ordinary fear of the Beyond shown by a man of ordinarily evil life."

I shifted restlessly. The dark implications of this statement sent a chill of nameless apprehension trickling down my spine.

"I know the country people always claimed that in his youth he sold his soul to the Devil, and that his sudden epileptic attacks were merely a visible sign of the Fiend's power over him; but such talk is foolish, of course, and belongs in the Dark Ages. We all know that John Grimlan's life was a peculiarly evil and vicious one, even toward his last days. With good reason he was universally detested and feared, for I never heard of his doing a single good act. You were his only friend."

"And that was a strange friendship," said Conrad. "I was attracted to him by his unusual powers, for despite his bestial nature, John Grimlan was a highly educated man, a deeply cultured man. He had dipped deep into occult studies, and I first met him in this manner; for as you know, I have always been strongly interested in these lines of research myself.

"But, in this as in all other things, Grimlan was evil and perverse. He had ignored the white side of the occult and delved into the darker, grimmer phases of it — into devil-worship and voodoo and Shintoism. His knowledge of these foul arts and sciences was immense and unholy. And to hear him tell of his researches and experiments was to know such horror and repulsion as a venomous reptile might inspire. For there had been no depths to which he had not sunk, and some things he only hinted at, even to me. I tell you, Kirowan, it is easy to laugh at tales of the black world of the unknown, when one is in pleasant company under the bright sunlight, but had you sat at ungodly hours in the silent bizarre library of John Grimlan and looked on the ancient musty volumes and listened to his grisly talk as I did, your tongue would have cloven to your palate with sheer horror as mine did, and the supernatural would have seemed very real and near to you — as it seemed to me!"

"But in God's name, man!" I cried, for the tension was growing unbearable; "come to the point and tell me what you want of me."

"I want you to come with me to John Grimlan's house and help carry out his outlandish instructions in regard to his body."

I had no liking for the adventure, but I dressed hurriedly, an occasional shudder of premonition shaking me. Once fully clad, I followed Conrad out of the house and up the silent road which led to the house of John Grimlan. The road wound uphill, and all the way, looking upward and forward, I could see that great grim house perched like a bird of evil on the crest of the hill, bulking black and stark against the stars. In the west pulsed a single dull red smear where the young moon had just sunk from view behind the low black hills. The whole night seemed full of brooding evil, and the persistent swishing of a bat's wings somewhere overhead caused my taut nerves to jerk and thrum. To drown the quick pounding of my own heart, I said:

"Do you share the belief so many hold, that John Grimlan was mad?"

We strode on several paces before Conrad answered, seemingly with a strange reluctance. "But for one incident, I would say no man was ever saner. But one night in his study, he seemed suddenly to break all bonds of reason.

"He had discoursed for hours on his favorite subject — black magic — when suddenly he cried, as his face lit with a weird unholy glow: 'Why should I sit here babbling such child's prattle to you? These voodoo rituals — these Shinto sacrifices — feathered snakes — goats without horns — black leopard cults — bah! Filth and dust that the wind blows away! Dregs of the real Unknown-the deep mysteries! Mere echoes from the Abyss!

"'I could tell you things that would shatter your paltry brain! I could breathe into your ear names that would wither you like a burnt weed! What do you know of Yog-Sothoth, of Kathulos and the sunken cities? None of these names is even included in your mythologies. Not even in your dreams have you glimpsed the black cyclopean walls of Koth, or shriveled before the noxious winds that blow from Yuggoth!

"'But I will not blast you lifeless with my black wisdom! I cannot expect your infantile brain to bear what mine holds. Were you as old as I — had you seen, as I have seen, kingdoms crumble and generations pass away — had you gathered as ripe grain the dark secrets of the centuries — '

"He was raving away, his wildly lit face scarcely human in appearance, and suddenly, noting my evident bewilderment, he burst into a horrible cackling laugh.

"'Gad!' he cried in a voice and accent strange to me, 'methinks I've frightened ye, and certes, it is not to be marveled at, sith ye be but a naked savage in the arts of life, after all. Ye think I be old, eh? Why, ye gaping lout, ye'd drop dead were I to divulge the generations of men I've known — '

"But at this point such horror overcame me that I fled from him as from an adder, and his high-pitched, diabolical laughter followed me out of the shadowy house. Some days later I received a letter apologizing for his manner and ascribing it candidly — too candidly — to drugs. I did not believe it, but I renewed our relations, after some hesitation."

"It sounds like utter madness," I muttered.

"Yes," admitted Conrad, hesitantly. "But — Kirowan, have you ever seen anyone who knew John Grimlan in his youth?"

I shook my head.

"I have been at pains to inquire about him discreetly," said Conrad. "He has lived here — with the exception of mysterious absences often for months at a time — for twenty years. The older villagers remember distinctly when he first came and took over that old house on the hill, and they all say that in the intervening years he seems not to have aged perceptibly. When he came here he looked just as he does now — or did, up to the moment of his death — of the appearance of a man about fifty.

"I met old Von Boehnk in Vienna, who said he knew Grimlan when a very young man studying in Berlin, fifty years ago, and he expressed astonishment that the old man was still living; for he said at that time Grimlan seemed to be about fifty years of age."

I gave an incredulous exclamation, seeing the implication toward which the conversation was trending.

"Nonsense! Professor Von Boehnk is past eighty himself, and liable to the errors of extreme age. He confused this man with another." Yet as I spoke, my flesh crawled unpleasantly and the hairs on my neck prickled.

"Well," shrugged Conrad, "here we are at the house."

The huge pile reared up menacingly before us, and as we reached the front door a vagrant wind moaned through the nearby trees, and I started foolishly as I again heard the ghostly beat of the bat's wings. Conrad turned a large key in the antique lock, and as we entered, a cold draft swept across us like a breath from the grave — moldy and cold. I shuddered.

We groped our way through a black hallway and into a study, and here Conrad lighted a candle, for no gas lights or electric lights were to be found in the house. I looked about me, dreading what the light might disclose, but the room, heavily tapestried and bizarrely furnished, was empty save for us two.

"Where — where is — *It?*" I asked in a husky whisper, from a throat gone dry.

"Upstairs," answered Conrad in a low voice, showing that the silence and mystery of the house had laid a spell on him also. "Upstairs, in the library where he died."

I glanced up involuntarily. Somewhere above our head, the lone master of this grim house was stretched out in his last sleep — silent, his white face set in a grinning mask of death. Panic swept over me and I fought for control. After all, it was merely the corpse of a wicked old man, who was past harming anyone — this argument rang hollowly in my brain like the words of a frightened child who is trying to reassure himself.

I turned to Conrad. He had taken a time-yellowed envelope from an inside pocket.

"This," he said, removing from the envelope several pages of closely written, time-yellowed parchment, "is, in effect, the last word of John Grimlan, though God alone knows how many years ago it was written. He gave it to me ten years ago, immediately after his return from Mongolia. It was shortly after this that he had his first seizure.

"This envelope he gave me, sealed, and he made me swear that I would hide it carefully, and that I would not open it until he was dead, when I was to read the contents and follow their directions exactly. More, he made me swear that no matter what he said or did after giving me the envelope, I would go ahead as first directed. 'For,' he said with a fearful smile, 'the flesh is weak but I am a man of my word, and though I might, in a moment of weakness, wish to retract, it is far, far too late now. You may never understand the matter, but you are to do as I have said.'"

"Well?"

"Well," again Conrad wiped his brow, "tonight as he lay writhing in his death-agonies, his wordless howls were mingled with frantic admonitions to me to bring him the envelope and destroy it before his eyes! As he yammered this, he forced himself up on his elbows and with eyes staring and hair standing straight up on his head, he screamed at me in a manner to chill the blood. And he was shrieking for me to destroy the envelope, not to open it; and once he howled in his delirium for me to hew his body into pieces and scatter the bits to the four winds of heaven!"

An uncontrollable exclamation of horror escaped my dry lips.

"At last," went on Conrad, "I gave in. Remembering his commands ten years ago, I at first stood firm, but at last, as his screeches grew unbearably desperate, I turned to go for the envelope, even though that meant leaving him alone. But as I turned, with one last fearful convulsion in which blood-flecked foam flew from his writhing lips, the life went from his twisted body in a single great wrench."

He fumbled at the parchment.

"I am going to carry out my promise. The directions herein seem fantastic and may be the whims of a disordered mind, but I gave my word. They are, briefly, that I place his corpse on the great black ebony table in his library, with seven black candles burning about him. The doors and windows are to be firmly closed and fastened. Then, in the darkness which precedes dawn, I am to read the formula, charm or spell which is contained in a smaller, sealed envelope inside the first, and which I have not yet opened."

"But is that all?" I cried. "No provisions as to the disposition of his fortune, his estate — or his corpse?"

"Nothing. In his will, which I have seen elsewhere, he leaves estate and fortune to a certain Oriental gentleman named in the document as — Malik Tous!"

"What!" I cried, shaken to my soul. "Conrad, this is madness heaped on madness! Malik Tous — good God! No mortal man was ever so named! That is the title of the foul god worshipped by the mysterious Yezidees — they of Mount Alamout the Accursed — whose Eight Brazen Towers rise in the mysterious wastes of deep Asia. His idolatrous symbol is the brazen peacock. And the Muhammadans, who hate his demon-worshipping devotees, say he is the essence of the evil of all the universes — the Prince of Darkness — Ahriman — the old Serpent — the veritable Satan! And you say Grimlan names this mythical demon in his will?"

"It is the truth." Conrad's throat was dry. "And look — he has scribbled a strange line at the corner of his parchment: 'Dig me no grave; I shall not need one.'"

Again a chill wandered down my spine.

"In God's name," I cried in a kind of frenzy, "let us get this incredible business over with!"

"I think a drink might help," answered Conrad, moistening his lips. "It seems to me I've seen Grimlan go into this cabinet for wine —" He bent to the door of an ornately carved mahogany cabinet, and after some difficulty opened it.

"No wine here," he said disappointedly, "and if ever I felt the need of stimulants — what's this?"

He drew out a roll of parchment, dusty, yellowed and half-covered with spiderwebs. Everything in that grim house seemed, to my nervously excited senses, fraught with mysterious meaning and import, and I leaned over his shoulder as he unrolled it.

"It's a record of peerage," he said, "such a chronicle of births, deaths and so forth, as the old families used to keep, in the Sixteenth Century and earlier."

"What's the name?" I asked.

He scowled over the dim scrawls, striving to master the faded, archaic script.

"G-r-y-m — I've got it — Grymlann, of course. It's the records of old John's family — the Grymlanns of Toad's-heath Manor, Suffolk — what an outlandish name for an estate! Look at the last entry."

Together we read, "John Grymlann, borne, March 10, 1630." And then we both cried out. Under this entry was freshly written, in a strange scrawling hand, "Died, March 10, 1930." Below this there was a seal of black wax, stamped with a strange design, something like a peacock with a spreading tail.

Conrad stared at me speechless, all the color ebbed from his face. I shook myself with the rage engendered by fear.

"It's the hoax of a madman!" I shouted. "The stage has been set with such great care that the actors have overstepped themselves. Whoever they are, they have heaped up so many incredible effects as to nullify them. It's all a very stupid, very dull drama of illusion."

And even as I spoke, icy sweat stood out on my body and I shook as with an ague. With a wordless motion Conrad turned toward the stairs, taking up a large candle from a mahogany table.

"It was understood, I suppose," he whispered, "that I should go through with this ghastly matter alone; but I had not the moral courage, and now I'm glad I had not."

A still horror brooded over the silent house as we went up the stairs. A faint breeze stole in from somewhere and set the heavy velvet hangings rustling, and I visualized stealthy taloned fingers drawing aside the tapestries, to fix red gloating eyes upon us. Once I thought I heard the indistinct clumping of monstrous feet somewhere above us, but it must have been the heavy pounding of my own heart.

The stairs debouched into a wide dark corridor, in which our feeble candle cast a faint gleam which but illuminated our pale faces and made the shadows seem darker by comparison. We stopped at a heavy door, and I heard Conrad's breath draw in sharply as a man's will when he braces himself physically or mentally. I involuntarily clenched my fists until the nails bit into the palms; then Conrad thrust the door open.

A sharp cry escaped his lips. The candle dropped from his nerveless fingers and went out. The library of John Grimlan was ablaze with light, though the whole house had been in darkness when we entered it.

This light came from seven black candles placed at regular intervals about the great ebony table. On this table, between the candles — I had braced myself against the sight. Now in the face of the mysterious illumination and the sight of the thing on the table, my resolution nearly gave way. John Grimlan had been unlovely in life; in death he was hideous. Yes, he was hideous even though his face was mercifully covered with the same curious silken robe, which, worked in fantastic bird-like designs, covered his whole body except the crooked claw-like hands and the bare withered feet.

A strangling sound came from Conrad. "My God!" he whispered; "what is this? I laid his body out on the table and placed the candles about it, but I did not light them, nor did I place that robe over the body! And there were bedroom slippers on his feet when I left —"

He halted suddenly. We were not alone in the deathroom.

At first we had not seen him, as he sat in the great armchair in a farther nook of a corner, so still that he seemed a part of the shadows cast by the heavy tapestries. As my eyes fell upon him, a violent shuddering shook me and a feeling akin to nausea racked the pit of my stomach. My first impression was of vivid, oblique yellow eyes which gazed unwinkingly at us. Then the man rose and made a deep salaam, and we saw that he was an Oriental. Now, when I strive to etch him clearly in my mind, I can resurrect no plain image of him. I only remember those piercing eyes and the yellow, fantastic robe he wore.

We returned his salute mechanically and he spoke in a low, refined voice, "Gentlemen, I crave your pardon! I have made so free as to light the candles — shall we not proceed with the business pertaining to our mutual friend?"

He made a slight gesture toward the silent bulk on the table. Conrad nodded, evidently unable to speak. The thought flashed through our minds at the same time, that this man had also been given a sealed envelope — but how had he come to the Grimlan house so quickly? John Grimlan had been dead scarcely two hours and to the best of our knowledge no one knew of his demise but ourselves. And how had he got into the locked and bolted house?

The whole affair was grotesque and unreal in the extreme. We did not even introduce ourselves or ask the stranger his name. He took charge in a matter-of-fact way, and so under the spell of horror and illusion were we that we moved dazedly, involuntarily obeying his suggestions, given us in a low, respectful tone.

I found myself standing on the left side of the table, looking across its grisly burden at Conrad. The Oriental stood with arms folded and head bowed at the head of the table, nor did it then strike me as being strange that he should stand there, instead of Conrad who was to read what Grimlan had written. I found my gaze drawn to the figure worked on the breast of the stranger's robe, in black silk — a curious figure, somewhat resembling a peacock and somewhat resembling a bat, or a flying dragon. I noted with a start that the same design was worked on the robe covering the corpse.

The doors had been locked, the windows fastened down. Conrad, with a shaky hand, opened the inner envelope and fluttered open the parchment sheets contained therein. These sheets seemed much older than those containing the instructions to Conrad, in the larger envelope. Conrad began to read in a monotonous drone which had the effect of hypnosis on the hearer; so at times the candles grew dim in my gaze and the room and its occupants swam strange and monstrous, veiled and distorted like an hallucination. Most of what he read was gibberish; it meant nothing; yet the sound of it and the archaic style of it filled me with an intolerable horror.

"To ye contract elsewhere recorded, I, John Grymlann, herebye sweare by ye Name of ye Nameless One to keep goode faithe. Wherefore do I now write in blood these wordes spoken to me in thys grim & silent chamber in ye dedde citie of Koth, whereto no mortal manne hath attained but mee. These same wordes now writ down by mee to be rede over my bodie at ye appointed tyme to fulfill my parte of ye bargain which I entered intoe of mine own free will & knowledge beinge of rite mynd & fiftie years of age this yeare of 1680, A. D. Here begynneth ye incantation:

"Before manne was, ye Elder ones were, & even yet their lord dwelleth amonge ye shadows to which if a manne sette his foote he maye not turn upon his track."

The words merged into a barbaric gibberish as Conrad stumbled through an unfamiliar language — a language faintly suggesting the Phoenician, but shuddery with the touch of a hideous antiquity beyond any remembered earthly tongue. One of the candles flickered and went out. I made a move to relight it, but a motion from the silent Oriental stayed me. His eyes burned into mine, then shifted back to the still form on the table.

The manuscript had shifted back into its archaic English.

" — And ye mortal which gaineth to ye black citadels of Koth & speaks with ye Darke Lord whose face is hidden, for a price maye he gain hys heartes desire, ryches & knowledge beyond countinge & lyffe beyond mortal span even two hundred and fiftie yeares."

Again Conrad's voice trailed off into unfamiliar gutturals. Another candle went out.

"— Let not ye mortals flynche as ye tyme draweth nigh for payement & ye fires of Hell laye hold upon ye vytals as the sign of reckoninge. For ye Prince of Darkness taketh hys due in ye endde & he is not to bee cozened. What ye have promised, that shall ye deliver. *Augantha na shuba* —"

At the first sound of those barbaric accents, a cold hand of terror locked about my throat. My frantic eyes shot to the candles and I was not surprised to see another flicker out. Yet there was no hint of any draft to stir the heavy black hangings. Conrad's voice wavered; he drew his hand across his throat, gagging momentarily. The eyes of the Oriental never altered.

" — Amonge ye sonnes of men glide strange shadows for ever. Men see ye tracks of ye talones but not ye feete that make them. Over ye souls of men spread great black wingges. There is but one Black Master though men calle hym Sathanas & Beelzebub & Apolleon & Ahriman & Malik Tous —"

Mists of horror engulfed me. I was dimly aware of Conrad's voice droning on and on, both in English and in that other fearsome tongue whose horrific import I scarcely dared try to guess. And with stark fear clutching at my heart, I saw the candles go out, one by one. And with each flicker, as the gathering gloom darkened about us, my horror mounted. I could not speak, I could not move; my distended eyes were fixed with agonized intensity on the remaining candle. The silent Oriental at the head of that ghastly table was included in my fear. He had not moved nor spoken, but under his drooping lids, his eyes burned with devilish triumph; I knew that beneath his inscrutable exterior he was gloating fiendishly — but why — *why?*

But I *knew* that the moment the extinguishing of the last candle plunged the room into utter darkness, some nameless, abominable thing would take place. Conrad was approaching the end. His voice rose to the climax in gathering crescendo.

"Approacheth now ye moment of payement. Ye ravens are flying. Ye bats winge against ye skye.

There are skulls in ye starres. Ye soul & ye bodie are promised and shall bee delivered uppe. Not to ye dust agayne nor ye elements from which springe lyfe —"

The candle flickered slightly. I tried to scream, but my mouth gaped to a soundless yammering. I tried to flee, but I stood frozen, unable even to close my eyes.

" — Ye abysse yawns & ye debt is to paye. Ye light fayles, ye shadows gather. There is no god but evil; no lite but darkness; no hope but doom —"

A hollow groan resounded through the room. *It seemed to come from the robe-covered thing on the table!* That robe twitched fitfully.

"Oh winges in ye black darke!"

I started violently; a faint swish sounded in the gathering shadows. The stir of the dark hangings? It sounded like the rustle of gigantic wings.

"Oh redde eyes in ye shadows! What is promised, what is writ in bloode is fulfilled! Ye lite is gulfed in blackness! Ya — Koth!"

The last candle went out suddenly and a ghastly unhuman cry that came not from my lips or from Conrad's burst unbearably forth. Horror swept over me like a black icy wave; in the blind dark I heard myself screaming terribly. Then with a swirl and a great rush of wind something swept the room, flinging the hangings aloft and dashing chairs and tables crashing to the floor. For an instant, an intolerable odor burned our nostrils, a low hideous tittering mocked us in the blackness; then silence fell like a shroud.

Somehow, Conrad found a candle and lighted it. The faint glow showed us the room in fearful disarray — showed us each other's ghastly faces — and showed us the black ebony table — empty! The doors and windows were locked as they had been, but the Oriental was gone — and so was the corpse of John Grimlan.

Shrieking like damned men we broke down the door and fled frenziedly down the well-like staircase where the darkness seemed to clutch at us with clammy black fingers. As we tumbled down into the lower hallway, a lurid glow cut the darkness and the scent of burning wood filled our nostrils.

The outer doorway held momentarily against our frantic assault, then gave way and we hurtled into the outer starlight. Behind us the flames leaped up with a crackling roar as we fled down the hill. Conrad, glancing over his shoulder, halted suddenly, wheeled and flung up his arms like a madman, and screamed, "Soul and body he sold to Malik Tous, who is Satan, two hundred and fifty years ago! This was the night of payment — and my God — look! *Look!* The Fiend has claimed his own!"

I looked, frozen with horror. Flames had enveloped the whole house with appalling swiftness, and now the great mass was etched against the shadowed sky, a crimson inferno. And above the holocaust hovered a gigantic black shadow like a monstrous bat, and from its dark clutch dangled a small white thing, like the body of a man, dangling limply. Then, even as we cried out in horror, it was gone and our dazed gaze met only the shuddering walls and blazing roof which crumpled into the flames with an earth-shaking roar.

SONG AT MIDNIGHT

The Phantagraph, August 1940

I heard an old gibbet that crowned a bare hill
Creaking a song in the midnight chill;
And I shivered to hear that grisly refrain
That moaned in the night through the fog and the rain.

"Oh, where are the men who came to me
"And danced all night on the gallows tree?
"Gallant and peasant, man and maid,
"Many have walked in that long parade.
"My chains are broken and red with rust,
"My wood is sealed with the moldy crust.
"Have men forgotten their debt to me,
"That they come no more to the gallows tree?"

The drear wind moaned for a dark refrain,
And a raven called in the drifting rain:
"Oh, where are the feasts that awaited me
"Long, long ago on the gibbet tree?"

A slow-worm spoke from the gallows foot:
"Death is spoils for a crow to loot.
"The winds and the rain they worked their will,
"The kites and the ravens have had their fill,
"But last of all when the chains broke free,
"The fruit of the gallows came to me.
"Men and their works, so swiftly past,
"Come to a feast for the worms at last.

"*Here I have gnawed on this marrow good,*
"*Where now I gnaw on this crumbling wood.*
"*For men and their works are a feast for me—*
"*The bones, and the noose, and the gallows tree.*"

WITCH FROM HELL'S KITCHEN

Avon Fantasy Reader #18, 1952

"Has he seen a night-spirit, is he listening to the whispers of them who dwell in darkness?"

Strange words to be murmured in the feast-hall of Naram-ninub, amid the strain of lutes, the patter of fountains, and the tinkle of women's laughter. The great hall attested the wealth of its owner, not only by its vast dimensions, but by the richness of its adornment. The glazed surface of the walls offered a bewildering variegation of colors — blue, red, and orange enamels set off by squares of hammered gold. The air was heavy with incense, mingled with the fragrance of exotic blossoms from the gardens without. The feasters, silk-robed nobles of Nippur, lounged on satin cushions, drinking wine poured from alabaster vessels, and caressing the painted and bejeweled playthings which Naram-ninub's wealth had brought from all parts of the East.

There were scores of these; their white limbs twinkled as they danced, or shone like ivory among the cushions where they sprawled. A jeweled tiara caught in a burnished mass of night-black hair, a gem-crusted armlet of massive gold, earrings of carven jade — these were their only garments. Their fragrance was dizzying. Shameless in their dancing, feasting and lovemaking, their light laughter filled the hall in waves of silvery sound.

On a broad cushion-piled dais reclined the giver of the feast, sensuously stroking the glossy locks of a lithe Arabian who had stretched herself on her supple belly beside him. His appearance of sybaritic languor was belied by the vital sparkling of his dark eyes as he surveyed his guests. He was thick-bodied, with a short blue-black beard: a Semite — one of the many drifting yearly into Shumir.

With one exception his guests were Shumirians, shaven of chin and head. Their bodies were padded with rich living, their features smooth and placid. The exception among them stood out in startling contrast. Taller than they, he had none of their soft sleekness. He was made with the economy of relentless Nature. His physique was of the primitive, not of the civilized athlete. He was an incarnation of Power, raw, hard, wolfish — in the sinewy limbs, the corded neck, the great arch of the breast, the broad hard shoulders. Beneath his tousled golden mane his eyes were like blue ice. His strongly chiselled features reflected the wildness his frame suggested. There was about him nothing of the measured leisure of the other guests, but a ruthless directness in his every action. Whereas they sipped, he drank in great gulps. They nibbled at tidbits, but he seized whole joints in his fingers and tore at the meat with his teeth. Yet his brow was shadowed, his expression moody. His magnetic eyes were introspective. Wherefore Prince Ibi-Engur lisped again in Naram-ninub's ear: "Has the lord Pyrrhas heard the whispering of night-things?"

Naram-ninub eyed his friend in some worriment. "Come, my lord," said he, "you are strangely distraught. Has any here done aught to offend you?"

Pyrrhas roused himself as from some gloomy meditation and shook his head. "Not so, friend; if I seem distracted it is because of a shadow that lies over my own mind." His accent was barbarous, but the timbre of his voice was strong and vibrant.

The others glanced at him in interest. He was Eannatum's general of mercenaries, an Argive whose saga was epic.

"Is it a woman, lord Pyrrhas?" asked Prince Ena-kalli with a laugh. Pyrrhas fixed him with his gloomy stare and the prince felt a cold wind blowing on his spine.

"Aye, a woman," muttered the Argive. "One who haunts my dreams and floats like a shadow between me and the moon. In my dreams I feel her teeth in my neck, and I wake to hear the flutter of wings and the cry of an owl."

A silence fell over the group on the dais. Only in the great hall below rose the babble of mirth and conversation and the tinkling of lutes, and a girl laughed loudly, with a curious note in her laughter.

"A curse is upon him," whispered the Arabian girl. Naram-ninub silenced her with a gesture, and was about to speak, when Ibi-Engur lisped: "My lord Pyrrhas, this has an uncanny touch, like the vengeance of a god. Have you done aught to offend a deity?"

Naram-ninub bit his lip in annoyance. It was well known that in his recent campaign against Erech, the Argive had cut down a priest of Anu in his shrine. Pyrrhas' maned head jerked up and he glared at Ibi-Engur as if undecided whether to attribute the remark to malice or lack of tact. The prince began to pale, but the slim Arabian rose to her knees and caught at Naram-ninub's arm.

"Look at Belibna!" She pointed at the girl who had laughed so wildly an instant before.

Her companions were drawing away from this girl apprehensively. She did not speak to them, or seem to see them. She tossed her jeweled head and her shrill laughter rang through the feast-hall. Her slim body swayed back and forth, her bracelets clanged and jangled together as she tossed up her white arms. Her dark eyes gleamed with a wild light, her red lips curled with her unnatural mirth.

"The hand of Arabu is on her," whispered the Arabian uneasily.

"Belibna!" Naram-ninub called sharply. His only answer was another burst of wild laughter, and the girl cried stridently: "To the home of darkness, the dwelling of Irhalla; to the road whence there is no return; oh, Apsu, bitter is thy wine!" Her voice snapped in a terrible scream, and bounding from among her cushions, she leaped up on the dais, a dagger in her hand. Courtesans and guests shrieked and scrambled madly out of her way. But it was at Pyrrhas the girl rushed, her beautiful face a mask of fury. The Argive caught her wrist, and the abnormal strength of madness was futile against the barbarian's iron thews. He tossed her from him, and down the cushion-strewn steps, where she lay in a crumpled heap, her own dagger driven into her heart as she fell.

The hum of conversation which had ceased suddenly, rose again as the guards dragged away the body, and the painted dancers came back to their cushions. But Pyrrhas turned and taking his wide crimson cloak from a slave, threw it about his shoulders.

"Stay, my friend," urged Naram-ninub. "Let us not allow this small matter to interfere with our revels. Madness is common enough."

Pyrrhas shook his head irritably. "Nay, I'm weary of swilling and gorging. I'll go to my own house."

"Then the feasting is at an end," declared the Semite, rising and clapping his hands. "My own litter shall bear you to the house the king has given you — nay, I forgot you scorn to ride on other men's backs. Then I shall myself escort you home. My lords, will you accompany us?"

"Walk, like common men?" stuttered Prince Urilishu. "By Enlil, I will come. It will be a rare novelty. But I must have a slave to bear the train of my robe, lest it trail in the dust of the street. Come, friends, let us see the lord Pyrrhas home, by Ishtar!"

"A strange man," Ibi-Engur lisped to Libit-ishbi, as the party emerged from the spacious palace, and descended the broad tiled stair, guarded by bronze lions. "He walks the streets, unattended, like a very tradesman."

"Be careful," murmured the other. "He is quick to anger, and he stands high in the favor of Eannatum."

"Yet even the favored of the king had best beware of offending the god Anu," replied Ibi-Engur in an equally guarded voice.

The party was proceeding leisurely down the broad white street, gaped at by the common folk who bobbed their shaven heads as they passed. The sun was not long up, but the people of Nippur were well astir. There was much coming and going between the booths where the merchants spread their wares: a shifting panorama, woven of craftsmen, tradesmen, slaves, harlots, and soldiers in copper helmets. There went a merchant from his warehouse, a staid figure in sober woolen robe and white mantle; there hurried a slave in a linen tunic; there minced a painted hoyden whose short slit skirt displayed her sleek flank at every step. Above them the blue of the sky whitened with the heat of the mounting sun. The glazed surfaces of the buildings shimmered. They were flat roofed, some of them three or four stories high. Nippur was a city of sun-dried brick, but its facings of enamel made it a riot of bright color.

Somewhere a priest was chanting: "Oh, Babbar, righteousness lifteth up to thee its head —"

Pyrrhas swore under his breath. They were passing the great temple of Enlil, towering up three hundred feet in the changeless blue sky.

"The towers stand against the sky like part of it," he swore, raking back a damp lock from his forehead. "The sky is enameled, and this is a world made by man."

"Nay, friend," demurred Naram-ninub. "Ea built the world from the body of Tiamat."

"I say men built Shumir!" exclaimed Pyrrhas, the wine he had drunk shadowing his eyes. "A flat land — a very banquet-board of a land — with rivers and cities painted upon it, and a sky of blue enamel over it. By Ymir, I was born in a land the gods built! There are great blue mountains, with valleys lying like long shadows between, and snow peaks glittering in the sun. Rivers rush foaming down the cliffs in everlasting tumult, and the broad leaves of the trees shake in the strong winds."

"I, too, was born in a broad land, Pyrrhas," answered the Semite. "By night the desert lies white and awful beneath the moon, and by day it stretches in brown infinity beneath the sun. But it is in the swarming cities of men, these hives of bronze and gold and enamel and humanity, that wealth and glory lie."

Pyrrhas was about to speak, when a loud wailing attracted his attention. Down the street came a procession, bearing a carven and painted litter on which lay a figure hidden by flowers. Behind came a train of young women, their scanty garments rent, their black hair flowing wildly. They beat their naked bosoms and cried: "*Ailanu!* Thammuz is dead!" The throngs in the street took up the shout. The litter passed, swaying on the shoulders of the bearers; among the high-piled flowers shone the painted eyes of a carven image. The cry of the worshippers echoed down the street, dwindling in the distance.

Pyrrhas shrugged his mighty shoulders. "Soon they will be leaping and dancing and shouting, 'Adonis is living!', and the wenches who howl so bitterly now will give themselves to men in the streets for exultation. How many gods are there, in the devil's name?"

Naram-ninub pointed to the great zikkurat of Enlil, brooding over all like the brutish dream of a mad god.

"See ye the seven tiers: the lower black, the next of red enamel, the third blue, the fourth orange, the fifth yellow, while the sixth is faced with silver, and the seventh with pure gold which flames in the sunlight? Each stage in the temple symbolizes a deity: the sun, the moon, and the five planets Enlil and his tribe have set in the skies for their emblems. But Enlil is greater than all, and Nippur is his favored city."

"Greater than Anu?" muttered Pyrrhas, remembering a flaming shrine and a dying priest that gasped an awful threat.

"Which is the greatest leg of a tripod?" parried Naram-ninub.

Pyrrhas opened his mouth to reply, then recoiled with a curse, his sword flashing out. Under his very feet a serpent reared up, its forked tongue flickering like a jet of red lightning.

"What is it, friend?" Naram-ninub and the princes stared at him in surprise.

"What is it?" He swore. "Don't you see that snake under your very feet? Stand aside and give me a clean swing at it —"

His voice broke off and his eyes clouded with doubt. "It's gone," he muttered.

"I saw nothing," said Naram-ninub, and the others shook their heads, exchanging wondering glances.

The Argive passed his hand across his eyes, shaking his head.

"Perhaps it's the wine," he muttered. "Yet there was an adder, I swear by the heart of Ymir. I am accursed."

The others drew away from him, glancing at him strangely.

There had always been a restlessness in the soul of Pyrrhas the Argive, to haunt his dreams and drive him out on his long wanderings. It had brought him from the blue mountains of his race, southward into the fertile valleys and sea-fringing plains where rose the huts of the Mycenaeans; thence into the isle of Crete, where, in a rude town of rough stone and wood, a swart fishing people battered with the ships of Egypt; by those ships he had gone into Egypt, where men toiled beneath the lash to rear the first pyramids, and where, in the ranks of the white-skinned mercenaries, the Shardana, he learned the arts of war. But his wanderlust drove him again across the sea, to a mud-walled trading village on the coast of Asia, called Troy, whence he drifted south-ward into the pillage and carnage of Palestine where the original dwellers in the land were trampled under by the barbaric Canaanites out of the East. So by devious ways he came at last to the plains of Shumir, where city fought city, and the priests of a myriad rival gods intrigued and plotted, as they had done since the dawn of Time, and as they did for centuries after, until the rise of an obscure frontier town called Babylon exalted its city-god Merodach above all others as Bel-Marduk, the conqueror of Tiamat.

The bare outline of the saga of Pyrrhas the Argive is weak and paltry; it can not catch the echoes of the thundering pageantry that rioted through that saga: the feasts, revels, wars, the crash and splintering of ships and the onset of chariots. Let it suffice to say that the honor of kings was given to the Argive, and that in all Mesopotamia there was no man so feared as this golden-haired barbarian whose war-skill and fury broke the hosts of Erech on the field, and the yoke of Erech from the neck of Nippur.

From a mountain hut to a palace of jade and ivory Pyrrhas' saga had led him. Yet the dim half-animal dreams that had filled his slumber when he lay as a youth on a heap of wolfskins in his shaggy-headed father's hut were nothing so strange and monstrous as the dreams that haunted him on the silken couch in the palace of turquoise-towered Nippur.

It was from these dreams that Pyrrhas woke suddenly. No lamp burned in his chamber and the moon was not yet up, but the starlight filtered dimly through the casement. And in this radiance something moved and took form. There was the vague outline of a lithe form, the gleam of an eye. Suddenly the night beat down oppressively hot and still. Pyrrhas heard the pound of his own blood through his veins. Why fear a woman lurking in his chamber? But no woman's form was ever so pantherishly supple; no woman's eyes ever burned so in the darkness. With a gasping snarl he leaped from his couch and his sword hissed as it cut the air — but only the air. Something like a mocking laugh reached his ears, but the figure was gone.

A girl entered hastily with a lamp.

"Amytis! I saw *her*! It was no dream, this time! She laughed at me from the window!"

Amytis trembled as she set the lamp on an ebony table. She was a sleek sensuous creature, with long-lashed, heavy-lidded eyes, passionate lips, and a wealth of lustrous black curly locks. As she stood there naked the voluptuousness of her figure would have stirred the most jaded debauchee. A gift from Eannatum, she hated Pyrrhas, and he knew it, but found an angry gratification in possessing her. But now her hatred was drowned in her terror.

"It was Lilitu!" she stammered. "She has marked you for her own! She is the night-spirit, the mate of Ardat Lili. They dwell in the House of Arabu. You are accursed!"

His hands were bathed with sweat; molten ice seemed to be flowing sluggishly through his veins of blood.

"Where shall I turn? The priests hate and fear me since I burned Anu's temple."

"There is a man who is not bound by the priest-craft, and could aid you," she blurted out.

"Then tell me!" He was galvanized, trembling with eager impatience. "His name, girl! His name!"

But at this sign of weakness, her malice returned; she had blurted out what was in her mind, in her fear of the supernatural. Now all the vindictiveness in her was awake again.

"I have forgotten," she answered insolently, her eyes glowing with spite.

"Slut!" Gasping with the violence of his rage, he dragged her across a couch by her thick locks. Seizing his sword-belt he wielded it with savage force, holding down the writhing naked body with his free hand. Each stroke was like the impact of a drover's whip. So mazed with fury was he, and she so incoherent with pain, that he did not at first realize that she was shrieking a name at the top of her voice. Recognizing this at last, he cast her from him, to fall in a whimpering heap on the mat-covered floor. Trembling and panting from the excess

of his passion, he threw aside the belt and glared
down at her.

"Gimil-ishbi, eh?"

"Yes!" she sobbed, grovelling on the floor in her
excruciating anguish. "He was a priest of Enlil, until
he turned diabolist and was banished. Ahhh, I faint! I
swoon! Mercy! Mercy!"

"And where shall I find him?" he demanded.

"In the mound of Enzu, to the west of the city.
Oh, Enlil, I am flayed alive! I perish!"

Turning from her, Pyrrhas hastily donned his garments and armor, without calling for a slave to aid
him. He went forth, passed among his sleeping servi-
tors without waking them, and secured the best of his
horses. There were perhaps a score in all in Nippur,
the property of the king and his wealthier nobles;
they had been bought from the wild tribes far to the
north, beyond the Caspian, whom in a later age men
called Scythians. Each steed represented an actual
fortune. Pyrrhas bridled the great beast and strapped
on the saddle — merely a cloth pad, ornamented and
richly worked.

The soldiers at the gate gaped at him as he drew
rein and ordered them to open the great bronze portals, but they bowed and obeyed without question.
His crimson cloak flowed behind him as he galloped
through the gate.

"Enlil!" swore a soldier. "The Argive has drunk
over-much of Naram-ninub's Egyptian wine."

"Nay," responded another; "did you see his face

that it was pale, and his hand that it shook on the rein? The gods have touched him, and perchance he rides to the House of Arabu."

Shaking their helmeted heads dubiously, they listened to the hoof-beats dwindling away in the west.

North, south and east from Nippur, farm-huts, villages and palm groves clustered the plain, threaded by the networks of canals that connected the rivers. But westward the land .lay bare and silent to the Euphrates, only charred expanses telling of former villages. A few moons ago raiders had swept out of the desert in a wave that engulfed the vineyards and huts and burst against the staggering walls of Nippur. Pyrrhas remembered the fighting along the walls, and the fighting on the plain, when his sally at the head of his phalanxes had broken the besiegers and driven them in headlong flight back across the Great River. Then the plain had been red with blood and black with smoke. Now it was already veiled in green again as the grain put forth its shoots, uncared for by man. But the toilers who had planted that grain had gone into the land of dusk and darkness.

Already the overflow from more populous districts was seeping back into the man-made waste. A few months, a year at most, and the land would again present the typical aspect of the Mesopotamian plain, swarming with villages, checked with tiny fields that were more like gardens than farms. Man would cover the scars man had made, and there would be forgetfulness, till the raiders swept again out of the desert. But now the plain lay bare and silent, the canals choked, broken and empty.

Here and there rose the remnants of palm groves, the crumbling ruins of villas and country palaces. Further out, barely visible under the stars, rose the mysterious hillock known as the mound of Enzu — the moon. It was not a natural hill, but whose hands had reared it and for what reason none knew. Before Nippur was built it had risen above the plain, and the nameless fingers that shaped it had vanished in the dust of time. To it Pyrrhas turned his horse's head.

And in the city he had left, Amytis furtively left his palace and took a devious course to a certain secret destination. She walked rather stiffly, limped, and frequently paused to tenderly caress her person and lament over her injuries. But limping, cursing, and weeping, she eventually reached her destination, and stood before a man whose wealth and power was great in Nippur. His glance was an interrogation.

"He has gone to the Mound of the Moon, to speak with Gimil-ishbi," she said.

"Lilitu came to him again tonight," she shuddered, momentarily forgetting her pain and anger. "Truly he is accursed."

"By the priests of Anu?" His eyes narrowed to slits.

"So he suspects."

"And you?"

"What of me? I neither know nor care."

"Have you ever wondered why I pay you to spy upon him?" he demanded.

She shrugged her shoulders. "You pay me well; that is enough for me."

"Why does he go to Gimil-ishbi?"

"I told him the renegade might aid him against Lilitu."

Sudden anger made the man's face darkly sinister.

"I thought you hated him."

She shrank from the menace in the voice. "I spoke of the diabolist before I thought, and then he forced me to speak his name; curse him, I will not sit with ease for weeks!" Her resentment rendered her momentarily speechless.

The man ignored her, intent on his own somber meditations. At last he rose with sudden determination.

"I have waited too long," he muttered, like one speaking his thoughts aloud. "The fiends play with him while I bite my nails, and those who conspire with me grow restless and suspicious. Enlil alone knows what counsel Gimil-ishbi will give. When the moon rises I will ride forth and seek the Argive on the plain. A stab unaware — he will not suspect until my sword is through him. A bronze blade is surer than the powers of Darkness. I was a fool to trust even a devil."

Amytis gasped with horror and caught at the velvet hangings for support.

"You? You?" Her lips framed a question too terrible to voice.

"Aye!" He accorded her a glance of grim amusement. With a gasp of terror she darted through the curtained door, her smarts forgotten in her fright.

Whether the cavern was hollowed by man or by Nature, none ever knew. At least its walls, floor and ceiling were symmetrical and composed of blocks of greenish stone, found nowhere else in that level land. Whatever its cause and origin, man occupied it now. A lamp hung from the rock roof, casting a weird light over the chamber and the bald pate of the man who sat crouching over a parchment scroll on a stone table before him. He looked up as a quick sure footfall sounded on the stone steps that led down into his abode. The next instant a tall figure stood framed in the doorway.

The man at the stone table scanned this figure with avid interest. Pyrrhas wore a hauberk of black leather and copper scales; his brazen greaves glinted in the lamplight. The wide crimson cloak, flung loosely about him, did not enmesh the long hilt that jutted from its folds. Shadowed by his horned bronze helmet, the Argive's eyes gleamed icily. So the warrior faced the sage.

Gimil-ishbi was very old. There was no leaven of Semitic blood in his withered veins. His bald head was round as a vulture's skull, and from it his great nose jutted like the beak of a vulture. His eyes were oblique, a rarity even in a pure-blooded Shumirian, and they were bright and black as beads. Whereas

Pyrrhas' eyes were all depth, blue deeps and changing clouds and shadows, Gimil-ishbi's eyes were opaque as jet, and they never changed. His mouth was a gash whose smile was more terrible than its snarl.

He was clad in a simple black tunic, and his feet, in their cloth sandals, seemed strangely deformed. Pyrrhas felt a curious twitching between his shoulder-blades as he glanced at those feet, and he drew his eyes away, and back to the sinister face.

"Deign to enter my humble abode, warrior," the voice was soft and silky, sounding strange from those harsh thin lips. "I would I could offer you food and drink, but I fear the food I eat and the wine I drink would find little favor in your sight." He laughed softly as at an obscure jest.

"I come not to eat or to drink," answered Pyrrhas abruptly, striding up to the table. "I come to buy a charm against devils."

"To buy?"

The Argive emptied a pouch of gold coins on the stone surface; they glistened dully in the lamplight. Gimil-ishbi's laugh was like the rustle of a serpent through dead grass.

"What is this yellow dirt to me? You speak of devils, and you bring me dust the wind blows away."

"Dust?" Pyrrhas scowled. Gimil-ishbi laid his hand on the shining heap and laughed; somewhere in the night an owl moaned. The priest lifted his hand. Beneath it lay a pile of yellow dust that gleamed dully in the lamplight. A sudden wind rushed down the steps, making the lamp flicker, whirling up the golden heap; for an instant the air was dazzled and spangled with the shining particles. Pyrrhas swore; his armor was sprinkled with yellow dust; it sparkled among the scales of his hauberk.

"Dust that the wind blows away," mumbled the priest. "Sit down, Pyrrhas of Nippur, and let us converse with each other."

Pyrrhas glanced about the narrow chamber; at the even stacks of clay tablets along the walls, and the rolls of papyrus above them. Then he seated himself on the stone bench opposite the priest, hitching his sword-belt so that its hilt was well to the front.

"You are far from the cradle of your race," said Gimil-ishbi. "You are the first golden-haired rover to tread the plains of Shumir."

"I have wandered in many lands," muttered the Argive, "but may the vultures pluck my bones if I ever saw a race so devil-ridden as this, or a land ruled and harried by so many gods and demons."

His gaze was fixed in fascination on Gimil-ishbi's hands; they were long, narrow, white and strong, the hands of youth. Their contrast to the priest's appearance of great age otherwise, was vaguely disquieting.

"To each city its gods and their priests," answered Gimil-ishbi; "and all fools. Of what account are gods whom the fortunes of men lift or lower? Behind all gods of men, behind the primal trinity of Ea, Anu and Enlil, lurk the elder gods, unchanged by the wars or ambitions of men. Men deny what they do not see.

The priests of Eridu, which is sacred to Ea and light, are no blinder than them of Nippur, which is consecrated to Enlil, whom they deem the lord of Darkness. But he is only the god of the darkness of which men dream, not the real Darkness that lurks behind all dreams, and veils the real and awful deities. I glimpsed this truth when I was a priest of Enlil, wherefore they cast me forth. Ha! They would stare if they knew how many of their worshippers creep forth to me by night, as you have crept."

"I creep to no man!" the Argive bristled instantly. "I came to buy a charm. Name your price, and be damned to you."

"Be not wroth," smiled the priest. "Tell me why you have come."

"If you are so cursed wise you should know already," growled the Argive, unmollified. Then his gaze clouded as he cast back over his tangled trail. "Some magician has cursed me," he muttered. "As I rode back from my triumph over Erech, my warhorse screamed and shied at Something none saw but he. Then my dreams grew strange and monstrous. In the darkness of my chamber, wings rustled and feet padded stealthily. Yesterday a woman at a feast went mad and tried to knife me. Later an adder sprang out of empty air and struck at me. Then, this night, she men call Lilitu came to my chamber and mocked me with awful laughter —"

"Lilitu?" the priest's eyes lit with a brooding fire; his skull-face worked in a ghastly smile. "Verily, warrior, they plot thy ruin in the House of Arabu. Your sword can not prevail against her, or against her mate Ardat Lili. In the gloom of midnight her teeth will find your throat. Her laugh will blast your ears, and her burning kisses will wither you like a dead leaf blowing in the hot winds of the desert. Madness and dissolution will be your lot, and you will descend to the House of Arabu whence none returns."

Pyrrhas moved restlessly, cursing incoherently beneath his breath.

"What can I offer you besides gold?" he growled.

"Much!" the black eyes shone; the mouth-gash twisted in inexplicable glee. "But I must name my own price, after I have given you aid."

Pyrrhas acquiesced with an impatient gesture.

"Who are the wisest men in the world?" asked the sage abruptly.

"The priests of Egypt, who scrawled on yonder parchments," answered the Argive.

Gimil-ishbi shook his head; his shadow fell on the wall like that of a great vulture, crouching over a dying victim.

"None so wise as the priests of Tiamat, who fools believe died long ago under the sword of Ea. Tiamat is deathless; she reigns in the shadows; she spreads her dark wings over her worshippers."

"I know them not," muttered Pyrrhas uneasily.

"The cities of men know them not; but the waste places know them, the reedy marshes, the stony deserts, the hills, and the caverns. To them steal the winged ones from the House of Arabu."

"I thought none came from that House," said the Argive.

"No *human* returns thence. But the servants of Tiamat come and go at their pleasure."

Pyrrhas was silent, reflecting on the place of the dead, as believed in by the Shumirians; a vast cavern, dusty, dark and silent, through which wandered the souls of the dead forever, shorn of all human attributes, cheerless and loveless, remembering their former lives only to hate all living men, their deeds and dreams.

"I will aid you," murmured the priest. Pyrrhas lifted his helmeted head and stared at him. Gimil-ishbi's eyes were no more human than the reflection of firelight on subterranean pools of inky blackness. His lips sucked in as if he gloated over all woes and miseries of mankind. Pyrrhas hated him as a man hates the unseen serpent in the darkness.

"Aid me and name your price," said the Argive.

Gimil-ishbi closed his hands and opened them, and in the palms lay a gold cask, the lid of which fastened with a jeweled catch. He sprung the lid, and Pyrrhas saw the cask was filled with grey dust. He shuddered without knowing why.

"This ground dust was once the skull of the first king of Ur," said Gimil-ishbi. "When he died, as even a necromancer must, he concealed his body with all his art. But I found his crumbling bones, and in the darkness above them, I fought with his soul as a man fights with a python in the night. My spoil was his skull, that held darker secrets than those that lie in the pits of Egypt.

"With this dead dust shall you trap Lilitu. Go quickly to an enclosed place — a cavern or a chamber — nay, that ruined villa which lies between this spot and the city will serve. Strew the dust in thin lines across threshold and window; leave not a spot as large as a man's hand unguarded. Then lie down as if in slumber. When Lilitu enters, as she will, speak the words I shall teach you. Then you are her master, until you free her again by repeating the conjure backwards. You can not slay her, but you can make her swear to leave you in peace. Make her swear by the dugs of Tiamat. Now lean close and I will whisper the words of the spell."

Somewhere in the night a nameless bird cried out harshly; the sound was more human than the whispering of the priest, which was no louder than the gliding of an adder through slimy ooze. He drew back, his gash-mouth twisted in a grisly smile. The Argive sat for an instant like a statue of bronze. Their shadows fell together on the wall with the appearance of a crouching vulture facing a strange horned monster.

Pyrrhas took the cask and rose, wrapping his crimson cloak about his somber figure, his horned helmet lending an illusion of abnormal height.

"And the price?"

Gimil-ishbi's hands became claws, quivering with lust.

"Blood! A life!"

"Whose life?"

"Any life! So blood flows, and there is fear and agony, a spirit ruptured from its quivering flesh! I have one price for all — a human life! Death is my rapture; I would glut my soul on death! Man, maid or infant. You have sworn. Make good your oath! A life! A human life!"

"Aye, a life!" Pyrrhas' sword cut the air in a flaming arc and Gimil-ishbi's vulture head fell on the stone table. The body reared upright, spouting black blood, then slumped across the stone. The head rolled across the surface and thudded dully on the floor. The features stared up, frozen in a mask of awful surprise.

Outside there sounded a frightful scream as Pyrrhas' stallion broke its halter and raced madly away across the plain.

From the dim chamber with its tablets of cryptic cuneiforms and papyri of dark hieroglyphics, and from the remnants of the mysterious priest, Pyrrhas fled. As he climbed the carven stair and emerged into the starlight he doubted his own reason.

Far across the level plain the moon was rising, dull red, darkly lurid. Tense heat and silence held the land. Pyrrhas felt cold sweat thickly beading his flesh; his blood was a sluggish current of ice in his veins; his tongue clove to his palate. His armor weighted him and his cloak was like a clinging snare. Cursing incoherently he tore it from him; sweating and shaking he ripped off his armor, piece by piece, and cast it away. In the grip of his abysmal fears he had reverted to the primitive. The veneer of civilization vanished. Naked but for loincloth and girded sword he strode across the plain, carrying the golden cask under his arm.

No sound disturbed the waiting silence as he came to the ruined villa whose walls reared drunkenly among heaps of rubble. One chamber stood above the general ruin, left practically untouched by some whim of chance. Only the door had been wrenched from its bronze hinges. Pyrrhas entered. Moonlight followed him in and made a dim radiance inside the portal. There were three windows, gold-barred. Sparingly he crossed the threshold with a thin grey line. Each casement he served in like manner. Then tossing aside the empty cask, he stretched himself on a bare dais that stood in deep shadow. His unreasoning horror was under control. He who had been the hunted was now the hunter. The trap was set, and he waited for his prey with the patience of the primitive.

He had not long to wait. Something threshed the air outside and the shadow of great wings crossed the moonlit portal. There was an instant of tense silence in which Pyrrhas heard the thunderous impact of his own heart against his ribs. Then a shadowy form framed itself in the open door. A fleeting instant it was visible, then it vanished from view. The thing had entered; the night-fiend was in the chamber.

Pyrrhas' hand clenched on his sword as he heaved up suddenly from the dais. His voice crashed in the stillness as he thundered the dark enigmatic conjurement whispered to him by the dead priest. He was answered by a frightful scream; there was a quick stamp of bare feet, then a heavy fall, and something was threshing and writhing in the shadows on the floor. As Pyrrhas cursed the masking darkness, the moon thrust a crimson rim above a casement, like a goblin peering into a window and a molten flood of light crossed the floor. In the pale glow the Argive saw his victim.

But it was no were-woman that writhed there. It was a thing like a man, lithe, naked, dusky-skinned. It differed not in the attributes of humanity except for the disquieting suppleness of its limbs, the changeless glitter of its eyes. It grovelled as in mortal agony, foaming at the mouth and contorting its body into impossible positions.

With a blood-mad yell Pyrrhas ran at the figure and plunged his sword through the squirming body. The point rang on the tiled floor beneath it, and an awful howl burst from the frothing lips, but that was the only apparent effect of the thrust. The Argive wrenched forth his sword and glared astoundedly to see no stain on the steel, no wound on the dusky body. He wheeled as the cry of the captive was re-echoed from without.

Just outside the enchanted threshold stood a woman, naked, supple, dusky, with wide eyes blazing in a soulless face. The being on the floor ceased to writhe, and Pyrrhas' blood turned to ice.

"Lilitu!"

She quivered at the threshold, as if held by an invisible boundary. Her eyes were eloquent with hate; they yearned awfully for his blood and his life. She spoke, and the effect of a human voice issuing from that beautiful unhuman mouth was more terrifying than if a wild beast had spoken in human tongue.

"You have trapped my mate! You dare to torture Ardat Lili, before whom the gods tremble! Oh, you shall howl for this! You shall be torn bone from bone, and muscle from muscle, and vein from vein! Loose him! Speak the words and set him free, lest even this doom be denied you!"

"Words!" he answered with bitter savagery. "You have hunted me like a hound. Now you can not cross that line without falling into my hands as your mate has fallen. Come into the chamber, bitch of darkness, and let me caress you as I caress your lover — thus! — and thus! — and thus!"

Ardat Lili foamed and howled at the bite of the keen steel, and Lilitu screamed madly in protest, beating with her hands as at an invisible barrier.

"Cease! Cease! Oh, could I but come at you! How I would leave you a blind, mangled cripple! Have done! Ask what you will, and I will perform it!"

"That is well," grunted the Argive grimly. "I can not take this creature's life, but it seems I can hurt him, and unless you give me satisfaction, I will give him more pain than even he guesses exists in the world."

"Ask! Ask!" urged the were-woman, twisting with impatience.

"Why have you haunted me? What have I done to earn your hate?"

"Hate?" she tossed her head. "What are the sons of men that we of Shuala should hate or love? When the doom is loosed, it strikes blindly."

"Then who, or what, loosed the doom of Lilitu upon me?"

"One who dwells in the House of Arabu."

"Why, in Ymir's name?" swore Pyrrhas. "Why should the dead hate me?" He halted, remembering a priest who died gurgling curses.

"The dead strike at the bidding of the living. Someone who moves in the sunlight spoke in the night to one who dwells in Shuala."

"Who?"

"I do not know."

"You lie, you slut! It is the priests of Anu, and you would shield them. For that lie your lover shall howl to the kiss of the steel —"

"Butcher!" shrieked Lilitu. "Hold your hand! I swear by the dugs of Tiamat my mistress, I do not know what you ask. What are the priests of Anu that I should shield them? I would rip up all their bellies — as I would yours, could I come at you! Free my mate, and I will lead you to the House of Darkness itself, and you may wrest the truth from the awful mouth of the dweller himself, if you dare!"

"I will go," said Pyrrhas, "but I leave Ardat Lili here as hostage. If you deal falsely with me, he will writhe on this enchanted floor throughout all eternity.

Lilitu wept with fury, crying: "No devil in Shuala is crueler than you. Haste, in the name of Apsu!"

Sheathing his sword, Pyrrhas stepped across the threshold. She caught his wrist with fingers like velvet-padded steel, crying something in a strange inhuman tongue. Instantly the moon-lit sky and plain were blotted out in a rush of icy blackness. There was a sensation of hurtling through a void of intolerable coldness, a roaring in the Argive's ears as of titan winds. Then his feet struck solid ground; stability followed that chaotic instant, that had been like the instant of dissolution that joins or separates two states of being, alike in stability, but in kind more alien than day and night. Pyrrhas knew that in that instant he had crossed an unimaginable gulf, and that he stood on shores never before touched by living human feet.

Lilitu's fingers grasped his wrist, but he could not see her. He stood in darkness of a quality which he had never encountered. It was almost tangibly soft, all-pervading and all-engulfing. Standing amidst it, it was not easy even to imagine sunlight and bright rivers and grass singing in the wind. They belonged to that other world — a world lost and forgotten in the dust of a million centuries. The world of life and light was a whim of chance — a bright spark glowing momentarily in a universe of dust and shadows. Darkness and silence were the natural state of the cosmos, not light and the noises of Life. No wonder the dead hated the living, who disturbed the grey stillness of Infinity with their tinkling laughter.

Lilitu's fingers drew him through abysmal blackness. He had a vague sensation as of being in a titanic cavern, too huge for conception. He sensed walls and roof, though he did not see them and never reached them; they seemed to recede as he advanced, yet there was always the sensation of their presence. Sometimes his feet stirred what he hoped was only dust. There was a dusty scent throughout the darkness; he smelled the odors of decay and mould.

He saw lights moving like glowworms through the dark. Yet they were not lights, as he knew radiance. They were more like spots of lesser gloom, that seemed to glow only by contrast with the engulfing blackness which they emphasized without illuminating. Slowly, laboriously they crawled through the eternal night. One approached the companions closely and Pyrrhas' hair stood up and he grasped his sword. But Lilitu took no heed as she hurried him on. The dim spot glowed close to him for an instant; it vaguely illumined a shadowy countenance, faintly human, yet strangely birdlike.

Existence became a dim and tangled thing to Pyrrhas, wherein he seemed to journey for a thousand years through the blackness of dust and decay, drawn and guided by the hand of the were-woman. Then he heard her breath hiss through her teeth, and she came to a halt.

Before them shimmered another of those strange globes of light. Pyrrhas could not tell whether it illumined a man or a bird. The creature stood upright like a man, but it was clad in grey feathers — at least they were more like feathers than anything else. The features were no more human than they were bird-like.

"This is the dweller in Shuala which put upon you the curse of the dead," whispered Lilitu. "Ask him the name of him who hates you on earth."

"Tell me the name of mine enemy!" demanded Pyrrhas, shuddering at the sound of his own voice, which whispered drearily and uncannily through the unechoing darkness.

The eyes of the dead burned redly and it came at him with a rustle of pinions, a long gleam of light springing into its lifted hand. Pyrrhas recoiled, clutching at his sword, but Lulitu hissed: "Nay, use this!" and he felt a hilt thrust into his fingers. He was grasping a scimitar with a blade curved in the shape of the crescent moon, that shone like an arc of white fire.

He parried the bird-thing's stroke, and sparks showered in the gloom, burning him like bits of flame. The darkness clung to him like a black cloak; the glow of the feathered monster bewildered and baffled him. It was like fighting a shadow in the maze of a nightmare. Only by the fiery gleam of his enemy's blade did he keep the touch of it. Thrice it sang death in his ears as he deflected it by the merest fraction, then his own crescent-edge cut the darkness and grated on the other's shoulder-joint. With a strident screech the thing dropped its weapon and slumped down, a milky liquid spurting from the gaping wound. Pyrrhas lifted his scimitar again, when the creature gasped in a voice that was no more human than the grating of wind-blown boughs against one another: "Naram-ninub, the great-grandson of my great-grandson! By black arts he spoke and commanded me across the gulfs!"

"Naram-ninub!" Pyrrhas stood frozen in amazement; the scimitar was torn from his hand. Again Lilitu's fingers locked on his wrist. Again the dark was drowned in deep blackness and howling winds blowing between the spheres.

He staggered in the moonlight without the ruined villa, reeling with the dizziness of his transmutation. Beside him Lilitu's teeth shone between her curling red lips. Catching the thick locks clustered on her neck, he shook her savagely, as he would have shaken a mortal woman.

"Harlot of Hell! What madness has your sorcery instilled in my brain?"

"No madness!" she laughed, striking his hand

aside. "You have journeyed to the House of Arabu, and you have returned. You have spoken with and overcome with the sword of Apsu, the shade of a man dead for long centuries."

"Then it was no dream of madness! But Naram-ninub —" he halted in confused thought. "Why, of all the men of Nippur, he has been my staunchest friend!"

"Friend?" she mocked. "What is friendship but a pleasant pretense to while away an idle hour?"

"But why, in Ymir's name?"

"What are the petty intrigues of men to me?" she exclaimed angrily.

"Yet now I remember that men from Erech, wrapped in cloaks, steal by night to Naram-ninub's palace."

"Ymir!" Like a sudden blaze of light Pyrrhas saw reason in merciless clarity. "He would sell Nippur to Erech, and first he must put me out of the way, because the hosts of Nippur cannot stand before me! Oh, dog, let my knife find your heart!"

"Keep faith with me!" Lilitu's importunities drowned his fury. "I have kept faith with you. I have led you where never living man has trod, and brought you forth unharmed. I have betrayed the dwellers in darkness and done that for which Tiamat will bind me naked on a white-hot grid for seven times seven days. Speak the words and free Ardat Lili!"

Still engrossed in Naram-ninub's treachery, Pyrrhas spoke the incantation. With a loud sigh of relief, the were-man rose from the tiled floor and came into the moonlight. The Argive stood with his hand on his sword and his head bent, lost in moody thought. Lilitu's eyes flashed a quick meaning to her mate. Lithely they began to steal toward the abstracted man. Some primitive instinct brought his head up with a jerk. They were closing in on him, their eyes burning in the moonlight, their fingers reaching for him. Instantly he realized his mistake; he had forgotten to make them swear truce with him; no oath bound them from his flesh.

With feline screeches they struck in, but quicker yet he bounded aside and raced toward the distant city. Too hotly eager for his blood to resort to sorcery, they gave chase. Fear winged his feet, but close behind him he heard the swift patter of their feet, their eager panting. A sudden drum of hoofs sounded in front of him, and bursting through a tattered grove of skeleton palms, he almost caromed against a rider, who rode like the wind, a long silvery glitter in his hand. With a startled oath the horseman wrenched his steed back on its haunches. Pyrrhas saw looming over him a powerful body in scale-mail, a pair of blazing eyes that glared at him from under a domed helmet, a short black beard.

"You dog!" he yelled furiously. "Damn you, have you come to complete with your sword what your black magic began?"

The steed reared wildly as he leaped at its head

and caught its bridle. Cursing madly and fighting for balance, Naram-ninub slashed at his attacker's head, but Pyrrhas parried the stroke and thrust upward murderously. The sword-point glanced from the corselet and plowed along the Semite's jawbone. Naram-ninub screamed and fell from the plunging steed, spouting blood. His leg bone snapped as he pitched heavily to earth, and his cry was echoed by a gloating howl from the shadowed grove.

Without dragging the rearing horse to earth, Pyrrhas sprang to its back and wrenched it about. Naram-ninub was groaning and writhing on the ground, and as Pyrrhas looked, two shadows darted from the darkened grove and fastened themselves on his prostrate form. A terrible scream burst from his lips, echoed by more awful laughter. Blood on the night air; on it the night-things would feed, wild as mad dogs, making no difference between men.

The Argive wheeled away, toward the city, then hesitated, shaken by a fierce revulsion. The level land lay quiescent beneath the moon, and the brutish pyramid of Enlil stood up in the stars. Behind him lay his enemy, glutting the fangs of the horrors he himself had called up from the Pits. The road was open to Nippur, for his return. His return? — to a devil-ridden people crawling beneath the heels of priest and king; to a city rotten with intrigue and obscene mysteries; to an alien race that mistrusted him, and a mistress that hated him.

Wheeling his horse again, he rode westward toward the open lands, flinging his arms wide in a gesture of renunciation and the exultation of freedom. The weariness of life dropped from him like a cloak. His mane floated in the wind, and over the plains of Shumir shouted a sound they had never heard before — the gusty, elemental, reasonless laughter of a free barbarian.

BUT THE HILLS
WERE ANCIENT THEN

Amra, *Vol. 2, No. 8*, Nov.-Dec. 1959

Now is a summer come out of the sea,
 And the hills that were bare are green.
They shower the petals and the bee
 On the valleys that laze between.

So it was in the dreaming past,
 And life is a shifting maze,
Summer on summer fading fast,
 In a mist of yesterdays.

Out of the East, the tang of smoke,
 The flight of a startled deer,
A ringing axe the silence broke,
 The tread of the pioneer.

Saxon eyes in a weathered face,
 Cabins where trees had been,
Hard on the heels of a fading race,
 But the hills were ancient then.

Up from the South a haze of dust,
 The pack mules' steady pace,
Armor tarnished and red with rust,
 Stern eyes in a sun-bronzed face.

The mesquite mocked the flag of Spain,
 That the wind flung out again,
The grass bent under the pack mule train—
 But the hills were ancient then.

THE ONE BLACK STAIN

The Howard Collector #2, Spring 1962

(Sir Thomas Doughty, executed at St. Julian's Bay, 1578)

They carried him out on the barren sand where the rebel captains
    died;
Where the grim grey rotting gibbets stand as Magellan reared
    them on the strand,
And the gulls that haunt the lonesome land wail to the lonely tide.

Drake faced them all like a lion at bay, with his lion head upflung:
"Dare ye my word of law defy, to say this traitor shall not die?"
And his captains dared not meet his eye but each man held his
    tongue.

Solomon Kane stood forth alone, grim man of sober face:
"Worthy of death he may well be, but the trial ye held was mockery,
"Ye hid your spite in a travesty where justice hid her face.

"More of the man had ye been, on deck your sword to cleanly draw
"In forthright fury from its sheath and openly cleave him to the
    teeth—
"Rather than slink and hide beneath a hollow word of the Law."

Hell rose in the eyes of Francis Drake. "Puritan knave!" swore he,
"Headsman! Give him the axe instead! HE shall strike off yon
    traitor's head!"
Solomon folded his arms and said, darkly and somberly:

*"I am no slave for your butcher's work." "Bind him with triple
    strands!"*
*Drake roared in wrath and the men obeyed, hesitantly, as men
    afraid,*
*But Kane moved not as they took his blade and pinioned his
    iron hands.*

They bent the doomed man to his knees, the man who was to die;
*They saw his lips in a strange smile bend; one last long look they
    saw him send*
*At Drake, his judge and his one-time friend, who dared not meet
    his eye.*

The axe flashed silver in the sun, a red arch slashed the sand;
*A voice cried out as the head fell clear, and the watchers flinched
    in sudden fear,*
Though 'twas but a sea bird wheeling near above the lonely strand.

"This be every traitor's end!" Drake cried, and yet again;
*Slowly his captains turned and went, and the admiral's stare was
    elsewhere bent*
*Than where the cold scorn with anger blent in the eyes of Solo-
    mon Kane.*

Night fell on the crawling waves; the admiral's door was closed;
*Solomon lay in the stenching hold; his irons clashed as the ship
    rolled,*
*And his guard, grown weary and overbold, lay down his pipe
    and dozed.*

*He woke with a hand at his corded throat that gripped him like
    a vise;*
*Trembling he yielded up the key, and the somber Puritan stood
    up free,*
*His cold eyes gleaming murderously with the wrath that is slow
    to rise.*

THE MADNESS
OF CORMAC

Undated

Lock your arm of iron
Around the reeling moon,
Draw your sword, the grey sword, the sword of Fin, the fey sword,
Carved with a nameless rune.

Brace your feet like talons
On the dreaming world,
Break the shapes, the dread shapes, the dragon-things, the red apes,
Out of the abyss hurled.

Ghost of all the ages
Fill the ancient skies,
Red queens and white kings, nameless forms and night things,
Men fools and wise.

UNTITLED

("I Am the Spirit of War")

1925

I am the Spirit of War!
My hands are red with gore.
They know my heel
Where the clash of steel
Matches the cannon's roar!
My hands are gory red
Ranks crumple beneath my stride
O'er vanquished heaps I tread,
On the wings of the wind I ride.

ADVENTURE

("I Am the Spur . . .")

1926

I am the spur
That rides men's souls.
The glittering lure
That leads around the world.

THE DANCER
1926

A gibbering wind that whoops and drones
A clank of chains and a clatter of bones;
Vultures that circle and swoop and fly
And a glimmer of white against the sky!
And a ghost that rides on the winds that dree,
To dance with the bones on the gallows tree!

With a swing and a fling and a merry prance,
Will you not join in the mirthsome dance?
Why, here is a maid, though her bones are bare,
And the raven has long since reft her hair.
Yet she is as fair as a maid may be,
Come dance with her on the gallows tree!

The gibbering wind shall smite his lute,
And the horned owl shall add his hoot.
There shall be music and tunes enow,
If ye but come to the dance, I trow!
And the chains shall clatter most merrilee!
Come ye, and dance on the gallows tree!

UNTITLED

("Against the Blood Red Moon")

1927

Against the blood red moon a tower stands;
An everlasting silence haunts the place.
It was not reared by any human hands,
The silent symbol of a shadowy race.
There, long ago, I stole through ancient night
My footsteps woke strange echoes through the hour;
Strange specters walked with me through mazy light.
I left my soul, a ghost to haunt the tower.

UNTITLED

("The East Is Red and I Am Dead")

1927

The east is red and I am dead, stark on a silent host
The day breaks and the kite wakes and laughter thrills my ghost.

UNTITLED

("The Seeker Thrust")

1928

The Seeker thrust warily at a door. It opened with a mutter of iron hinges, and he stepped through. Behind him the door closed with a jar of grim finality which sent shivers through the Seeker's soul. He stood looking up a monstrously high staircase which went up and up until it seemed to mingle with the stars. The Seeker mounted, until after what seemed an age, he came out upon a sort of roof, where a great black iron idol brooded and incense smoke drifted up from a red-stained altar.

The Seeker fixed his eyes upon this smoke and soon it began to take shadowy form. A face gleamed vaguely and then before him stood a tall smooth-limbed man, of blond hair, clad in the garments of a cavalier.

"You —" began the Seeker, but the other raised a hand.

"Silence! The Night glides about us with a million eyes, and the triangle is not yet complete."

Silence fell like a silvery fog. The Seeker heard the grisly whisperings of the night wind, and the rustling of the heavy velvet tapestries upon the roofless walls.

The stars gleamed like silver, but one was a dark sinister red and then the Seeker realized with a cold, crawling fear, that this star hovered above the ape-like misshapen skull of the idol. Then the star was gone and before the Seeker stood a tall, broad-shouldered man, even taller than the first. His hair was black and his eyes were deep as ice and cold as fire. Somewhere in the great terrible building below sounded the tread of stealthy great inhuman feet.

"Listen —" the Seeker was cold with fear.

"Silence!" the newcomer raised a halting hand; he was clad like a Roman soldier. "The Night of the Night is Horror and the triangle is not yet complete."

Silence reigned. A panther with gleaming eyes came silently from behind the idol — then there was no panther, but a heavily-built man of medium height, clad like an Atlantean gladiator.

"Hangor, goram, raamo and goreth," droned the Roman, cutting the air with strange intricate patterns, mysterious sinister gestures.

The Seeker shuddered. The moon had come up like a silver wave above the black hills afar and the stars paled like ghosts at a banquet of Hades.

"The sword, the book and the full moon," said the Atlantean.

"The altar, the rhyme and the crescent moon," said the Cavalier.

"The moon on the altar, the star on the moon, the dagger on the star," intoned the Roman, and the cold sweat beaded the Seeker's brow.

There was evil in the air. Evil, nameless and age-less, he read in the eyes of the Three, evil that tran-scended the sins of men and had no part thereof. In the face and the crimson garments of the Cavalier he read it, in the armor of the Roman, in the sword-belt of the Atlantean. Evil that reached taloned fingers down the ages, out of the deeps, that stretched blind black arms into the cosmic gulfs of screaming black insanity and doom. Even the moon now gleamed red and grisly.

"You are old," said the Seeker.

"Older than the world," they answered. "We saw the making and the breaking of the gods."

"Do ye live?" the Seeker gasped, for a cold hand was on his heart.

"We are not dead; yet surely we are not alive."

Night and Silence and the threat of unearthly doom hung like a fog. Below sounded the footfalls of demoniac feet; above the sweep of unseen bat-like wings. Three pairs of deep eyes, cold with ancient death and vibrant with undying life, stared fixedly at the Seeker.

"Back, fiends!" he gasped, reeling up. "Back to the lost ages whence ye came! Back to the doom ye have cheated, the oblivion ye have broken! Mock ye the laws of gods and men, dark demons from the abyss?"

"By the long road of Yesterday we come," said they, "and on that road there is no returning. Like bats in the night, like winds beneath the moon, we come. And there be none who may stay our comings and goings."

"I know you now," screamed the Seeker wildly, as a man who is lost. "The Eon's Eternal Rebels are you, accursed of God and man." And high across the shuddering land sounded his frenzied laughter which rose and rose till the stars shook.